THE GIRL IN THE SONG

SARAH WATTS

To my husband Jay, for always believing

1

ED

Now

Musical Muses: The Girl in the Song
A NETFLIX ORIGINAL SERIES

Ed "Nasher" Nash, the charismatic lead singer of indie rock band, The Mountaineers sits in an oversized black leather chair, preparing to be interviewed by the renowned and respected music journalist, Mick Kennedy. An attractive dark-haired make-up artist puts the finishing touches to Ed's make-up to eliminate any potential shine on his handsome face. Ed thanks the girl, flashing her one of his smiles and she flushes slightly and then hurriedly leaves the set.

Mick Kennedy glances briefly down at his notes just before the camera starts recording and he welcomes Ed, with a smile.

MK: This interview is the first in our series of Musical Muses: The Girl in the Song where we look at songs that were inspired by some quite remarkable women and today we have Ed Nash, writer of 'Used to Be' and lead singer of indie band The Mountaineers. Hello, Ed. Great to see you again. So, you've finally got the success you deserve.

EN: Thanks Mick, yeah. It's been one hell of a ride to get here!

Ed shifts slightly in his chair and takes a sip of water from the glass tumbler placed on the small coffee table which separates the two men.

MK: What do you mean by that Ed?

EN: Well, we've been writing and playing music for years but after Observance, the BBC series about the cult asked if they could use our track "Used to Be" as their theme tune, people have started to really see and hear us. It's let us reach a much wider audience and we're extremely thankful.

MK: We're here today to talk to you about your inspiration for that particular song, Evie Del Rio - your muse, if you like. Tell me a bit about her.

EN: Well, when I was in sixth form, I met Evie through some friends and we started a very intense relationship. We did everything together.

MK: Would you say that she was the inspiration behind many of your songs?

Ed enthusiastically nods in agreement, warming to his theme.

EN: Yes. Definitely. She was and still is my muse. She has inspired all of my song writing.

MK: Are you still in touch with her?

The camera does a close up of Ed, capturing his handsome face, etched with regret.

EN: No, unfortunately we lost touch as her parents moved away from where we lived in South West London.

MK: That's got to be over thirty years ago! Mick gives Ed a sympathetic smile.

Ed nods.

EN: Yes, it was.

MK: No one's ever matched up to Evie Del Rio then?

EN: No. Never.

MK: What made Evie so special?

EN: Well, she was a one off. Different to other girls my age, you know. I always described her as the female version of me. She got me and I got her. She completed me and inspired me with my songwriting. It was such a shock when she disappeared without a word to anyone.

MK: You have no idea where she went or where she is now?

Ed Nash shakes his head sadly, pushing his hand distractedly through his dark hair.

EN: No. I have no idea, but I'd love to be reunited with her one day, to see if the spark is still there.

Ed smiles full on to the camera, his hypnotic blue eyes staring straight into the lens.

MK: Tell me a bit more about the song "Used to Be" after we've had a look at a short clip from the video.

Camera cuts from Ed and Mick straight to the video which shows a young couple embracing and then later it shows them being apart, while the camera cuts to Ed singing along with the rest of the band.

MK: That's such an iconic video. I mean, I've probably seen it about a hundred times, but I take something new away from it, every time.

EN: Thanks Mick. I appreciate that. I wrote this song originally when Evie and I were together but after she left, I rewrote the lyrics slightly to represent what we'd had together and to show her how much I missed her.

Mick nods briefly and sympathetically, before pushing ahead with more questions.

MK: Am I right in saying that your entire debut album, Past Times was inspired by Evie Del Rio?

EN: Yes. Every single song was inspired by Evie. I know it was a long time ago, but I've never forgotten her. I just hope she's ok and that she's had a happy and

3

fulfilling life. I'm just gutted that I couldn't be part of it.

MK: You've never married or had kids, have you, Ed?

Ed shakes his head as Mick continues, like a dog with a bone not quite ready to give up the question that everyone wants to know.

MK: Do you think not knowing where Evie is has held you back, how can I put this….

Mick pauses for dramatic effect. He continues.

MK: ….from forming future long-term relationships?

Ed answers immediately.

EN: Yes. Absolutely yes. None of my relationships have ever matched up to what I had with Evie.

MK: Don't you think it's just some kind of teenage romanticised nostalgic memory?

EN: Not at all. The feelings I had all those years ago are as real and raw as they were when Evie and I were still together. It was that heady kind of first love that I think would have lasted a lifetime. If she hadn't gone, I think we would still be together.

MK: Wow! That's very honest and candid of you. There's every likelihood that Evie has probably moved on.

EN: In reality, yes, she probably has but there is always that slight possibility that she is still single. And I really hope that she still thinks about me and what we had together.

MK: What would you say to her if you had the chance to speak to her today?

EN: I'd ask her why she left as it's the one question that I've never had the answer to.

MK: She knew where you lived all those years ago. Don't you ever wonder why she never got in touch with you?

EN: Yes, constantly. There's got to be a legitimate reason as to why she disappeared. That's one of the reasons I agreed to being part of this documentary. I want to find Evie and hear from her own mouth as to why she left. I mean I completely respect that she may well be married but I just want some sort of explanation from her, some closure really.

MK: You must surely have tried looking for her via social media.

EN: Yes, frequently but without success unfortunately. There's no trace of her.

MK: If you could say something to Evie right now. What would it be?

The camera zooms in on Ed's face and he looks straight into the lens.

EN: Please Evie, just reach out to me, I just want to understand why you left.

Ed breathes deeply and then composes himself.

MK: Thanks Ed, for your time today.

EN: Thanks Mick. And thank you for including "Used to Be" in the documentary. We, as a band are so honoured. It's just mad to be included with such other amazing songwriters and bands. I can't wait to watch the rest of the series.

MK: Our pleasure Ed. Any last words, before we wrap?

EN: Yes, um, I'd just like to put it out there that if anyone knows where Evie is or knows what happened to her, please do get in touch.

MK: Well, that's quite the ask, isn't it? British public – you know what to do! Let's find Evie Del Rio. Someone must know where she is. Next week I'll be talking to Noel Gallagher and his inspiration behind Oasis' epic anthem Wonderwall. And interestingly, it's not quite what everyone thinks!

Mick reaches over to shake Ed's hand and the camera pans away from the two men as they chat quite amicably in the background until just their two shadows remain and the last few verses of *Used to Be* play out.

2

GENIE

Now

I've worked hard to become Genie McNamara, a respectable mother of two and a devoted wife to my husband Gray, a successful self-made businessman who has always worked hard for his family. From the outside we look like the picture-perfect family; with our two teenage children, a daughter, Cassie and a younger son called Will. Having been together since I just turned nineteen, we've lived a charmed life so far but there has always been that dread that one day my long-kept secret would come back to haunt me.

Friday night in the McNamara household is always Netflix night; we each take turns to choose something to watch. Most Fridays Gray and I order a takeaway when he gets back from work to make the most of our evening together. It's Gray's choice tonight, he's chosen a Netflix documentary which has just come out today called *Musical Muses: The Girl in the Song.*

I'm snuggled comfortably up against Gray's familiar, solid body, as the credits begin. I've already had a glass of wine with dinner, and I feel sleepy and content but as soon as I see who's being interviewed, I'm completely wide awake.

Ed Nash. My 'Ed', my ex-boyfriend is here in my living room in crystal clear HD looking straight at me and my husband. Ed's song "Used to Be" has been everywhere recently and so far I've managed to avoid the subject with Gray, but here tonight my anxiety is building that tonight I'm going to be found out.

'Can you pause it for a sec? I just need the loo.' I say, extricating myself as quickly as I can from Gray.

'You always do this when we're about to watch something!' Gray calls out as I leave the room, chuckling to himself, so used to my idiosyncrasies, after a lifetime together.

'Sorry! Won't be long!' I shout back as I close the downstairs bathroom door behind me, giving me a few minutes to myself to try and work out what to say to Gray once he puts two and two together about me and Ed.

What on earth was Ed doing on that show I wondered. He looked good, though older, obviously, but he was no match for Gray. I splash my face with cold water and wonder just how long it was before Gray and everyone else starts asking me questions about my former life as teenage Evie Del Rio? It doesn't bear thinking about. I briefly contemplate feigning illness to avoid Gray seeing Ed's interview, but I realise that he will inevitably watch or hear about this documentary sooner or later.

I return to the sitting room and resume my position cuddled up, close and safe against my husband's comfortable body and watch the screen intently at the man who once meant everything to me open his heart to the world in his search for me. I'm convinced that Gray can hear my racing heartbeat.

Ed was being interviewed by music journalist Mick

Kennedy who seemed to be very well acquainted with Ed. They had that casual, blokey banter between them that seemed so popular nowadays on television.

I'd hoped that Gray would have nodded off by now, like he often does after a hard week at work but unfortunately for me he's wide awake and takes in every single word of the interview.

After what seems an age, the interview is at an end and as the credits roll, I find myself letting out a breath that I wasn't even aware that I was holding.

'What do you fancy watching now?' Gray asks casually.

'I don't mind. Maybe Squid Game? I know you're desperate to watch the new series.' I suggest, relieved that on this occasion, my secret is still safe. I start to relax and settle down to watch Squid Game, despite the extreme violence, it's a welcome distraction from my own life.

3

EVIE

Then

Evie's parents were fuming, having just been called into school by Sister Maria, Evie's headmistress, yet again. Evie and her best friend Ginny always joked that Sister Maria was a frigid old cow who just hated her pupils because they were young and pretty and had the world at their feet, whereas she chose to be married to the church. Evie had been caught with Ed, from St Augustine's School, kissing at the bus stop around the corner from her school, and although they'd managed to get away from her by jumping on the bus, they had certainly been clocked by her. Ed and Evie had run up the stairs to the upper deck and managed to get the back seat of the bus, where they had a bird's-eye view of Sister Maria shaking her fist like she was possessed by the Devil, rather than being a devout sister of Christ. Ed didn't help things, as he flipped her the finger. They thought she was going to have a fit.

They got off the bus a couple of stops later, quite close to Ed's house, and walked the last few minutes, hand in hand. Amazingly, his mum and dad were out, so they had the whole place to themselves. Evie loved being at Ed's house – as it seemed so cool and bohemian, compared to hers, complete with her sanctimonious mother insisting on having a crucifix displayed in the hallway. It gave Evie the creeps. Both Ed's parents were artists, although his mum was also a teacher and his dad was a part-time singer in a band, so there was always something happening. Sometimes his dad had his mates round for a smoke and a jam. Evie loved it when Ed joined in, and his dad let him play guitar. He'd promised Evie that he was going to write a song for her one day so everyone would know just how much she meant to him.

As soon as they got in and Ed realised no one was around, he suggested going upstairs to his bedroom. He put one of his mixtapes into his stereo. With the melancholy and haunting sound of The Smiths singing "This Charming Man", he gently pushed Evie onto his bed, with his kisses becoming more and more forceful. Evie enjoyed being with Ed but made it clear that that was a far as she was willing to go. After the kissing stopped, Ed rolled a joint, took a big drag and passed it to Evie. She tried to copy what he'd just done but ended up coughing her guts up.

'You really do have to put in a bit more practice, you know?' Ed laughed as he sat up in bed and traced his finger around the contours of her face, finally resting on her lips. He kissed her mouth once again and smiled at her.

'Christ! I'd best get going before mum sends out a search party for me!' Evie said, breaking the sexual tension.

'You sure you're off now?' Ed said, pulling her so close she could feel his heart beating next to hers.

'Yeah. I gotta go.' she replied, trying half-heartedly to release herself from his tight embrace.

'One more kiss.'

'Just one more.' she agreed, knowing she had to get home

quickly, her body betraying her by just wanting to stay there with Ed.

Ed grabbed her again, pushing her back down on the bed. They kissed again, Ed only releasing her when he heard a key in the door.

'Wait here.' instructed Ed, placing his finger on his lip to indicate to Evie to keep quiet.

'Mum, Dad? he called out, stumbling out into the hallway.

'Hi, Ed. It's Paul.' a gruff voice replied. 'Your dad said to use the spare key, as I need to lay low for a couple of nights.'

Ed continually talked about Paul. He was Ed's uncle, his dad's half-brother. He was cool and never treated Ed like his parents did. He was nearer in age to Ed than he was to his own brother, as Ed's dad and Paul had different mums. Ed always said that Paul was more like an older brother to him than an uncle.

'Alright, mate. Just coming down.' Ed signalled for Evie to follow him.

She grabbed her bag and followed Ed downstairs.

'This is my girlfriend Evie.' Ed said proudly introducing Evie to Paul.

'Pleased to meet you, Evie.' Paul said as he cast his eyes appreciatively over her body. 'You've done well there, Ed.'

'Hi Paul. Great to meet you. I've heard so much about you.' Evie replied politely, wanting to make a good impression on the man who Ed thought so much of. 'But, I'd best be off.'

Ed walked Evie to the door, planting a passionate kiss firmly on her lips and watched her until she was out of sight.

Evie had never run so fast in her life to get home. All that training she'd done for Borough Sports had clearly paid off. As she turned the corner, her bus had just arrived at the stop. She did a final sprint and managed to jump on just as the bus started to move. She sat downstairs on one of the long seats near where the conductor stood and daydreamed about her afternoon with Ed and how she couldn't wait to see him again. *Just wait until I tell Ginny*, Evie thought. *She'll be fuming.* Ginny had always fancied Ed, but he'd decided that it was Evie he wanted to be with.

4

AMIRA

Now

Being one of the UK's most popular and successful investigative TikTokers is starting to take its toll on me. I haven't had many exclusives since my explosive reveal on former 'Telepathy' boyband member Atticus Blythe's full on drug addiction. His squeaky-clean image has been left in tatters, stripped from his many ad endorsements that highlighted his supposed healthy lifestyle. Since my exposé on Atticus, we've become good friends and I often feature him on my TikTok but since he's become clean, interest in him has faded. So, when the press interest intensified on rock god Ed Nash's missing former girlfriend, Evie Del Rio, after his appearance on the smash hit Netflix documentary Musical Muses: The Girl in the Song, I just knew I had to be the one that finds Evie - whether she wants to be found or not.

I don't do much TV work, preferring to appear on my own TikTok account, but the recent requests to appear on TV have been too good to pass up. I'm already booked to appear on Loose Women in the coming weeks and I've even managed to have a few names to drop as to the identity of the real Evie Del Rio. Ed's story has everything that appeals to my viewers; a mysterious missing girlfriend, an iconic love song and a lovelorn rock god who just can't let go of the past. It has instant classic TikTok appeal that my followers will just lap up.

In anticipation of my upcoming TV appearance, I book appointments to have my hair done along with a mani-pedi and a facial. I simply must keep up appearances if I'm to maintain my popularity.

My last TikTok about Ed went viral and I expect after my forthcoming TV appearance, the hype and hysteria will only increase. I'm determined to retain my title as the UK's top TikTok sleuth and influencer, whatever it takes......

5

ED

Then

Ed Nash and his mates had always had great success with the girls from the local Catholic girls' sixth form. There was this one blonde called Ginny who had the most amazing curvy figure. Ginny always made a beeline for Ed. She was nice enough, but Ed only kept her sweet, because he really fancied her friend Evie. Evie was just one of those girls that everyone wanted as their girlfriend. She also had blonde hair, but hers looked more natural against Ginny's brassy peroxide colour.

Evie really was a classic beauty. The type of girl who looked good dressed in anything. As her and Ginny were always together, Ed managed to get to know her quite well. There was a small group of boys and girls from both sixth forms who kind of hung out together in the local park, smoking and sometimes sharing a couple of cans of Fosters one of them had managed to take from home without their parents noticing.

Eventually, Ed and Evie started hanging back from the rest of the group. They would meet from school and Ed would wait with Evie at the bus stop, passionately kissing until her bus arrived. Neither of them cared about people looking as they were just lost in the moment until the day Evie's headmistress caught them kissing at the bus stop. They gave her the slip and then went back to Ed's house. Thankfully, his parents were out, and the kissing continued while they listened to one of Ed's mixtapes upstairs in his bedroom. That was until Paul showed up at the house unannounced. Ed was always fascinated by Paul, as he never seemed to work but always had loads of cash. He would often push a crumpled fiver into Ed's hand with a wink, being careful that his parents didn't see. Ed was happy to have finally introduced Evie to Paul before she went home.

Not long after Evie left, Paul asked if there was any beer. He was obsessed with booze. He was continually drinking and smoking.

'Yeah, sure. Dad's got a load in the fridge. Just help yourself.' Ed replied.

He then sat down on the leather sofa and put his muddy old Dr. Martens on one of Ed's mum's new cushions. She'd be fuming if she found out. She wasn't overly keen on Paul at the best of times, as she thought that he always got her husband into trouble. She was probably right, because every time that Paul was with them, there was kind of an air of excitement in the house - well, it seemed that way for both Ed and his dad.

From the overflowing ashtray and the tower of empty lager cans building up on the coffee table it was clear just how Paul and Ed had spent their afternoon, just in time for Ed's mum to see as she returned from work.

'Paul, Ed, what on earth do you think you're doing? Ed, have you been smoking and drinking?' she shouted.

Ed went to stand up but, in his drunken and stoned state, lost his balance and fell flat on the floor, which in turn made Paul collapse on top of him in a fit of laughter. Ed's mum looked at them both in disgust, turned on her heel and stormed out of the house. They just lay there laughing uncontrollably.

'Fancy another beer, Ed?'

'Yeah, why not?' He readily agreed.

'How about another joint?'

'Sure.'

'Tell you what, you get the beers, and I'll teach you how to roll a joint properly. I think you could do with the practice.' He slurred.

6

GENIE

Now

I'm sick to the back teeth of Ed Nash. I really do wish that he would crawl back under the rock from which he came. I know we have history together, but to be honest it's a history I would like to forget. I'm also getting quite anxious about what Ed's going to reveal next if the price is right from the press. I've got to tell Gray absolutely everything about my past, which is something that I really don't want to do. I don't think I can bear him finding out the truth about me. It will be just like when my parents found out what I was really like.

Grown-up Genie McNamara is going to have to sort out Evie Del Rio's youthful mess once and for all. I still haven't quite worked out when or how I'm going to do it, but I really want my nice, safe, ordinary life back. I'll start by calling Maura. She's always such a positive breath of fresh air. I could have done with having Maura in my life sooner but she's with me now and she's always on my side. I think I'll tell her everything and see what she thinks I should do. I'm hopeful that she won't judge me too harshly. I reach for my mobile and call her.

Gray's out tonight, a leaving do for one of his long-serving salesmen so it's a great excuse for him to enjoy a few drinks. Cassie's staying at her friend Mel's house, so that just leaves Will here, who will be so engrossed in his Xbox he wouldn't even notice if the roof caved in. With a near empty house, I'll tell Maura to pack an overnight bag too, just in case.

The press interest is getting intense now since the Netflix documentary aired as more and more people have watched it and each day another amateur sleuth on TikTok posts another theory as to my identity, so I'm sure it won't be too long before someone realises that I'm #thegirlinthesong. Can you believe I've even got my very own hashtag? The children are obsessed with TikToker Amira Malik who day by day seems to come closer to revealing my identity. Her last TikTok went viral, and she's been teasing that she has identified a few possibilities who could be Ed's Evie Del Rio. It won't be long before Amira Malik finds me or gets to me via Gray or the children.

Gray's old mate Jonesy says his villa in Florida is free for most of July and August, so I may be able to persuade Gray to take some time off so we can spend some family time together. It will be good for the kids to get away from London, especially after Cassie's GCSEs and to put some distance between us and the UK's current media obsession of all things #thegirlinthesong

Maura arrives in a taxi in typical "Maura style" - her unruly curly red hair is loosely tied up in a scrunchie. She flashes a big smile at her driver as he dutifully carries her overnight bag all the way to our front door.

'Thanks a million, Ahmed. You're a real star.'

'You are most welcome, Miss Maloney. Have a pleasant evening.'

'I'm sure I will. Now, don't you work too hard. I'll see you again soon.'

I open the front door before Maura has even pressed our Ring doorbell.

'Thanks so much for coming over. I…' I start to say but my tears cut me off.

'You're fine, my love. You're fine. I've got you.' says Maura, enveloping me into her enormous bosom. 'Let's get ourselves inside and open one of Gray's expensive bottles of wine.' She cajoles me with a conspiratorial wink.

Maura knows my house almost as well as she knows her own, and she soon has me sat on the sofa, a large glass of rosé in my hand. She sits beside me, takes a big sip from her glass and waits until I'm ready to talk.

Before I can even say one word, I start to cry, letting out big, loud sobs. Maura rushes immediately to console me. The tears keep coming but eventually they subside as I take a big breath. Maura rubs my back, and my breathing starts to go back to normal. We both sit there in silence as I try to compose myself and that's when we both hear a loud creak from the stairs.

'Will? Is that you?' Maura calls out.

'Oh, Auntie Maura. I was just getting some snacks.' Will's voice replies from midway up the stairs.

'Come on down and say hello.' Maura calls out to Will.

Will retreats from the stairs and gives Maura a big hug, his now tall frame making Maura seem even shorter than usual.

'Have you eaten yet, Will?' Maura probes.

Will shakes his head.

'Well in that case, let's order in, my treat.'

I immediately feel guilty that I haven't even remembered to feed Will. Thank God Maura is here to help maintain some normality to our lives.

Maura hands him her phone to choose a takeaway. I remain sitting on the sofa, trying to look engrossed on my phone, discreetly wiping the tears away from my face, keen not to worry Will unnecessarily

'Let's have Chinese. I know it's your favourite.'

'You're a great, thoughtful lad Will. Now choose plenty. It's my treat, as long as we get some of that crispy aromatic duck with the plum sauce that your Mum and I like!' Maura chatters on.

With a few swipes and clicks we were sorted for dinner and Will helpfully suggests getting some plates and cutlery from the kitchen. As soon as he's out of earshot Maura continues to calm me down and suggests that we can chat again after dinner if that's still what I want to do. As my mind starts to clear, I decide to shelve telling all to Maura for now. I owe it to Gray to tell him first. There should be no secrets between a husband and his wife.

7

ED

Now

I can't believe my luck and change of fortune over the last year, and it's all thanks to that TV series using my song "Used to Be" and then the Netflix documentary featuring it together with classics like "Layla" and "Wonderful Tonight" by Eric Clapton, written about Pattie Boyd. It has certainly stirred up quite a media storm, which I'm really benefitting from, but I've also started thinking back to those heady days when I was with Evie. It's such a shame we were forced apart, but I guess we were so young. I do sometimes wonder if we would have got married and had kids had we stayed together. That's my one regret not having kids. Or perhaps our relationship would have just run its course.

After pretty much coasting along in life - just like my uncle Paul, as Mum always used to say - I've suddenly got a purpose. The band have been offered a reunion tour, and the lads and I are well up for it. We're not young anymore, we're all nearly pushing fifty, but I'm convinced we've still got the stamina to go on tour. It's all going to be televised by the Netflix documentary makers. Perhaps Evie might come along and listen to her song? Somehow, I don't think that's going to happen though.

I've just been contacted by Ginny (or Virginia, as she now goes by), who used to be good friends with Evie way back. I feel a bit guilty about the way I used her to get to Evie all those years ago, but she doesn't seem to hold a grudge. She's even suggested meeting up privately, as she's just discovered some old photos of us all from when Evie and I were together. She thinks the press will be really interested to see them, but she wants to run them by me first. I asked her to message me the photos privately, but she was very insistent in meeting up to show me the photos in person. And to be honest, I'm quite intrigued to see Virginia again and see how life has treated her, so we've been messaging each other on Instagram to arrange a meeting. She seems keen to meet me at my flat but I'm not so sure, so I may try and arrange to meet at hers or somewhere more neutral. The press is all over me currently and they are closely monitoring who goes in and out of my flat, so I need to think of a way for us to meet up discreetly. Quite a few of our old school friends have sold stories already with a few old photos, which is fine as far as I'm concerned. Why should I be the only one to make a few bob out of the current hysteria? But Virginia has hinted that the recent photos she's found could be interesting. I'll sleep on it.

I need a good night's sleep, as I'm being interviewed by the morning TV magazine show called *Wake Up and Smell the Coffee*. I'm looking forward to showing them a bit of the Ed "Nasher" Nash charm. I'll give Virginia and her photos some more thought tomorrow.

8

GENIE

Then

I've always had a soft spot for Gray's best mate, Jonesy, because if it wasn't for him, then Gray and I would never have met. They first met a secondary school, and Jonesy was studying art at Brighton Polytechnic when he first started coming into the bar where I worked, whereas Gray had just secured his first job in advertising sales in London, so he used to work all week in Soho and then would go and visit Jonesy in Brighton on Friday nights. They'd be partying all weekend and then Gray would leave on the Sunday to get ready for work on Monday. It was like being a student, but with money. He'd lived for his weekends.

Jonesy had introduced Gray to The Hidden Snicket, named as such because to get there you had to cut through the narrowest of alleyways and it was fairly off the beaten track of all the normal traditional pubs and cheesy wine bars. It was on Gray's first visit to The Hidden Snicket that we first met as I was lucky enough to have been hired by Maura to work there when I first arrived in Brighton, first as a cleaner as I was underage and then when I finally turned eighteen, she trained me up to help out behind the bar.

Gray purposely chose to be served by me, but it was hard back then to even get me to crack a smile. Since leaving Bournemouth so abruptly, I tended to keep myself to myself, always wondering if my old life was going to catch up with me. He for some reason thought I was worth persevering with and, obviously, eventually it paid off. I still remember the first thing he ever said to me.

'Two Sapporos, please.' He later told me he had been trying to appear sophisticated with his choice of Japanese beer. 'And a drink for yourself.'

'Thanks.' I'd replied with only a hint of a smile. 'I'll have mine later on if that's ok?'

'Of course. What time do you finish?'

I remember looking at him as if trying to work out if he was just your normal lecherous Friday night punter or an ok kind of guy. Luckily, I gave him a chance.

'The bar closes at eleven, but I've got a break in five minutes. I might have a drink then.'

'Fancy some company?' He'd boldly asked. I just played it cool.

'If you like.' I'd gestured with my head towards Jonesy. 'You'd better give your friend his drink, otherwise he'll think you've ditched him.'

He passed a Sapporo to Jonesy, who was mid-conversation with a couple of Italian girls. It was clear they didn't have a clue what he was saying with their basic knowledge of English and his lack of Italian, coupled with his strong Welsh accent.

'Cheers, Gray. This is Carla and Sofia. Did I get that right?' he'd asked the giggling girls.

'Si, si.' they'd both replied, excitedly.

'I'll leave you to it, Jonesy.'

'Please yourself, mate.' Jonesy had replied as he returned his attention to his newfound friends.

Gray managed to get a seat at the bar, close to where I was, and he patiently waited. After a while, I came around to the other side of the bar with half a lager. I lifted my glass towards him and took a sip.

I remember thanking him and smiling at his kind, handsome face.

He'd made some jokey comment about different blokes trying to buy me drinks every night of the week and I'd replied with an equally jokey comment about just being thirsty.

'Oh, and I thought I was special.' He'd replied, pretending to clutch at his imaginary wounded heart.

'Maybe you are, or maybe you're not.' I'd replied trying to come over all mysterious. My idea of flirting was truly atrocious back then, as I really hadn't a clue, but Gray was already smitten.

'I'm Gray.' He'd formally announced, holding out his hand. I remember returning his handshake and introduced myself.

'Genie.' As soon as I'd left Bournemouth, I'd changed my name to Genie. I met a girl on the coach who had asked me my name and I just panicked so I said Genie as I didn't want to call myself Evie in case my parents came looking for me. And I had never liked being called by my real name, Genevieve, so Genie seemed like a good compromise. And it obviously stuck.

'Nice to meet you, Genie.'

'Good to meet you too, Gray, but I've got to get back behind that bar, as we're really short-staffed at the moment.' And with that, I took another sip of my drink and returned to my side of the bar.

Gray also says that the rest of the evening went by in a

blur. He'd politely chatted a bit to Jonesy and the Italian girls, who were so Jonesy's type, but he always says that I had completely turned his head. Last orders were called, and Jonesy got another round in, served by me. We chatted a bit and I could tell he really had Gray's back.

'Your barmaid wants to get you a drink after closing.' he'd whispered in Gray's ear as he handed him yet another beer and returned to his Italian girls.

'Really?'

'Really.'

Gray chatted a bit more with Jonesy and the girls until Maura rang the final bell to indicate it was time for everyone to go home.

After what seemed an age and we'd managed to shoo away the last of the Friday night stragglers, including Jonesy and his Italian girls, it was then time for the staff and their chosen friends to enjoy a late-night drink.

'Another Sapporo?' I'd asked Gray.

'Yes please. That would be great.'

I passed him a Sapporo, and this time my drink of choice was a vodka and tonic, with my glass full to the brim with crushed ice. I shyly took Gray's arm and ushered him to a couple of seats slightly tucked away from the main bar.

We started with some small talk, and he told me all about how he worked in advertising in Soho in the week but came down to visit Jonesy most weekends.

'I've seen your mate in here before. He's one of our regulars, but I've never seen him with the same girl twice. He seems like a bit of a player to me.' I'd said. I hadn't been too impressed with Jonesy and his antics back then.

'He just hasn't met the right girl yet.' Gray replied, taking another sip of his beer.

'How about you? Have you got a nice girl waiting for you

27

back in London?' I'd asked him cheekily, fiddling with one of the alcohol-soaked beer mats.

'Me? No such luck. Just me and my black cat Woody.'

'Woody? Cute name.' I'd replied and I'd meant it.

'I thought so. He was a stray.' he continued. 'Kept hanging around in my garden, so I started feeding him, and now we're inseparable.'

'Who looks after Woody when you're in Brighton?'

'Oh, my neighbour Bessie pops in and feeds him. I think she loves him as much as I do.' He laughed then, a proper hearty laugh.

I paused and took a breath; all the cheekiness had dropped from my face. 'And what's this Bessie like?'

'Oh, she's adorable. Not only does she look after Woody, but she also even leaves me a loaf of her delicious homemade bread whenever I've been away.' He replied with a big smile.

I'd swirled my drink around the glass, as if I'd suddenly gone off the idea of alcohol. 'How come you two aren't dating? She sounds like perfect girlfriend material to me.'

Gray almost spat out a mouthful of his overpriced beer. 'Maybe because she's as old as my grandma.'

'Oh.' I'd replied, looking somewhat sheepish.

'Were you imagining some busty blonde with a penchant for home baking?' Gray had teased.

'Err, no. Well, possibly.' I'd stammered as my face flushed cherry red with embarrassment. We'd both looked at each other and just burst out laughing.

9

ED

Now

Set of daytime magazine show Wake up and Smell the Coffee

Ed Nash's charming smile fills the screen as they cut to a short clip of The Mountaineers smash hit "Used to Be".

'Let's all give a very big Wake Up and Smell the Coffee welcome to Ed Nash, lead singer of indie band The Mountaineers and he also wrote the single "Used to Be" which just happens to be my current earworm!' presenter Rachel Peters announces as the crew and the small studio audience clap.

'Aww thank you. That's a great welcome.' Ed Nash says with his ever-familiar smile.

And it doesn't take too much time until Rachel mentions Evie Del Rio, the name on everyone's lips currently.

'So, Ed, how's your search going for Evie Del Rio or as we all now know her as #thegirlinthesong?' Rachel says, her eyes shining bright as she warms to her theme.

'Well... No one seems to be able to find her. I appreciate she has her reasons for not getting in touch, but who's to say that if we met up again one day the spark wouldn't still be

there?' Ed shrugs but the shrug comes off as overconfident... almost cocky.

'Would you say Evie Del Rio was your first true love?' asks Rachel. *'I'm sure lots of our viewers would love to know.'* She stares right into the camera and smiles, her teeth gleaming white, as if she's looking into the eyes of each viewer, giving them exactly what they want.

'Well, of course. When we were an item, we were always together. Almost inseparable.

'Oh, we all know what that young love feeling is like.' Ethan laughs and sighs reflectively. *'Why do you think "Used to Be" has been such a popular song?'*

'As you just touched on, I think it's because we all know what first love is like.' Ed places his hand on his heart. *'There's nothing more real than the first time you fall in love,'* Ed continues. *"All your senses come alive, and you're counting the hours, the minutes, the seconds until you can see that special someone again.'*

'Oh, you are spot on with your analogy of first love. I think everyone can identify with that.' Rachel says encouragingly. Ed flashes her another one of his killer smiles as Ethan interjects.

'Do you remember your first love, Rachel?' Ethan teases to his partner on TV and in real life too and as she replies, he pretends to be outraged.

'Well, yes, I do actually.' Rachel replies, blushing ever so slightly.

'Enough said about that until we get home.' Ethan concludes, faking a grin. *'So, Ed, if Evie Del Rio were to get in touch, you'd definitely be up for meeting up again?'*

'Of course I would. It would be great to catch up after all these years, but I completely respect that she has most probably moved on, but I still need to know why she left.'

'Good point! She may well have got herself a gorgeous husband by now.' adds Rachel somewhat provocatively.

'Err, yes. Yes, of course, she could be married. I, er, am completely aware that's a possibility.' Ed clears his throat and scratches the side of his head. 'Some of the gang from the old days are hoping to have some sort of reunion around the time The Mountaineers are starting their reunion tour, you know, catch up, find out what's been going on, so it would be great if Evie could join us.'

'Oh, that sounds interesting. Any idea what date that might be?' gushes Rachel, fiddling self-consciously with her hair.

'I'm just in the process of sorting something out with an old friend.'

'And does this old friend have a name?' Ethan coaxes him.

'I couldn't possibly say right now, but rest assured you'll be the first to know.' Ed cleverly retorts.

'Well, that's something to look forward to. And the reunion tour starts in October?' asks Rachel, seeking clarification.

'Yeah, that's right. We're starting in Newcastle on the eighth.'

'We'll make sure to put a link to all the tour dates on our website.' adds Ethan.

'Perhaps you and Rachel would like to come along to one of our London dates?' suggests Ed generously.

'We might just do that. Thanks, Ed.'

'Unfortunately, that's about all we have time for right now with Ed, as we've got to go to the news. Please do come back and see us again soon.' says Rachel, somewhat over enthusiastically under the watchful gaze of her husband.

'Thank you.' replies Ed, flashing a huge smile to the camera.

After the news and a further segment of how to keep your relationship fresh after the birth of your first child, the studio goes straight to the *Loose Women* studio who are doing a piece on how the hashtag #thegirlinthesong has been trending on social media and just what the TikTok generation are making of the mystery of Evie Del Rio by interviewing the influencer and TikTok sleuth Amira Malik.

10

EVIE

Then

Evie was so relieved that finally it was the Christmas holidays. Ed and her were still going strong, spending every available spare moment together. It was difficult though, as both Evie's parents and her school were really ramping up the amount of study she had to do for her exams, which she was due to take the following summer. Ed's parents were much more chilled and relaxed about his revision schedule, but as his mum was a teacher, Ed almost had a ready-made tutor on hand if he needed it. He was also one of those students who didn't really have to try too much with their studies, unlike Evie. If she didn't study, she simply wouldn't pass.

Ginny, Evie's best friend, was having a birthday party just before Christmas. She'd hired out the local church hall and invited nearly all the boys that they knew from St Augustine's. The plan was that Ed and Jamie (Ginny's boyfriend) were going to smuggle in a load of alcohol with Ed's uncle Paul's DJ kit, as he had been booked to DJ at Ginny's party. Paul had also promised that he'd supply them with some weed for the after-party at Ed's house. None of their parents had a clue about their plans and that was half the fun of it.

Ginny and Evie had spent months planning what to wear and, in the end, they were both very pleased with their choices. They'd bought their outfits from Kensington Market over several happy, lazy Saturday afternoons, mooching around the different stalls, soaking up the atmosphere. Even the food smells seemed exotic. They looked in awe at the eclectic bunch of stallholders - who seemed so mature and sophisticated to a couple of young and impressionable girls from Barnes. Evie had chosen the shortest black dress you had ever seen, which had a scooped low-cut back, so there was no chance of her wearing a bra. She'd teamed it with some cowboy boots and a black leather biker jacket. Ginny had a Grecian-style red dress. Her boobs looked even more enormous than usual, thrust forward in a gravity defying bra. Her peroxide hair was piled high on her head. She looked stunning.

The plan for after the official party was that Ginny had told her parents that she was staying with Evie and Evie had told a similar story to her parents, when in fact they were all staying at Ed's house. Ed's parents were away for the night, but Ed's Uncle Paul would be there. Paul seemed cool. He wasn't like any of their parents.

The party was amazing. Paul's choice of music was incredible, so the dance floor was never empty as he played all the latest hits from The Smiths to The Police, The Cure, Siouxsie and the Banshees to New Order. There was some-thing for everyone. You could almost smell the testosterone in the air as the single boys vied for the prettiest of the single girls, plying them with cheap booze as they pulled them closer as the music started to slow down towards the end of the evening. God knows how Ginny's parents didn't have a clue about what was going on, but they had mainly stayed in the little kitchenette area, handing out cokes and lemonades, which little did they know were being mixed with varieties of Cinzano and Bacardi. The tension mounted as Ed and his band, The Propellers, did their soundcheck and Paul helped them set up their kit. Ed was fairly drunk by now, but he still knew how to work a crowd.

Towards the end of their set, Ed decided to say a few words to the audience.

'Thanks to everyone for always supporting us and to the lovely birthday girl Ginny for allowing us to play at her party. I've just written a new song, and I'd like to dedicate it to my girlfriend, Evie.' Ed slurred to the audience, swaying ever so slightly.

He threw Evie one of his special smiles, and suddenly everyone's eyes were on her. The band started with the beginning of the song being just a riot of loud drumming from Mark coupled with Jez's bass guitar repeating the same riff over and over again, before Ed cut in with his vocals, his voice was slightly gruff and husky from an evening of smoking and drinking. The words were raw and personal, and Ed didn't take his eyes off Evie for a second as he sang every word directly to her. It was as if no one else existed in that moment.

The song ended in the same way that it had started - with Mark's heavy drumming and Jez's repetitive riff as Ed's voice repeated the same chorus line of "Forever mine, forever mine" again and again until the music came to an abrupt stop. The crowd clapped and cheered for the band, and Ginny and Evie just looked at each other in complete awe.

'Oh my God, Evie. That song was just beautiful. Have you heard it before?' asked Ginny, giving Evie's hand a squeeze.

'No, never.' Evie shook her head, still in complete shock, her face beaming.

'Ed's always saying he writes songs about me, but I'd never heard any of them until just then. That really was kinda cool.'

Ed sauntered towards Evie, wrapped his arms around her waist and kissed her so passionately he nearly knocked Ginny's mum over, complete with a sagging tray of soggy egg mayonnaise sandwiches. Once they came up for breath, Ginny's mum looked at them both, slightly wide-eyed.

'Sandwich anyone? There are loads left over.' Ginny's mum asked, trying to regain composure after being taken aback by such a passionate kiss.

Ed flashed Ginny's mum one of his killer smiles, patted his taut stomach whilst muttering something about needing to keep his figure in check, politely declining the neglected egg sandwiches.

'Oh, Ed, you're such a lovely young man and a very good singer too. Although all that drumming and guitar noise has given me quite a headache.' wittered Ginny's mum.

Ed's uncle Paul managed to interject cleverly, saying that he would lock up and that her and her husband were to get themselves home and rest up after all their hard work putting on such a good spread. He even said that he would make sure that everyone would take a piece of Ginny's birthday cake home. They didn't need to be asked twice. Ginny's parents had never moved quite so fast. On their way out the door, Ginny's mum asked Evie to thank her parents for having Ginny to stay over. Evie nodded and smiled politely, stifling a giggle.

Paul played "Come on Eileen" for one of the closing songs and finished with "New York, New York", which typically resulted in most of the crowd falling over as everyone linked arms and kicked their legs higher and higher as the song came to an end. Thankfully, Ginny and Evie remained upright. It really was one of the most brilliant parties Evie had ever been to. Ginny had begged her parents to let her have one of her presents early. She'd been hankering after a Polaroid instant camera so she could take loads of photos at the party. Of course, her parents caved in, and the latest must-have camera was in Ginny's possession just in time for the party. They'd had great fun taking photos of each other in various stages of undress while they got ready. The boys had managed to get hold of the Polaroid for a while and took some photos of the band together with quite a few shots of them generally larking about. They spent ages poring over the photos later that night back at Ed's.

11

ED

Then

After they packed Paul's DJ equipment and the band's kit safely away, they all left the church hall to go back to Ed's house. Ed's parents were away, thankfully. Ed's Dad would have been fine about Paul and everyone else staying over but anything whatsoever to do with Paul then Ed's mum always disapproved. So, Ed said that he was staying at Jamie's, and she seemed happy with that. She'd always thought that Jamie's parents were very respectable, what with Mr O'Connor owning his own garage and Mrs O'Connor being a dentist. Ed's parents were staying with his mum's sister in North London for a pre-Christmas party, so she was far too preoccupied to think too much about Ed.

They managed to store Paul's DJing equipment in his van together with their kit. He had a crook lock on the steering wheel, so everything was fairly safe overnight. Ed and the rest of the lads carried the rest of the booze back to Ed's and filled up every spare space in their fridge with the leftover drink from the party.

With the excitement of the party, Ginny had gained a newfound confidence and was drinking and smoking whatever she could lay her hands on. Evie was the same. They cranked up Ed's parents' old stereo and put on one of Paul's mixtapes. They took to the makeshift dance floor in the living room, dancing and gyrating provocatively to Siouxsie and the Banshees' version of "Dear Prudence". Every single guy in the room was transfixed by the girls' antics, and it felt good as Ed smugly thought that Evie was his girl. Jamie looked at Ginny with a wry grin, obviously harbouring similar feelings about Ginny. The boys turned to each other, clinked their drinks together and smiled, as if to say that they really couldn't believe their luck.

The partying continued late into the night and then a few people started to head home. Soon enough, there was just the usual crowd left: Ed and Evie, Jamie and Ginny, Mark and Jez from the band and a few girls from Evie and Ginny's sixth form who had kind of latched on. Paul had hooked up with one of the barmaids from the local pub, and she seemed perfectly happy serving drinks to everyone despite having just finished her shift. It might have something to do with Paul providing her with enough speed to last most people a whole weekend. Every time he, or indeed anyone else, wanted a drink, she was there, content with a little arse squeeze from him as a reward for all her sterling efforts. Paul was in his absolute element.

By 3 a.m. both Evie and Ginny were starting to flag, so the boys decided it was time for bed. Jamie and Ed made several attempts to get both girls upstairs but due to the amount of drink that everyone had consumed, it proved near impossible. Jamie gave up, and Ginny and Jamie ended up crashing on the sofa. Ed eventually picked Evie up and carried her up the remaining stairs to his bedroom. He lay her down gently on his bed and removed her cowboy boots, leaving her dress on. Ed stripped off to his boxer shorts and t-shirt and joined Evie in bed.

It took him some time to drop off, as he was completely wired after the gig and all the drinking. He could still hear Paul and his barmaid friend talking downstairs and the distant hum of Paul's mixtape as he eventually drifted off to sleep.

It seemed like he'd only just dropped off when he felt Evie's arms around him. She was now completely naked, tugging at Ed's boxer shorts. He turned towards her, and they started to kiss with more and more urgency.

'Are you sure this is what you want?' Ed whispered in Evie's ear, as she nodded, kissing him again.

'Of course I do.' Evie replied as they took their time, experimenting and exploring each other's bodies properly for the very first time. Ed reached for a condom from his bedside drawer and debated using it but was too caught up in the moment. Afterwards, Evie gave Ed one final kiss and they both settled back down to sleep, their bodies cuddled close together not wanting this special night to end.

'I love you, Evie Del Rio.' He whispered.

'I know you do. Me too.' Evie sleepily replied as she drifted back off to sleep.

12

ED

Now

I have to say that I think my appearance on *Wake Up and Smell the Coffee* with Rachel and Ethan went extremely well. I managed to flirt a little with Rachel, but not too much as to upset Ethan, and I managed to plug the band's reunion tour. I hope I seemed considerate regarding Evie's feelings, but our teenage relationship, although brief, still seems to make headlines, so I'm going to milk it for as long as I can. The studio provides a car to take me home. I'm keen to get away, so I'm still covered in makeup, the colour on my face resembling a young David Dickinson I think to myself. I sit in the taxi and get ready to watch the much hyped and anticipated *Loose Women* interview with Amira Malik, the influencer and one of the most popular current TikTok sleuths as they were doing a feature about how the hashtag #thegirlinthesong has gained popularity over social media on the back of my appearance on *Wake Up and Smell the Coffee*. Perhaps Amira has had more luck in finding Evie than I have. I put my earphones in and get ready to see what Amira has to say as I watch the titles for Loose Women appear on the screen of my phone.

The show anchor, Kaye Adams starts by introducing Amira Malik and she explains exactly who she is, as the studio and home audiences are not quite the right demographic for TikTok but they are certainly aware of all #thegirlinthesong furore. Amira's poker straight and glossy black hair is tied back in a neat ponytail, her makeup immaculate with her dark eyes accentuated by black kohl and mascara, her full lips covered in a dark red shiny lip gloss. She smiles in all the right places as Kaye Adams starts to put Amira through her paces.

'Welcome Amira. It's so good to finally have you on the show and we are privileged to have you on to talk about the ever trending #thegirlinthesong hashtag, the rockstar Ed Nash from the indie rock band The Mountaineers and his relentless pursuit of trying to find his ex-girlfriend Evie Del Rio.' Kaye begins.

'Thank you for having me, Kaye. Ladies.' Amira replies, remembering to thank everyone, smiling at the rest of the panel.

'It's a fascinating story. A lost love, a load of conspiracy theories, an epic indie love anthem and a rock star who refuses to give up his search for his ex-girlfriend. Back in the eighties it was much easier to disappear as there were no mobile phones or social media, but the thing I'm most surprised about is that Evie Del Rio hasn't come forward herself.' Amira explains straight towards the camera.

The rest of the panel start to join the conversation.

'If a rock god like Ed Nash wrote a love song for me, I wouldn't be hiding away. I'd be right out there!' Colleen Nolan says with her trademark cheeky grin and the audience erupts with laughter.

'Now, I remember interviewing Ed Nash back in the early nineties when The Mountaineers had just changed their band name from The Propellers. They had just released their debut album, and I always found him to be a pleasure to interview. The band hadn't really had much commercial success back then, but he told me all the songs he'd written were about his ex-girlfriend Evie.' Janet Street Porter says, sharing her memories about me.

'I've met him a couple of times at a few award ceremonies.' Brenda Edwards interjects. 'And I agree with Janet, he's one of the good guys who's just curious as to why his ex-girlfriend left without saying goodbye. Obviously, if he hadn't written all those songs about her, then we probably wouldn't be having this conversation. And it's such a great album.'

Amira smiles and nods as the panel talk about their experiences of meeting me and then Kaye takes control of the interview once again.

'So, Amira, you said there were loads of conspiracy theories about just what did happen to Evie Del Rio?'

'Yes, there have been. Some people say that she must have left the UK and there have even been sightings of her as far away as Australia and Thailand, but I think that's just people wanting to have their fifteen minutes of fame. I have it on good authority that Evie Del Rio is still in this country but living under another name.' Amira reveals as both the audience, and the panel make a collective gasp.

'Wow! That's one bold statement.' Kaye says, echoing everyone's response. 'Can you tell us anymore? Where do you get all your information from?' she further probes.

'Much as I'd like to tell you Kaye, I never reveal my sources unless they want me to and on this occasion my source has decided to stay anonymous.' Amira confidently answers Kaye's question with her well-rehearsed off pat answer.

'So, we're not going to get another exclusive this lunchtime, then.' Kaye says with a twinkle in her eye.

'I'm afraid not, although I will be shortly making a couple of exclusive TikTok videos revealing some new information that has come to light.' Amira replies, somewhat smugly.

'It's quite incredible how the #thegirlinthesong hashtag continues to trend, isn't it? Kaye asks Amira.

'I know, as hashtags go, it has a catchy ring to it and until Ed Nash finds #thegirlinthesong, I don't think this story is going away in a hurry….' Amira replies mysteriously.

Loose Women cut to the much played "Used to Be" video and the audience clap along in time to the music as the camera pans back to Amira.

'I'd like to give a very big thank you to Amira for joining us today and here's a little message to Evie Del Rio #the-girlinthesong herself – You're welcome any time on our show, that's if Amira doesn't find you first!' Kaye says straight at the camera with a big smile, as the audience claps again, and the show goes straight to a break.

I'm almost home so I take out my earphones and put my phone in my pocket. I didn't come off too bad on Loose Women, but the most interesting thing is the fact that Evie is still in the UK but using a different name which is probably why it's been so difficult to find her. I tried to speak to Evie's parents after she first left to find out where she was, but no one ever answered the door and then their house was sold pretty quickly after that. Not that Evie's mum would have given me the time of day. She was never my greatest fan.

Once home, I make myself a coffee and take a seat on my balcony, taking advantage of another beautiful sunny day, and begin to scroll through my social media feeds. Perhaps now is the time to hire my own private detective to try and track Evie down myself. Virginia has privately messaged me on Instagram again, congratulating me on my appearance. She's keen to catch up and probing me to give a definitive date to do so. Virginia was always a nice enough girl, but not a patch on Evie. We did have a bit of a thing way back, not long after Evie left. I just remember it not feeling right at the time. It was too soon after Evie and we both regretted it as soon as it happened. I left the area where we all used to live not long after. I send her back a quick message confirming that I can meet her at her house one evening this week. It will be more discreet this way, and I also don't really want her to know exactly where I live just now.

The consensus generally was positive on social media after my TV appearance, which I'm happy with. Mission accomplished.

I look out over the balcony and admire the pleasing view of the carefully manicured gardens below. I could never have afforded to live somewhere like this if the TV series and then the documentary hadn't picked up on my song. Life is good but something is missing.

I glance at my DMs again to see if Virginia has replied yet. Nothing. It would be interesting to catch up after all these years. I've lost touch with most of the old gang except for my fellow band members. When we were growing up, it wasn't as easy as it is nowadays to keep in touch. If you moved without a forwarding address or a new telephone number, then you could just disappear. Which is exactly what happened with Evie and then again with me.

After Evie left, I just wanted to get away, to try and reinvent myself and not be reminded of her every single day. I spent a whole month after she went just answering questions as to her whereabouts. No one around me understood what it felt like to be me having your girlfriend just up sticks and leave without saying a word. It destroyed my self-confidence. When Paul offered me a way out, I took it. My mother was heartbroken when I left with him. My father, however, would have loved to have had the guts to come with us, but he knew it would break my mother's heart to lose both her only son and her husband. They're still together to this day. My relationship with them is somewhat strained, but we've been in touch since #thegirlinthesong media storm. My mother will never forgive Paul for taking me away, but at the time it seemed like my only choice: to get away and start over.

Paul, unfortunately, has been in and out of prison over the years. Not surprisingly mainly for dealing, some shoplifting and for being drunk and disorderly, as he's always getting into fights when he's drunk. I keep in touch, bung him a bit of money every now and again because I owe him for being there when I needed him. I also like to keep him away from the press. I don't need some journalist probing Paul about my past. Paul was the one who first introduced me to drugs. I was quite a mess by the time Paul went to prison. I couldn't hold down a job, as I was either pissed or high, usually both. I couldn't hold down a relationship, and I was always getting asked to leave bands that I'd joined. They used to love me at first, but once I'd made that first good impression and they got to know the real me, they would let me go. I just couldn't sustain being sober long enough to do the one thing that I'm good at; being the frontman in a rock band. Thankfully, I've had my second chance with being in a successful band.

It's strange to think that all my misfortune started with Evie leaving me and yet somehow my resurgence today is all to do with the song that I wrote for her all those years ago. I just wish I could talk to her to find out what happened. I'm almost fifty, and I've never been married or had a family. I feel like I've missed out. Don't get me wrong, I'm so grateful for a second shot at getting my music heard but my personal life's a mess.

My phone beeps with a DM from Virginia inviting me over to her house in Hampton Hill tonight, with the promise of a home-cooked meal. It does sound inviting. I message her back, agreeing to meet. I'm not meeting her until 8 p.m., so I have the rest of the day to myself. I decide to hit the gym, do some weights, go for a run and relax in the jacuzzi in readiness for dinner.

I reach Virginia's house just after 8p.m. and discover her to be a very pleasant surprise. Obviously, it's the first time we've seen each other in over thirty years but we've picked up quite effortlessly, and I'm really enjoying the evening. She's cooked an amazing roast beef dinner with all the trimmings. I haven't eaten such a delicious home-cooked meal in years. Virginia has two ex-husbands and two daughters, Sasha and Shannon, who she's mainly brought up single-handedly. You can easily tell how proud she is of them. They sound like a nice, tight family unit. The more I hear about her family, the more I regret the choices I've made over the years and the fact I'm fundamentally alone.

'I'll just go upstairs and get the photos.' says Virginia, leaving the kitchen. 'Help yourself to another beer if you like.'

She continues down the hallway. 'What are your plans for tomorrow? Do you have an early start?' Virginia asks, waiting for a response with her foot on the bottom step, ready to climb the stairs.

'We start our rehearsals for the upcoming tour, and we've got a meeting with our manager, so it will be busy but hopefully nice and productive but yes, thanks, I think I will have another beer.'

'Can you just top up my glass please? The bottle's in the fridge.' Virginia calls down from halfway up the stairs.

'Sure thing.' I call back, grabbing myself another beer and topping up Virginia's prosecco.

I sip my beer as Virginia returns from upstairs with a bunch of Polaroids. She's also carrying a tray. Within seconds, she's carefully arranged all the Polaroids in a row across the tray.

'I've tried to put them in date order as best I can. You might be able to shed some light on some of the ones that I can't remember the dates of.' Virginia continues.

We spend a few minutes laughing and joking about the state of our haircuts and clothing choices from the eighties until Virginia focuses our attention on a couple of the later photos of me and Evie. I remember the day quite vividly, as it was an unusually warm day in early April. A big crowd of us had gone to hang out at Mark's. His parents had installed their own swimming pool in their garden, inspired by their Spanish villa. It was a great novelty back then, and Mark's parents were more than happy to have us all over to share in the fun of having an outdoor swimming pool in London.

'Look at Evie in this photo.' says Virginia, pointing a carefully manicured nail at Evie, who was sitting on the side of the pool, dangling her legs in the water, watching and laughing as the rest of us splashed around in the pool. 'Don't you think it's odd that Evie is the only one of us not in swimwear?'

I shake my head. 'Not really. I think she forgot her swim-suit that day, if I remember. She'd had another argument with her mum about going out when she was grounded, and she stormed out of the house without it.'

'Well, the Evie I used to know would have just jumped in the pool in her underwear, but she seemed very hesitant on that day to undress and get in the water. Don't you think that's odd?'

'Err no, not really. Maybe she was on her period? I dunno. Evie was a girl with her own rules.' I say, feeling slightly uncomfortable as to where this conversation could be heading.

Virginia continues to scrutinise Evie in the photo. 'Don't you think she looks like she's got a bit of a tummy on her?'

I stare harder at the photo. 'Umm, I didn't really notice, to be fair.' I reply. I had forgotten that once Ginny has a bee in her bonnet, she won't let it go.

Virginia leans back, taking her eyes from the photo to me. 'Well, I have a theory. Pass me my glass, and I'll explain.'

Virginia doesn't waste any time once I pass over her glass. She takes a big swig, wrinkling her nose from the bubbles. 'I think Evie was pregnant. That's why she left. I guess her parents found out. Did you have any idea?'

Virginia's comments are like a sucker punch. A family is all I've ever wanted. Surely that can't be the reason Evie left?

'I don't think she was. I think I would have known.' I reply somewhat defensively, not really knowing quite what to say to Virginia but trying to shut down this awkward topic of conversation.

'No disrespect, but you were never and probably will never be an expert on pregnancy.' says Virginia, completely dismissing my view. 'I've had two babies. I know what it's like to be pregnant, the changes that your body goes through. You can see how her waist has slightly thickened here.' She points to it in the photo. 'She definitely looks bigger. Her boobs look bigger too. I'm surprised you didn't notice them. I can't believe we didn't notice all those years ago, but I guess we were young.' she concludes, staring at me, waiting for me to respond.

'Well, I'm not so sure. I'd like to think I would have noticed if Evie was pregnant, but I suppose it does explain a lot. I guess I'll never know. I can't exactly ask her, can I?' I eventually say, completely dumbfounded by Virginia's suggestion that Evie might have been pregnant. This is not what I expected from tonight's meet up. I just feel emotion-less, my brain struggling to process, still wanting to deny the whole thing because... the idea of nearly having everything I've ever wanted and losing it is harder than thinking I was never even close.

'I know it's a lot to digest, Ed and I may be wrong, but it does explain why Evie left in such a rush. I know you two were having sex, because you know, girls talk.' Virginia stated.

'We only had sex a handful of times. We were careful....' I begin before Virginia cuts me off abruptly.

'I know Evie wasn't on the pill, so it's very possible that you weren't as careful as you thought you were.' Virginia said, almost scolding me like I was one of her children.

'I guess it's a possibility, I suppose. But how will I ever know?' I ponder.

'You'll just have to hope that someone knows where Evie is, or she might reach out herself I guess.' Virginia says, before adding. 'Look I know this is a lot to take in, so I promise I won't say anything to the press or release the photos, ok?'

'Thanks Virginia. I really do appreciate that.' I say, hoping that our teenage friendship is enough for this now almost stranger not to take her thoughts about a possible pregnancy to the press. It's a risk I must take.

13

GENIE

Now

Ever since the first episode of Musical Muses: The Girl in the Song dropped on Netflix featuring Ed 'Nasher' Nash from the band The Mountaineers and his now iconic indie love song, my life has never been the same.

Being the inspiration behind the ever-popular song "Used to Be" by 90s indie band The Mountaineers is probably one of the most intrusive and mortifying things to ever happen to me in my adult life. And now the TikTok star Amira Malik has named me, along with two other women as the potential 'real' Evie Del Rio, both Gray and the kids are being hassled. The children have been taunted at school, and I know that there have been whispers at Gray's work too. As more and more people watch the Netflix documentary, the furore and hysteria as to exactly who the girl in the song really is, has only just intensified. Ever since that interview everyone has started searching for me, the hashtag #thegirlinthesong had been trending on all social media channels and "Used to Be" is currently one of the most popular songs used on TikTok.

The rumours of a supposed pregnancy have only added fuel to the fire.

Cassie and Will are just as obsessed with finding out the identity of Evie Del Rio as the rest of the country is and my story to them is that I knew him when I was younger. My song has been played everywhere: on the radio, at weddings and the original BBC2 TV drama series that used "Used to Be" as its' theme tune has just been repeated on BBC1 reaching a brand-new primetime audience. Everyone been using Shazam to find out who the song was by, and after Ed's appearance on the Netflix documentary, "Used to Be" is now one of the most downloaded songs of the year.

The catalyst must be the recent piece that The Daily Mail published, complete with some awful photos that they somehow got hold of, picturing myself, Ed and our assorted friends at a pool party in the mid 80s. That was the one sure way my parents were going to find out that Ed Nash was back in my life as my mother is an avid Daily Mail reader.

The Daily Mail
Who's That Girl?

Do you know the identity of #thegirlinthesong?
By Zane Peters, Showbusiness News Editor

Indie rock god, Ed 'Nasher' Nash, 49, lead singer of the band The Mountaineers is desperate to find his former girl-friend, Evie Del Rio who ever since the Netflix documentary Musical Muses: The Girl in the Song, is now known across social media as #thegirlinthesong. Ed last saw her in the mid 80s when they were just teenagers but unfortunately up until recently that's where the trail runs cold – until now.....

The Daily Mail has recently acquired some never seen

before photos of the possible last sighting of Evie Del Rio at a pool party at a friend's house.

Accompanying the article there are numerous photos showing Ed and I and our various friends enjoying ourselves at Mark's pool party. Most of the teenagers are in swimwear except for me as in most of the photos I'm seated on a sun lounger or otherwise can be seen dangling my feet in the pool, dressed in a white shirt and a grey skirt smiling into the camera, my blue eyes squinting against the April sunshine.

I really can't believe my past has come back to haunt me. And to be made so public too. I have worked so hard to reinvent myself as a respectable wife and mother, and I really thought I'd finally achieved a life that my parents could be truly proud of. If only Ed hadn't released that song. I remember him telling me that all the songs he'd written about me would one day make him famous, and I suppose he was right. I had to tell Gray that I did know Ed and that we had dated very briefly. He doesn't know the full story yet, and for now I want to keep it that way.

I've basically stopped going out. You see, Ed has really exaggerated and embellished our story, and although most of the stuff he has said has an element of truth to it, I really don't want to be reminded of my past.

Poor Gray and our children, along with the rest of the world are about to find out just who Evie Del Rio really is.

I thought my secrets would remain safe after all these years, but with Ed's resurgence of popularity, he's lit the touchpaper, sat back and watched it burn. Thankfully, his uncle Paul seems to have vanished off the face of the earth, so at least that's one less person to worry about selling his story to the press.

Ed is relentless in his pursuit of fame, and he's now got the recognition he always craved. I don't suppose he even realises how much I've changed over the years - I have so much to lose. I'm not the same wild Evie he met all those years ago who didn't give a damn about the future. Evie just lived for the moment and to hell with the consequences. It's only since I met, and married Gray and we had our children that I realised what real, true love is. What Ed and I had all those years ago was complete infatuation and pure lust.

14

ED

Now

Do you know where #thegirlinthesong is?
By Zane Peters, Showbusiness News Editor

I catch sight of the headline of The Daily Mail, accompanied by a series of very familiar photos, just a week after I'd seen the same photos at Virginia's house. She'd promised that she would keep them safe and not do anything with them for the moment, but I guess being on her own, she obviously needed the money. Virginia had hinted that she had thought there was the possibility that Evie was pregnant and that had been playing on my mind ever since. Was that the reason Evie left without saying goodbye? We'd only had sex a few times and had mainly used condoms as far as I could remember....

I open the TikTok app on my phone and watch TikTok's current queen, Amira Malik and her recent conspiracy theory about the possible identity of #thegirlinthesong. There were at least three names in the frame. One was a cashier called Evie Beckett who worked part-time in Tesco in Wandsworth, the second was a primary school teacher called Genevieve Ellis from Barnes where we all used to live, and the final one was an attractive well-heeled housewife from Richmond called Genie McNamara. All were around the right age, but I wasn't convinced that any of them were Evie, as it was hard to see their faces close up. It was Amira's second TikTok video that stopped me in my tracks, as she had picked up on the fact that the real reason that Evie had left all those years ago was because she was pregnant. She'd even circled in on Evie's slightly rounded tummy from Virginia's photos.

TikTok exploded with both Amira's videos going viral and #thegirlinthesong was once more trending on all social media channels and Evie's song, "Used to Be" continued to trend as more and more people used the song in their TikTok posts.

I close my TikTok app down and shoot a short curt WhatsApp to Virginia.

I thought we'd agreed that you wouldn't do anything with the Polaroids

A minute later she'd replied.

I'm so sorry Ed. It wasn't me. It was my ex – Callum, Shannon's dad. I think he took copies of the Polaroids the day after we met. Shannon must have mentioned that you were over the other night to him. I thought it was odd that he'd popped over. I'm really so very sorry. V

Her reply seemed genuine enough but maybe her and her ex-husband were in on it together.

I message her back.

Not a lot either of us can do about it now. Maybe with the photos being out there, Evie might get in touch and I can finally find out the truth

Virginia sent another message.

I would never have sold the photos, but I am sorry that this has happened. Hope you find what you're looking for. V

I just did a thumbs up emoji back. She seemed genuine

enough. If her and her ex had made some money out of it, then fair enough. I've exploited Evie enough since "Used to Be" has had a resurgence so I'm hardly blameless.

After Amira's TikTok video went viral, "Used to Be" was again one of the most streamed songs on ITunes and Spotify which I was sure our manager Toby Turner would be delighted by! It all helped but was I any nearer to finding out the real truth about Evie?

15

EVIE

Then

How the Christmas holidays dragged without Evie seeing either Ed or Ginny. Her parents had kept her under lock and key ever since Ginny's party. They'd had a deal: if they allowed her to go to the party, then she had to do loads of revision for her mock exams over the holidays once they returned from Auntie Maureen's house on the twenty-seventh. Ginny's party was amazing. Evie couldn't believe that they had all got away with staying at Ed's house. His uncle was a right laugh, and he certainly knew how to throw a party, and because he was older, all their parents seemed to trust him. Well, apart from Ed's mum, who'd always thought that he was an idiot. She'd have gone mad if she'd known that everyone had stayed at their house overnight.

Ginny had taken loads of photos with her new Polaroid camera at her party. Because of Evie's enforced incarceration, they still hadn't managed to catch up and go through them properly. Evie remembered taking one of Ginny where she was just going to blow out the candles on her cake. She'd looked amazing.

Evie hadn't even been able to use the phone to call Ginny. To be fair, their calls did go on a bit. They would chat about what they'd just been up to despite having just seen each other earlier that day. But Evie had formulated a plan to try and meet up with everyone.

Evie's Mum was in the kitchen, fastidiously ironing bedsheets, so Evie took out the remaining bottle of milk from the fridge and purposely knocked it all over the kitchen table. Evie's mum was completely outraged by her daughter's clumsiness, and as Evie half-heartedly cleared up the mess, she suggested popping to the corner shop to buy some more. Incredibly, her mother fell for it, mainly because of her coffee addiction. Evie was out that door before her mother had the chance to change her mind.

Evie ran to the corner shop and straight past it, hoping the fact that she was running had given her extra time away from the house. She planned to call in at the corner shop on the way back. She legged it over to Ginny's, as she lived the closest, and rang the bell impatiently.

A very sleepy-looking Ginny answered the door. 'Hello, stranger.' It was only 9:30 a.m., but clearly Ginny didn't have to get up at the crack of dawn like Evie had to, as she was still dressed in her nightclothes.

'Can I come in? I haven't got long.' Evie said breathlessly.

'Sure. Come in. Mum's gone to visit one of her friends, so she'll be ages.' Ginny yawned and stepped aside for her to enter.

They went through to the kitchen, and Ginny poured them both an orange juice.

'I've been wondering what happened to you.' said Ginny, handing Evie a glass.

'Well, you know there were conditions for me to go to your party, don't you?'

Ginny nodded.

'They've kept me indoors since we got back from my aunt's house so I can revise. I'm going mad. They won't even let me use the phone. Can you believe that? Mum's put a lock on it. I mean, I know I agreed to restrictions but... this is not what I thought at all.'

'Blimey, that's a bit extreme, isn't it? Oh, you poor thing.' said Ginny, giving Evie a hug.

'So, what have I missed?' Evie said, eager to catch up on all the latest gossip, knowing that she had limited time away from the house.

'Not a lot, to be honest. I'd have called round for you but we only got back from my nan's house late last night. Everyone's been forced to see family over the Christmas break, although there's talk about a party on New Year's Eve.'

'No, I can't believe it. Whose party?' Evie asked impatiently.

'Mark's. The band are going to play a few numbers.'

'It's so not fair that I'm locked in the house all over the holidays.' Evie pounded her fist on Ginny's kitchen table with pure frustration.

'I know. They are really being overstrict, aren't they?' agreed Ginny. 'Do you want my mum to have a word with your mum to see if you can stay here for the night?' she added, desperately trying to find a solution to Evie's latest set of rules.

'I don't think it will make any difference, to be honest. They have basically banned me from going out anywhere so I can study. I only managed to get out the house just now because I purposely spilt the remaining pint of milk and offered to buy a new one. Which reminds me. I'd better get to the shops, otherwise she'll be sending out a search party for me.' Evie explained, as she glanced at Ginny's kitchen clock.

'Why don't you take a pint from our fridge? We've got loads. Mum won't miss it.'

'Thanks, Ginny. You're a star.'

'No probs.' she said, opening the fridge. 'Listen, why don't we send letters as a way of contacting each other whilst you're grounded. Once I've found out a bit more about the New Year's Eve party, I will leave a note in some clingfilm under that big flowerpot where you keep your spare key outside your porch. If you want to contact me, you do the same. I'll pop along to check for messages when your mum's car isn't on the drive.'

'Sounds like a plan.' Evie agreed. 'I'd better run. Love you, Ginny.'

'Right back atcha.' she replied, thrusting the pint of milk into Evie's hand.

Evie ran as fast as she could to get back home, stopping at the end of her street to catch her breath. Once Evie reached her house, she spotted the curtain twitching. Her Mum was obviously looking out for her.

'You took your time.' she scolded as she opened the front door.

'I bumped into Ginny at the shop.'

'Well, get inside and make me a coffee. I trust you remembered the milk?' She snapped.

'Of course.' Evie replied, holding the pint of milk aloft triumphantly as she stepped past her, into the house.

She made her mum a coffee and a cup of tea for herself and spent the remainder of the day pretending to revise while listening to a compilation tape that Ed had made her. One side featured songs from bands like The Smiths, Depeche Mode, Aztec Camera and New Order. On the B-side, Ed had recorded some of his own music with The Propellers, including the song he played at Ginny's party. Listening to that tape helped to maintain Evie's sanity with her enforced incarceration.

It wasn't so bad when Evie's dad was at home. He could always be persuaded to see both sides of an argument or discussion. But that could also be a problem. It depended on who was the most persuasive. Evie or her Mum? Evie decided to try and get her dad on side once she knew a bit more about the New Year's Eve party. Evie thought that Ginny's secret letter idea was genius, but she was worried that they would get rumbled by her mum. She seemed to have a sixth sense whenever Evie was planning anything.

She'd been incarcerated in her bedroom for what seemed like an eternity, although it was only 12:30 p.m., so she decided to venture downstairs for some lunch. Her mum was busy meticulously ironing her dad's work shirts in the kitchen, almost trance-like. She couldn't work her mum out. She was a pillar of the community: she helped at church every Sunday, she always baked for the Holy Communion breakfasts, and she regularly did charity box collections for the local children's charity door to door. Evie used to help her when she was younger, carefully peeling off the smiley stickers to give to the people who'd kindly donated, but she was a cold fish towards her own family. Evie couldn't even remember the last time her mother had held her close or kissed her when she was upset. She often wondered why her dad stayed with her mum all those years, as she was as cold to him as she was to her. It was only Phillip, Evie's older brother, who had long since flown the nest, that made her mum happy and had a way of making her smile.

That's why Evie liked staying at other people's houses, as it was nice to see how other families lived. Ginny's parents, although a bit fuddy-duddy, always held hands whenever they went out, and you could see how Ginny was completely adored by them both - a kind of brightness shone from their eyes. Even Ed's parents were very tactile.

'Don't make a mess in the kitchen. I've only just finished cleaning it after you spilt the milk earlier.' snapped Evie's Mum, as she momentarily looked up from her beloved ironing.

'I won't.' Evie snapped back, as she reached up for the Breville toastie maker from one of the high cupboards.

'I asked you not to make a mess, Evie. Don't use the Breville, dear. It takes ages to clean, and I don't suppose you'll be the one cleaning it, will you?' she grumbled.

Evie gritted her teeth against what felt like the start of an argument. 'I will clean it out, Mum. Please, I just really fancy a toastie. I'm starving.'

'No, it's not happening today. Use the normal toaster.'

'What is the point in having a Breville if we can't use it?' Evie shouted, slamming the door of the cupboard with as much force as she could manage. The door bounced off its usual closed resting place due to the slam and settled slightly ajar.

'Don't use that tone with me, young lady. I have given you an option. If you don't like it, you can do without and go to your room.' Her mum crossed her arms and moved to stand right in front of her daughter.

'Stick your Breville, I'm going out.' Evie pushed past her mum and flounced out of the kitchen.

'You are not allowed out. We agreed. You have to…'

Evie didn't stay long enough to hear the rest of what her mum had to say, but she'd heard it all before. She grabbed her jacket, slamming the door behind her, making sure the whole house vibrated. Fuelled by pure rage, she ran all the way to Ginny's, cursing her mother, knowing full well that Ginny's mum would let her use their Breville. Despite ringing on

Ginny's doorbell numerous times, there was no reply. She sat on Ginny's doorstep in the hope that she'd reappear, but after about ten minutes, she gave up and walked over to Ed's house.

It had been ages since they'd seen each other, and Evie was really missing him. It took her a good twenty minutes to walk to Ed's house from Ginny's. She rang the bell and waited, and she was just about to leave when she heard someone walking towards the front door. The door opened. It was Paul.

'Who do we have here, then?' he said with a wry grin. 'Well, if it isn't the lovely Evie. Come in. Come in. Ed's not in right now, but please come in and wait.'

'Umm, don't worry, I'll come back later.' Evie smiled awkwardly and started to turn away.

'He won't be long. He said earlier that he wouldn't be late. We're going to have a bit of a jam when he gets back. He's been working on some new material. He'd be cross if I didn't insist that you stay.' Paul opened the door wider, the wry grin still on his face.

She bit her bottom lip, trying to decide what to do. She didn't have any other options currently, and it wasn't like she didn't know Paul. It couldn't do any harm to just wait for ten minutes or so.

'Thanks. I'll come in and wait if it's no bother.' she relented.

'No bother at all.' he said, ushering her through to the sitting room, the same smile plastered all over his face.

'Fancy a drink?'

'No, I'm fine thanks.' She replied as she sat down.

'You don't mind if I carry on, do you?' asked Paul, pointing at the guitar propped up in the corner of the room.

'No, go for it.'

Paul started to play his guitar as Evie stared out the window, wondering how much longer Ed would be. It seemed odd being in the same house as Paul without Ed or the usual hangers-on. Plus being sober. Evie didn't think she'd ever seen Paul without a drink in his hand or a spliff between his lips. He always looked quite cool, but that day, in the harsh daylight, he just looked old. She watched as Paul's yellow nicotine-stained fingers whizzed all over his guitar. She could definitely see where Ed got his musical talent from.

She glanced at the time: nearly 2p.m. She hadn't even had any lunch yet, and she was starving. Ed surely wouldn't be much longer?

'Do you play, Evie?' enquired Paul.

'No. I just like music in general. I wish I had a musical talent like you and Ed.'

'I'm sure you've got some other special talents.' Paul licked his top lip showing his yellowing teeth and Evie immediately pretended not to notice or indeed hear what he had just said. 'Well, I could always teach you the basics of playing the guitar if you ever wanted to learn, you know.' he added.

'Oh, I'm fine, thanks. How much longer do you think Ed will be?' she asked, swiftly changing the subject, slowly pulling her skirt down to cover her knees, feeling uncomfortable with Paul's change of tone.

I'm sure he won't be too long now.'

'I don't want to intrude. I might just go.' Evie stammered.

'Stop stressing. Here, have a beer. It will chill you out.' Paul said forcibly, as he opened a couple of cans of Foster's.

'It's a bit early for me, and I haven't had any lunch yet.'

'Well, just sip it. It will pass the time until Ed gets here.'

'Umm, ok. Thanks.' Evie said, reluctantly taking the can.

Paul took a big swig of his beer and then ran the tip of his tongue over his top lip suggestively, looking straight at Evie as he did it. Evie took a little sip from her can, feeling the bitterness of the beer burning the back of her throat as she swallowed it. This whole situation didn't feel right to her. Even being back at home being shouted at by her mum seemed preferable to this. She couldn't put her finger on it but for the first time ever Paul unsettled her.

Evie wasn't sure if it was telepathy or just good timing but within a minute or so, she heard a key in the door, and in came Ed. She was so pleased to see him that she nearly knocked him off his feet as she rushed towards the door to greet him.

'Woah, that's a great welcome.' said Ed, as he greeted her with a big kiss. 'How did you escape your mum?'

'We had a row, and I walked out.' She explained.

'I see good old Uncle Paul has been looking after you.' Ed remarked, noticing her beer.

'I always treat the ladies well. You know that, Eddy boy. Do you fancy joining us for a beer?' he said.

'I might later, but right now I'm starving. Have you eaten, Evie?'

She shook her head. 'Not yet. That was what the row was about. Mum wouldn't let me use the Breville.'

Ed frowned. 'What's up with that woman? I think we've still got one in the back of the cupboard. Let me have a look.'

It didn't take long for Ed to locate the sandwich maker, and they were soon happily eating delicious ham and cheese toasties together at the table in the living room. Evie was so relieved to be away from Paul and she'd purposely left her beer behind too. Although she enjoyed a drink with her friends, drinking in the middle of the day with a grown man didn't seem right.

They finished off the toasties and then Ed made them both a steaming hot chocolate, which they took upstairs, leaving Paul with just his beer and guitar for company. They laid back on Ed's bed and just enjoyed being together once again. Evie closed her eyes and snuggled up to Ed, feeling relaxed for the first time in ages.

'Evie, your mum phoned to see if you're here.'

The sound of Paul's voice, jolted Evie awake. She couldn't believe that they'd both fallen asleep.

'Did you tell her I'm here?' Evie anxiously shouted back, mouth dry, wishing she'd drunk her hot chocolate as she looked at it cold on the bedside table.

'No, of course not. Said I haven't seen you in ages.'

'Ok, thanks for that.'

'She sounded properly pissed off though.' he added, his voice getting quieter as he wandered away from the bottom of the stairs.

Ed yawned and stretched next to Evie. 'I suppose you'd better get going. Where are you going to say you've been?' he asked.

Evie sighed. 'I'll say I went window shopping. I can't say I was at Ginny's. My mum may well have phoned there as well, although she was out earlier when I called round.'

'I do hope I wasn't the second choice to hang out with today.' Ed said playfully, running his hand through his tousled hair.

Evie rolled her eyes. 'You know Ginny's house is closer than yours, you dingbat. That's why I tried her house first.'

'I'm only sorry I wasn't here earlier. I can think of loads of things we could have got up to this afternoon.' Ed says as he pushed Evie on his bed with a forceful and passionate kiss.

'Don't.' She tried to object, unlocking her lips from his. 'I really want to stay here with you. But this really isn't helping…'

Ed slipped his hand under her top and began kissing her with more and more urgency. Needless to say, she didn't leave Ed's house for at least another forty-five minutes. They slipped downstairs, greeted by the sounds of Paul playing guitar and singing the same lines over and over.

'Uncle Paul, Evie's leav—'

'Oh, don't disturb him on my account.' she said, trying to sound as though she was being polite, when in reality she just didn't want to have to see Paul again.

'He'll be annoyed if I don't let him know you're leaving; you know how much he likes having you around.' Ed grabbed Evie's hand to lead her to Paul, leaving her no chance to protest.

They walked through to the back room and Evie waved and mouthed "goodbye" to Paul, who had stopped singing and was busily rolling another joint.

'See ya, Evie. Don't worry, your secret is safe with me.' He grinned, and she faked a grin back.

She made a swift exit towards the front door and gave Ed one last kiss as she left to face her mother as she would still be fuming from earlier and the fact she'd stormed off and had spent the whole afternoon out. It also looked extremely unlikely that she'd be able to make it to Mark's New Year's Eve party, as her mum would certainly punish her for today. She'd have to try to make amends and get Dad onside. She could usually talk her dad round, as she'd always been the apple of his eye. Her mother and her, however, had never been close. It's as if she resented her daughter's youth. When her parents had first met, her mother was a natural blonde with aquamarine eyes and an hourglass figure. Her dad had always said that he'd had to fight off many an admirer to finally get Felicity to himself. She was still an attractive woman, but family life seemed to have sucked her dry. She never let herself have any fun.

They'd met at the local dance when they were both seventeen, and since that day, they'd never been apart. Felicity had never been a girl's girl. She had two much older brothers and her older sister Maureen, who was a bit of a religious nut. Felicity adored Evie's older brother Phillip but she always bemoaned that it was having Evie had ruined her figure. 'Sorry, I didn't ask to be born.' was always Evie's staple reply, much to the irritation of her mother.

A mere twenty minutes and Evie was back home again. An all-time record. It was amazing what an afternoon with Ed could do for a girl's energy levels. Evie pushed the garden gate open and walked up the path. She reached for the spare key, which was always kept under the flowerpot outside their porch, but it seemed to have mysteriously disappeared. She rang the bell and waited for her mum to let her in, but she didn't come to the door. Evie sighed and sat herself on the doorstep. There was no point ringing the bell again – she had realised that her Mum was definitely inside, definitely knew that she was here and was definitely ignoring her. Evie brought her knees to her chest and wrapped her arms around her legs, trying to protect herself from the cold December evening, Thankfully, her dad returned a little bit earlier than normal from work, although her whole body was practically numb at this point.

'Evie, what on earth are you doing outside in the cold?' Her dad frowned, taking his coat off and gently draping it around his daughter's shoulders.

'I had an argument with Mum, and she's locked me out.' She said as she wiped her runny nose with the back of her hand as her dad's coat enveloped her like a warm hug.

'I'm sure your mum wouldn't have locked you out on purpose. There must be a logical explanation why she hasn't answered, her dad said, who never thought the worst of his wife. He opened the door, ushering her into the warmth. 'Put the kettle on and make some tea to get yourself warmed up.'

Evie went through to the kitchen. The kettle was still warm, so her mum couldn't be too far away. She busied herself while her dad called out for his wife. With no sign of her downstairs, her dad sprinted up the stairs. Evie listened to his footsteps and could tell by the different creaks that he'd gone straight to their bedroom. She heard her mum's raised voice being softened by her dad's hushed tones. Evie made herself and her dad a cuppa, remembering to add two sugars into his favourite mug, which she'd bought for him a few years ago for Father's Day, emblazoned with "World's Greatest Dad".

She sat at the table, drank her tea, enjoying the feeling returning to her fingers and toes. Ten minutes later, her dad came back downstairs. He took a seat opposite his daughter and had a big swig of his tea.

'Thanks for this. You even remembered the extra sugar.' he said gratefully. 'Don't let your mum know; I'm supposed to be on a diet.' He added as he winked at his daughter.

'Your secret's safe with me.' she replied with a furtive smile, happy that he wanted her onside. 'Where's Mum?' Evie asked. She didn't want her dad to think she had listened in in any way, even though she couldn't hear what was being said.

'She's got one of her migraines, you know, the ones that keep her practically bedridden. That's why she didn't answer the door when you rang the bell.' her dad explained, and Evie thought sadly that he genuinely believed his own words. 'We'll talk later about what happened earlier because right now I want to change out of my suit and have some dinner. I'm starving. I don't think Mum had time to sort out any dinner, but we could pop down to Wimpy if you fancy?'

'I'd love that. We haven't done that for ages.' Evie said, as she stood up and put her empty mug in the sink. 'I'll just change into some warmer clothes.'

Evie popped upstairs to grab her new black and red stripy mohair jumper, and as she did so she glanced briefly through the crack in her parents' bedroom door. Her mum was propped up in bed, reading the latest Jackie Collins paperback. She clearly didn't have a migraine, as Evie had suspected, she was just sulking after today. Just an excuse not to have to spend time with Evie and her dad. Well, sod her, Evie thought. They would have a nice meal out without her. And Evie had decided that she would broach the subject of Mark's party. She was sure that she would be able to talk her dad round without her mum being there.

16

GENIE

Now

Well, tonight is the night I will finally tell Gray the whole truth. He deserves to know absolutely everything, and I think I'm just about ready to tell him everything. I am so grateful to Gray for rescuing me all those years ago. In fact, moving to Brighton was the catalyst in changing my life for the better, because not only did I meet my future husband, I also met my best friend, Maura. I never believed in fate until I moved to Brighton and met them both. They were clearly sent to save me.

I've got in a selection of beers and a couple of bottles of rosé. By the time Gray arrives home, I'm already halfway through my first glass of wine. Dutch courage, I suppose.

'Hi, gorgeous.' Gray says, planting a kiss on the top of my head. 'How are you doing?'

'I'm ok. Let me get you a drink. What's your poison?' I say, getting off the sofa.

'You always used to say that to me when we first met, you know.'

'Did I?' I reply, amazed still by what a caring and considerate man Gray is and how he always has a knack of remembering things about when we first met.

'I'll join you in a glass of wine although I must confess, I did have a couple of beers at work with the lads. You ok?' He pauses, as if listening for movement upstairs. 'No kids?'

'I'm fine. Cassie is at Mel's and Will is at Tommy's so we've got the house to ourselves but there is something I wanted to talk to you about.' I reply, nervously chewing on the side of my lip.

'Well, why don't we have something to eat first and then we can have a good catch up.'

'Sure.' I agree, knowing my secret's still all mine for now. To be honest, I'd probably prefer to talk to Gray alone first without the kids here.

I fetch some food I cooked earlier from the kitchen and bring it to the conservatory, placing it on the table that I've already set up in there. I put the radio on low, hoping "Used to Be" doesn't make an appearance tonight.

'Do you want to chat now or after we've eaten?' Gray asks, clearly keen to start eating, as he crams a piece of salami into his mouth.

'No, we'll talk after. We have the whole evening to talk.' I reply, taking a seat opposite him. I know I'm holding the inevitable off. Maybe a glass or two of wine will lighten him up in preparation for the news. I mean, he seems to be in a good mood anyway but just to be sure.

Gray eats heartily, he's probably worked through lunch again, knowing him, while I pick at a bit of salad, pushing the same couple of leaves around my plate, my throat dry and prickly with apprehension.

We mostly eat in silence. Luckily, silences between us have never felt awkward. I don't think Gray has time to talk between the amount he's shovelling in per mouthful and the quickness at which he's eating. His second plate of food is nearly empty and he's drinking quickly. Our talk is looking less and less likely to happen.

'Come on, Genie. What's the great revelation, then?' Gray slurs, trying to pour me another drink. I put my hand over my glass to show I don't want any more, but Gray doesn't notice and manages to pour the wine all over my hand and partly over the table. I go to the kitchen to get a cloth to clear up the mess.

When I return, Gray isn't there. I watch him pacing at the bottom of the garden. I walk down to join him, wrapping my arms around his waist. He envelops me in one of his special big bear hugs.

'Sorry, Genie, the drinking's got to my head, and I just needed some air. I'm feeling a bit better now.' His words are coming out less slurred. 'Now, what did you want to tell me? I guess it's important, and my guess is that it's probably got something to do with Ed Nash.' He huffs, letting go of me.

Gray's handsome face looks flushed and I'm not sure I should reveal all while he's drunk. 'I-I-I don't know that now is the right time after all. You've had quite a lot to drink and—'

'Oh, for God's sake, Genie, I'm sick to the back teeth of pussyfooting around you. Spit it out, woman. Perhaps you should have another glass of wine to loosen you up a bit. I only want to help you and look after you. That's all I've ever wanted to do. But time and time again, you close me down, and I feel as though you've never fully given yourself to me.' Gray leans back against the fence and looks up, clearly agitated. 'I've always been honest with you, but you have always held something back. I'm giving you that opportunity here and now. Yes, maybe I've had a little too much to drink tonight but I'm here and I'm ready to listen to whatever you need to tell me.'

I've never seen him so riled up, so passionate and so

brutally honest. I love that man with every bone of my body, and here I am ready to break his heart. But he needs to know the truth. I owe him that much.

I take a deep breath. 'If I tell you everything Gray, I ask you one thing. Just let me talk without saying anything. I'll answer any questions that you have afterwards. It all started when I was in sixth form when I first met Ed Nash…' I begin, knowing that once I say these words out loud to Gray there is no taking them back and Gray more than likely will never look at me in the same way.

'It was just after my best friend Ginny's birthday party and my parents had said that if they allowed me to go to her party I would then have to stay in and study up until my exams. After Christmas I became stir crazy being incarcerated at home and would make excuses to try and escape. I also really wanted to go to Mark's New Year's Eve party. He's the drummer from Ed's band. Somehow, I managed to talk Dad round, but my mum was furious. Of course, the party turned into complete chaos as you can imagine with a bunch of teenagers in charge. We all got so drunk that I ended up crashing out with Ed in one of Mark's spare bedrooms. When I didn't come home my parents came looking for me at Mark's. I have never been so humiliated as I was dragged from upstairs, leaving Ed crashed out and alone. I was then completely grounded. My dad even drove me to school in the mornings, but I was allowed to come home on my own, mainly because it suited my mother, who did some sort of voluntary work at our local church in the afternoons. Obviously, I took advantage of this time without either of my parents being around and could be found either over at Ed's or Ginny's. It was one of those afternoons probably around late January early February when I called over to Ed's not knowing that he'd got a detention. I rang on the bell and his Uncle Paul opened the door, like he had many times before and welcomed me in. He insisted that I had a drink, and I remember asking him for a cup of tea as it was quite cold outside and typical of most teenagers, I wasn't wearing a coat. He made me a tea which I drank sitting on the sofa in their living room whilst Paul practiced guitar in their kitchen. I remember feeling an overwhelming desire to just sleep and I must have drifted off. I'm not sure how long I was asleep for but when I woke up, I felt groggy and disorientated, and I just didn't feel right. I went to stand up, but my legs buckled, and I sat right back down again. I called out to Paul but there was no reply. I managed to somehow get myself upright and went to the bathroom when I noticed that my school shirt had the buttons done up the wrong way which seemed odd. I splashed water on my face which seemed to help. I walked through to the kitchen but there was no sign of anyone, so I just let myself out of the house and went home. I just knew something was off as I just didn't feel right and the fact that Paul was nowhere to be seen unsettled me. Thankfully no one was home, so I went upstairs and had a shower which made me feel a bit better.'

Gray looks at me and raises his hand as if to ask permission to speak. I nod.

'Do you think Paul slipped something in your drink?'

'It's a possibility I suppose. I have no recollection of what happened that afternoon as I just felt so tired, but I made sure that I was never alone with Paul again. He just gave me the creeps. I always felt he was watching me whenever Ed and I were together. I never told Ed that I had called for him that afternoon and Paul obviously didn't mention it either. I just felt disorientated and quite frankly I just wanted to forget about it.' I said, taking a big breath to try and continue.

'Genie! That's an awful thing to have gone through. I had no idea. He was old enough to be your dad for God's sake. I'd rip a man to shreds if that ever happened to Cassie. Why on earth didn't you tell your parents?' said Gray, completely horrified, shaking his head in disbelief.

'I know it is. But at that time, I just put what had happened to the back of my mind because I didn't really know if anything had happened. We all thought Paul was so cool. He's a lot younger than Ed's Dad, as they are half-brothers. They had the same dad, but Paul's mum was much younger than their dad, so Paul was in fact closer in age to Ed than he was to his own brother. That's why he used to hang round with us lot so much. Ed and I still saw each other as much as we could within my curfew times. Around March time I missed my period but put it down to stress as I was studying hard for my exams. I didn't mention it to my parents, but my clothes started to feel a bit tight and certain foods made me feel sick. Looking back now I should have realised that I was pregnant, but the naiveté of youth pushed all those symptoms to one side. It was only in late April time when Mother and I had had another flaming row because I had pretended to go swimming with Ginny, and I had yet again stormed out of the house. I in fact had gone to Mark's pool party – the photos were in the papers - but there was no way I could ever have told my parents that that's what I wanted to do. I had snuck back home for a bath after being at Mark's when my mother caught sight of me coming out of the bathroom with a towel wrapped around me that she started to suspect. She had a good look at my stomach which at this stage wasn't huge, as I think I was probably only about twelve weeks or so, maybe a bit more, but my once nipped in waist had long since disappeared. She shouted at me again and again, asking me if I was pregnant and I kept shrugging my shoulders as I really didn't know if I was or not at that time. She was relentless and kept asking me who the father was. I just stood there silently hoping that Dad would get back early, just for once and stick up for me. She kept prodding me and prodding me, pushing me further and further across the landing shouting at me calling me every name under the sun. I never knew that Mum could be so foul mouthed. She was like a woman possessed. I honestly thought she was going to push me down the stairs. Just as she was gearing up for another slanging match, I heard Dad's key in the door and heaved a sigh of relief. At least he would be on my side. She called him upstairs and blurted out to Dad that I had gone and got myself pregnant. He asked her to calm down and made mother go downstairs. He sat me down and asked if it was true. I told him I wasn't sure. Dad was brilliant and arranged for me to see a friend of his who was a private doctor, and she confirmed that I was over three months pregnant. I was shocked to say the least. I thought we had been careful but obviously we hadn't. I wasn't allowed to see any of my friends, so Ed didn't even get to know that I was pregnant. They pulled me out of school immediately and my mother and I went to stay with her sister, Auntie Maureen in Bournemouth. They also got me a home tutor. Once the pregnancy was confirmed my whole life changed.'

I take a breath and look at Gray, who has tears in his eyes. I can tell he's heartbroken now he knows the truth. But I can't work out if he's heartbroken at what I went through or the fact I kept it from him. Maybe he thinks I don't trust him, which is not the case at all. I had to put my secret baby behind me and move on for my own sanity.

'Did you have the baby?' Gray said with barely a whisper as he struggles to get the words out.

'I had complications at just over eight months, and I lost a lot of blood as I gave birth. I had a blood transfusion. We were both very weak and poorly.' I reply. 'But yes, I had a little girl. Because I was so out of it, I didn't get to see her properly. Milly. At least, that's what I would have called her if I'd been able to keep her.'

'Oh, Genie. I'm so sorry.' he says as he pulls me in close. I breathe him in, tears coming to my own eyes.

'It was all my fault she was so small.' I murmur. 'I had smoked and had carried on drinking as I had no idea I was pregnant. She never stood a chance. And now Ed is back, I'm frightened that he'll find out. Have you seen the latest from TikTok? There's some influencer type with her conspiracy theories, speculating that I was pregnant. I feel bad that Ed never knew he was a dad, but I thought he'd never get the opportunity. At the time, I wished he knew, but now…' I bite my bottom lip. 'So much time has passed. I'm so sorry I never told you about Milly.' I say, as I wrap my arms around Gray, desperately hoping he won't judge me too harshly. Although, no one can judge me as hard as I've judged myself.

'I can't believe you went through all of that, and you never told me.' Gray says, shaking his head in disbelief.

I immediately feel my body clench at the words "you never told me".

'You've carried all that guilt for years, but it does make sense why you have such a fractured relationship with your parents.' he continues. 'What happened to Milly?'

'The original plan went ahead: she was adopted to a good Catholic family. Or, at least, that's what I was told. Apparently, they could give her all she'd ever need. Everything I couldn't provide.' I reply sadly.

'Kids need love. You could have provided that.'

I look up at Gray, love in my teary eyes. Part of me, a big part of me, wishes I'd told him years ago. He would have understood my erratic behaviour, fought with me through this mess and helped me emotionally in every way I needed. All this fear I've built up over the years is now crumbling before me. Fear that didn't even need to be there in the first place.

'And you've not had any further contact since then?' asks Gray.

'No.' I lean my forehead against his chest, shame running through me. 'I've always thought about her, but I try to remember that I gave her a good life by letting someone else bring her up. I was almost eighteen when she was born, and I had absolutely nothing to offer her.' I look up at him, trying to read his face. 'I'm sorry, Gray, that I wasn't honest with you when we first met. But the longer I left it, the harder it seemed to tell you the truth.'

'It's a lot to take in. You have another daughter. The kids have a grown-up half-sister. I can't quite get my head around it all. Does Maura know?' I shake my head. His arms loosen around me as the information sinks in. 'You've been so brave telling me about Milly. Thank you for being so honest. It explains so much…' says Gray, deep in thought, a single tear rolling down his cheek. A single tear for the stepdaughter he never had, or a single tear for my dishonesty.

The secret I've been harbouring for over thirty years is finally out, but this is just the beginning. I still must tell the kids, and Gray could still decide this is all too much and he can't be with me anymore. I just feel so emotionally drained.

'I'm so tired, Gray. I need to go to bed.'

'You go on up. I'll tidy up.' Gray replies, kissing my cheek gently.

Relieved that Gray finally knows my secret, I gratefully climb the stairs and half-heartedly attempt to take off my makeup. I go to close the shutters in our bedroom and catch sight of Gray in the garden. He sits down on the decking, lights a cigarette and sips at what looks like a neat whiskey. Gray gave up smoking years ago, but I know he's been having the odd one here and there as I'd seen a pack in his work bag the other day, when I was looking for a phone charger. I guess we all have our secrets. Some just aren't as big as others.

He necks the rest of his whiskey and stubs out his

cigarette and makes a move to go inside to lock up. He'll be upstairs soon so I quickly get into bed and feign sleep. Fifteen minutes later he walks to his side of the bed, slips in beside me, our bodies so perfectly in tune with each other, his legs fitting into the bend of mine as they do every night. He kisses the back of my head and settles down to sleep. I only hope that he can find it in his heart to forgive me. We need to explain everything to the children and fast before the media find out that I'm #thegirlinthesong that everyone has been looking for.

17

EVIE

Then

'What are you looking for in such a hurry?'

Evie jumped and turned to look at her mother, who was standing in her bedroom doorway, arms folded. Her mum should be out. She's meant to be out. She's meant to be doing charity work. What is she doing here? Evie thought, searching her brain for a story. One she would hopefully agree to. Not that Evie thought that she'd agree to anything – Evie is supposed to be grounded. Again.

'Ummm… my swimming costume. I'm going swimming with Ginny.' It's not a complete lie. She was looking for her swimming costume, and she was going swimming with Ginny, she just left out the fact it's at Mark's house in his newly built swimming pool.

'Have you forgotten you're grounded?' Her mum reminded her.

Evie was glad that she had her back to her mum as she searched through her drawers again. If her mum had seen the eyeroll, she would have been in deeper trouble than she already was. 'I just want a bit of fun, that's all. Everyone else's parents let them have a life, you know. It's just a trip to the swimming baths.' She spat back.

She had got incredibly used to lying. Unfortunately, her Mum had got incredibly used to her lies. Her mum had no idea what was truth or lie anymore when it came to Evie, so she just deemed everything a lie. Even when Evie told the truth, she couldn't win. Not that this was one of those times.

'You're *not* going.' She said it slowly, accentuating the "not".

'Oh, but I am going. You just try and stop me.' Evie almost growled back at her mum, finally locating her old swimsuit which she defiantly stuffed in her bag.

'Put that back.' Her mother shouted.

Evie had had enough, and with no detection of a motherly bond from her mum, she couldn't help but feel nothing but hate and an unwillingness to do anything she told her. 'No. Why should I? You can't keep me locked up like a prisoner forever, you know?' She replied, her cheeks flushed with rage.

Evie barged her way out of her room as her mother screamed obscenities after her. She ran down the stairs as quickly as she could - not that she thought that she would chase her, and even if she did, she knew she wouldn't be able to keep up. Evie slammed the door behind her. She was literally shaking as she sprinted all the way to Mark's house, knowing that this time her mother really would make her life a misery once she finally returned home. Not that she'd really notice; every day with her mother already felt like a misery.

Ginny was already at Mark's, parading in her new lime green bikini, which accentuated her fabulous figure. None of the boys could take their eyes off her. She looked amazing.

'Evie, you made it!' Ginny grinned and ushered her over to the side of the pool. 'Did you manage to get your swimsuit?'

'No.' she lied, thinking about her faded dowdy pale blue swimsuit that she'd just risked everything for, stuffed at the bottom of her bag. It was no match against Ginny's beautiful new bikini. 'Can you believe my mum was at home? She caught me red-handed looking for my swimsuit and kindly reminded me that I'm grounded. We rowed, as per usual, and I stormed out. At least I'm here though. I'll just roll up my skirt and shirt sleeves and dangle my legs in the pool. It'll be fine.'

'You know, Evie, you look great in whatever you wear anyway.' she said graciously, as she sashayed off towards the sun loungers, immediately making Evie feel guilty for coveting her beautiful bikini.

Ed soon appeared, grabbed Evie by the waist and passionately kissed her.

'Come on, you two lovebirds, let's get in the pool.' shouted Mark.

Ed and Evie reluctantly parted locked lips, and Evie went off to find Ginny. Ed, who was already wearing his swimming trunks, spectacularly divebombed into the pool with Mark, soaking all the girls, all of whom were sitting at the side of the pool. They all frowned and grumbled; their carefully styled hair ruined by the chlorinated water. Ginny had been clever enough to sit on one of the sun loungers slightly away from the pool, so both her and Evie's makeup and hair remained beautifully intact.

'Budge up, Ginny.' Evie said, as she perched on the end of the lounger.

'Did you see the boys' divebombs?' Ginny laughed. 'The look on Meredith Jenkins' face when her hair and makeup got ruined was priceless. She's had her eye on Mark for ages, you know. She doesn't stand a chance though. He only ever goes for dark-haired girls.'

'Yeah, I know what you mean.' Evie said, momentarily feeling a little sorry for poor mousey-haired Meredith.

Ginny and Evie moved to the side of the pool and dangled their toes in the water. Ed and Mark soon joined them at the side of the pool, Ed squeezed himself between Evie and Ginny while Mark started chatting up the very dark-haired Veronique, who'd just moved in next door after relocating from France. Her grasp of English was almost as limited as Mark's grasp of French, but within moments they were kissing quite passionately by the side of the pool while a heartbroken Meredith looked on despondently.

'You girls getting into the water?' Ed asked as he slipped back into the inviting pool.

'I haven't got my swimsuit with me. I forgot it this morning and then when I went back after school, Mum was there, so I just stormed out.' Evie explained to Ed.

'Another row? I thought she was supposed to be doing her charity work this afternoon?'

'She was. It must have been cancelled. I'm quite happy just soaking my feet in the water, to be honest.' Evie bluffed as Ed stood between her legs as they dangled in the water and leant in for a kiss, neither of them caring that her clothes were now completely soaked. They eventually pulled apart as Ed swam off to the other side of the pool.

'How about you, Ginny? Fancy a dip?' he called out.

'I'll be in in a minute. I just want to get some photos taken first. I'll ask Meredith to take some.'

Ginny walked over to where Meredith and her friends were sitting. 'Meredith?'

'Y-yes.' Meredith stammered, completely intimidated by the beautiful Ginny.

'Any chance you could take a few photos of us all? Would you mind?' Ginny asked in her most persuasive voice.

'Sure. Just show me what to do. I've never used a Polaroid before.' she replied nervously.

'It's really simple. You just look through here, point the camera and click. Then the photo pops out here.' Ginny explained patiently, pointing to where the photo came out.

Ed, Jamie, Ginny and Evie sat together at the side of the pool as Mark and Veronique knelt just behind them. Meredith took the first picture. As they waited for it to develop, Ginny encouraged her to take another one. Poor Meredith now seemed to have the job of "official photographer". By the end of the afternoon, Meredith had accumulated quite a collection of Polaroids for Ginny.

'Thanks, Meredith. These are awesome. Tell you what, as a thank you, I'll take one of you and your friends.' Ginny suggested, not taking no for an answer.

Meredith and her friends Dionne and Charmaine sat together on the sun loungers. Ginny took a quick photo of the girls as they squinted against the April sunshine. The photo developed, and Ginny handed it over to Meredith and her friends, who studied it religiously, anxiously looking at themselves in all their Polaroid glory.

Ed spent the rest of the afternoon alternating between sitting by the side of the pool with Evie and showed off his admirable diving skills while he messed about with Jez, Mark and Jamie in the water. Ginny and Evie spent most of the afternoon people-watching. Ginny and Jamie were still getting on famously. He was really into her in a big way and hung off her every word.

Evie glanced at her watch and realised that she would have to make a move, as her dad would be back from work soon and she wanted to get to him before her mum did.

'Ed, I've got to get back and face the music.' Evie shouted over to him.

'Give us a sec, and I'll walk you back.' Ed called out to Evie as he swam over in her direction.

'It's fine. Stay here and enjoy yourself. I don't want my mother shouting at you as well. She's going to be fuming as it is.' Evie replied.

'As long as you're sure?' Ed jumped out of the pool and half-heartedly dried himself off with a towel. He took Evie's hand and led her through the house to the front door.

'Are you sure you can't stay?' he asked, as he grabbed hold of her, leaving another damp patch on her shirt.

'You know I'd love to, but I've got to get back around the time Dad gets home. I have to at least try and get him onside.' She gave Ed a quick kiss on the lips, keen to get going.

'Evie Del Rio, that was a rubbish kiss. I want a proper one.' he demanded as he pulled her towards him for a far more passionate kiss.

Evie arrived back from Mark's house before her dad got back from work, and she even managed to get upstairs to the bathroom without her mother catching sight of her. She was having a lie down in her bedroom, probably suffering from another one of her imaginary "migraines" Evie thought.

She locked the door behind her and ran a bath, liberally pouring some of her mother's expensive bath oil into it that her dad had bought her mum at Christmas. She still hadn't bothered to use it. The bath somehow felt nicer having used the forbidden bath oil, the temperature was perfect, the feel of the water a pleasant change. As she immersed her whole head into the water, she wished she could wash away all her problems. She spent ages in the bath shaving her legs and then washed her hair using the special highlighting shampoo and conditioner set Ginny had bought her for Christmas.

Her skin was soon in danger of resembling a wrinkled old prune, so she got out of the bath, grabbing some fresh fluffy towels from the airing cupboard, and wrapped a towel around her body and then towel-dried her hair before combing it through. Letting the water drain away, she washed the bath out, erasing any evidence that she'd used her mother's bath oil. With her dad not home and her mother in bed with a "migraine", she chanced leaving her towel on the side of the bath to dry.

She'd just opened the bathroom door and was furtively walking across the landing when her mother came out of her bedroom. It had been years since she had last seen her daughter in any state of undress, let alone naked. Her mother's eyes popped, as Evie tried to protect her modesty as best she could by covering herself with her arms.

'You've put an awful lot of weight on, Evie.' she stated, as she took a long look at her daughter.

'Ummm, thanks.' Evie replied as she sprinted to her room. 'Apparently, I boredom eat when I'm grounded. Which happens an *awful* lot.' She opened her bedroom door.

'Stop!' she shrieked. 'Let me look at you properly.'

Evie paused in the doorway to her bedroom and turned around as she moved her hands away. 'Here. Is this what you want to see? What's your problem? Now, if you don't mind.'

Within moments, her mother started hurling abuse at her. For a woman who spent so much time in church, her language had become increasingly aggressive, littered with the most unchristian words that Evie had ever heard come out of her mouth.

'Change into your nightclothes and then get back here. Your father will be home soon.' her mother ordered.

'But—'

'Just do it.' she screamed at the top of her voice.

Already in enough trouble as it was, she did as she was told and nervously joined her back on the landing. She made her lift up her top, revealing her clearly expanding waistline.

She shook her head and laughed. But it was far from happy laughter.

'Are you pregnant?' She raised her thin, pencilled in eyebrows and stared at her expectantly for an answer. Evie focussed on her breathing and didn't respond. 'I said, *are you pregnant*?' Her spittle hit Evie's cheek as she screamed in her face.

'No. I mean, I'm not, am I? I can't be. I'm way too young.'

'We all know you've been spending time with that Ed boy. Clearly, you've been doing more than spending time with him, haven't you?' She put her hand on her forehead, as if she felt lightheaded. 'I can't believe it. My daughter is a sl—'

'Felicity, you stop right there before you say something you'll regret.' Evie's dad's voice boomed from the downstairs hallway. Caught up in their own world, neither of them had heard him come in. The stairs sounded louder than usual as he made his way up them. 'What on earth is going on?'

'Thank God you're home, Dad.' Evie said, relieved, as she tried to pull her top back down, but her mum grabbed hold of it and kept it lifted.

'Look at her stomach. She's pregnant!' Her mother shrieked.

"I'm not.' Evie yelled back.

'Calm down, Felicity. Shouting at Evie isn't going to get us anywhere.' Evie's dad said as he knelt in front of her, trying to remain expressionless at the sight of her swollen stomach, and asked calmly, 'Evie, sweetheart, are you sure you're not pregnant?'

'I…' She stopped. There was no point lying anymore. To herself or anyone else. 'I'm so sorry, Dad, but I'm not sure.' She replied quietly. She felt like she wanted to cry but her mum had this aura about her and Evie didn't want her to see that she was in shock.

'I'll book you an appointment with a friend of mine who's a private doctor tomorrow. Go and rest now, Evie, dry your hair, and I'll fix us all some dinner.' Her dad calmly said, as he took control of the situation. 'Felicity, let's have a bit of a chat downstairs.'

Amazingly, her mother obediently followed her dad downstairs after her foul-mouthed tirade as Evie retreated to the sanctuary of her bedroom.

18

ED

Then

Ed was really missing Evie. The last time any of them had seen her was at Mark's pool party. She had, of course, had another row with her mum and hadn't been able to get her swimming stuff. Once she'd arrived at the pool, she just dangled her feet in the water, with her skirt and shirt rolled up. The weather was brilliant, and Ed and the lads had had a right laugh as they dive-bombed into the pool, literally soaking anyone nearby. Evie stayed close to Ginny, as she watched everyone having a laugh in the pool. Towards the end of the afternoon, Evie then had to go home. They'd kissed briefly and then she was gone.

According to Ginny, she never showed at school the next day. About a week later, the teacher told her that Evie and her family had relocated due to her dad's job, but Ginny swore blind she had seen Mr Del Rio a couple of times at their house. Whenever Ginny or Ed ever rang on their bell, no one ever answered.

Ginny and Ed still saw each other from time to time because she was now officially going steady with Jamie. Ed poured all his emptiness and sadness into his music. He decided to rewrite "Used to Be", as it was always the song that everyone shouted out for at their gigs, and it was Evie's song after all, and singing it made him feel closer to her. Since Evie had left, many of the boys at St Augustine's took the piss out of him, as they continually asked him where his girlfriend was. With no word from Evie, Ginny and Ed both realised that they just had to get on with their lives, as best they could without her.

The Propellers had just done a gig at the local youth club where Jamie had somehow got absolutely wasted so Ed helped Ginny get him back home. His parents were pretty cool about the state that he was in and put Jamie's drunkenness down to a silly, youthful misdemeanor and thanked them both for getting him home safely. Not wanting the night to end, Ed invited Ginny back to his for a drink and a smoke as his parents were out and weren't due back for ages. Once back home he fixed them a couple of beers and rolled a joint which they shared sitting outside in the back garden. Although it had been a stifling hot and sunny day, now sitting on a bench in Ed's garden as the temperature had dropped, Ginny's thin denim jacket was no match for the plummeting temperature, so Ed took off his leather jacket and wrapped it around her shoulders.

'Thanks Ed. It's freezing. God isn't it strange without Evie being here?' Ginny said, as she took a drag from the joint, looking around the garden as if Evie was still there. 'It just doesn't seem right without her. I miss her so much, but it must be so hard for you as well. I mean you probably spent just as much time with her as I did!'

'You're right. It's so weird that she just left without telling either one of us. Something awful must have happened for her to leave so suddenly.' Ed agreed, taking another sip of his beer.

'I miss her every single day. Life's just not the same without her.' Ginny muttered, handing back the joint, as a big fat tear plopped on to her cheek.

'I understand Ginny, I really do. Come here, please don't get upset.' He said trying to console her with a big hug. She just stayed there on the bench with her head lying against his chest as he rubbed her back trying to comfort her. He wasn't sure who kissed who first, but he did remember an innocent, comforting chaste kiss which suddenly turned into a full-on proper one. Moments later they found themselves upstairs in Ed's bedroom, hands all over each other, clothes being removed and the kisses becoming more passionate. And after-wards, they just clung to each other, neither of them speaking as they knew that they had crossed a line, but it was definitely some sort of release for them both.

'Oh my God. I don't quite know how that happened.' Ginny whispered, as she pulled the sheets closely around her to protect her modesty. 'I'm supposed to be going out with Jamie, and you're supposed to be Evie's boyfriend!'

'I know. I'm sorry. I don't know what came over me.' He agreed, looking away from Ginny's sad eyes.

'It wasn't just you Ed. It was me as well. I just wanted to be comforted tonight. And you've certainly done that.' she said with a slightly embarrassed giggle.

'Listen.' He held her cheek and made her look at him, before quickly pulling his hand away, the innocent move not feeling quite so innocent in this moment. 'I won't say anything to anyone. You have my word. Now, let's get dressed and then I'll walk you home.'

He picked his clothes up off the floor and got changed quickly.

'I'm going to lock up and then I'll get you back home. OK?' he said, trying to take control of the situation and get them out of it as fast as possible.

'Thanks Ed. It'll be our secret. I won't breathe a word.' Ginny said, as she reached for his hand and squeezed it, as if to seal the deal.

It wasn't long before Ginny came downstairs, her smudged red lipstick freshly applied and her tousled hair in place once again. It took about twenty minutes to get back to Ginny's house. They walked together through the streets of South West London and to anyone who might have seen them, they looked just like any other teenage couple returning from a night out instead of two friends who had together just betrayed the most important person in both of their lives.

They reached Ginny's house and there was an awkward moment where neither of them was quite sure whether to kiss or hug goodbye, so they just stood there for a couple of seconds before Ed took the initiative and gave Ginny a chaste kiss on her cheek, as he whispered that he understood. She nodded, opened the front door of her house and went inside. Ed jogged all the way home, keen to get home before his parents. He tidied away the evidence of their smoke and beers and laid down in his bed where his sheets now smelt of Ginny's musky, heady perfume. He couldn't even remember what Evie's perfume smelt like. She'd been gone for exactly four weeks and two days, and it wasn't getting any better to deal with. What sort of boyfriend was he that he'd already slept with her best friend and betrayed one of his best friends in the process? No wonder she left. Evie deserved so much more.

19

EVIE

Then

The day after the visit with the private doctor, where they confirmed Evie's pregnancy, her dad took the day off work and drove her and her mum to Auntie Maureen's house in Bournemouth. Evie was told she was to stay until she gave birth.

Ever since her pregnancy had been confirmed, she felt like all the fight in her had gone and she found herself obediently agreeing to whatever her parents suggested about her future life. It was as if the baby was not only taking over her body, but her mind too.

Auntie Maureen's house was on one of the soulless, new housing estates about a twenty-minute walk from the seafront. There was a tiny, paved garden where she had a selection of uninspired planted containers and a plastic green patio set with an umbrella, where Evie was allowed to sit as long as she didn't speak to any of the neighbours. She often sat outside if the weather was warm enough and tried to revise or read one of Auntie Maureen's Mills & Boon books where some handsome, hunky doctor always came and rescued a damsel in distress. Evie knew no one was coming to rescue her.

She often wondered what Ed, Ginny and the rest of the gang thought when they realised she was gone. She guessed they would have been upset at first, but at least they all had each other, whereas she was stuck in an unfamiliar area with a couple of middle-aged mean-spirited sisters, with no money or means of escape.

Auntie Maureen and her mother made her go to church every Sunday. They always sat in the front row, as if being so close to the altar and the priest would help wash away her sins. She could almost feel the hostile parishioners' eyes burning into her swollen belly every time they went to church, which was further accentuated by the flowing gingham smocks Auntie Maureen had been obsessively sewing for her ever since she heard about Evie's pregnancy. As the weeks progressed, Evie began to recognise particular parishioners.

There was one family with two daughters - one a similar age to Evie and she had a younger sister who was about eleven. They would always smile at her when they thought their parents weren't looking.

The months in Bournemouth bizarrely flew by, despite her enforced incarceration. Her mother accompanied her to any hospital appointments that she had, and her dad visited every other weekend for dinner and sometimes for a quick walk along the seafront. Evie lived for those visits, as her dad was the only person in the family who treated her with any compassion. Evie openly cried when he returned to London on Sunday evenings.

Sometimes, Evie dreamt that Ed was with her, supporting her through her pregnancy. Other times, she became resentful that he was just carrying on with his life as if nothing had changed. She longed for her freedom. If giving away her baby gave her freedom, then surely it was the right thing to do? Auntie Maureen put them in contact with a Catholic adoption service that apparently had loads of worthy parents longing for a child. She didn't really have any choice in the matter and just silently agreed to anything Auntie Maureen and her mother suggested about the fate of her unborn child. If her parents hadn't insisted on moving her to Bournemouth, she felt that things might have been different. Perhaps she could have left a secret note for Ginny under the flowerpot and then Ginny could have let Ed know what had happened to her. But being cut off from her safe and familiar surroundings and network of friends with no access to a phone, all Evie's youthful rebellion had been sucked dry.

Her mother and her home tutor had arranged for her to take her exams at the local comprehensive school's sixth form, so the plan was that every day Evie had an exam, Auntie Maureen would drive her to the school in her beloved pale blue Ford Fiesta. During the revision sessions that Evie had joined, the other pupils just stared at her ever-expanding belly and whispered disapprovingly in the corridors when it was time for break or lunch. After each exam, Auntie Maureen would return to collect her. Today was the last of those days. Today was a bittersweet day for Evie. While she was glad to get away from pretty much all the other students, there was one who she was really going to miss: Emma. Emma, who just so happened to be one of the sisters in the church.

Evie spent the last couple of months looking forward to seeing Emma at breaktimes and again at lunch, as she made her feel like a normal teenager again. It was good to talk to someone her own age. They swapped music suggestions, and Emma had even made Evie a mixtape of all her favourite recent chart hits, which Evie listened to secretly on her Walkman. The words of "When Love Breaks Down" by Prefab

Sprout took on a new meaning as Ed clouded her thoughts by day and kept her from sleeping at night. Well, that and a baby who enjoyed wriggling and moving inside her constantly. And just when she got into a comfortable position, especially at night, the baby would give her a hearty big kick, as if to remind her that they were very much still there.

Emma never judged Evie, and she never once asked who the baby's dad was either. She just offered her friendship and bought her endless supplies of sweets to satisfy the sweet tooth she had developed throughout her pregnancy. They spent many a breaktime stuffing themselves silly with flying saucers, Fruit Salads and if Evie was really lucky, Emma produced a Curly Wurly, which they would happily share. As her mother allowed her to join in with the revision sessions at school in between exams, it gave the girls a bit more time together to hang out. Evie even had Emma's phone number. She knew that Evie was unable to use the telephone at Auntie Maureen's, but she had said that it was useful to have at least one person's telephone number when you moved to a new area. Evie stored the little piece of paper that Emma had neatly written out her telephone number on in her jewellery box, having folded it several times so that it would fit, hoping and praying her mother wouldn't find it.

Her last exam was history, and once it was over, Emma and Evie enjoyed their final lunchtime together before it was time to say goodbye, as the dreaded Auntie Maureen would be waiting to drive Evie back home. They managed to find an empty classroom, out of earshot from the other pupils. They both shared a ham sandwich and Emma threw the foil covering towards the bin, spectacularly missing. Neither of them bothered to pick it up or put it in the bin. Evie wasn't even sure that she could even bend down that far to do it.

'I can't believe we won't be able to hang out anymore now school is over.' Emma said, pulling Evie close.

'I know, but Mother doesn't want me forming any ties down here. God knows what plans she's got for me once I've had the baby.' Evie replied, enjoying the physical contact of Emma's much-needed hug. It had been months since anyone other than her dad had showed her any affection.

'We can still see each other at church though, can't we?' said Emma, linking one of her arms through Evie's.

She nodded. We can, although we won't be able to talk. We'd probably get excommunicated.' Evie joked, winking at Emma.

'Just imagine that. No more boring Sundays at church.' Emma laughed.

'Once I've had this baby, I'm never going to set foot in a church again.' Evie vowed.

'I know what you mean. They always go on about forgiveness, but your mother just seems to enjoy punishing you.' She paused, wondering if perhaps she'd overstepped the mark. Evie was just glad someone else saw things the same way as her. 'I've never asked you, and I hope you don't mind, but if you could, would you want to keep your baby?'

Evie looked down at her pregnant tummy and stroked it and sighed. 'Yes, but I realise I have nothing to offer them. The baby's dad doesn't even know he has a child. They made me leave London before I was able to tell him. I've been told my baby will be going to a good Catholic household through the church, so they will be loved and looked after. Who am I to prevent my baby having that sort of life?'

'You're so brave.' Emma stared at Evie with adoration. Evie wasn't sure whether she meant that she was so brave giving up her baby or being so brave coping with a pregnancy without the dad around.

'I'm not brave; I'm just a silly girl who got caught out. My boyfriend and I took a few too many risks, and this is the result.' She pointed at her swollen stomach.

'Well, I think you're brave, and you've got my number if you feel you ever need it.' Emma said loyally.

'Thanks, Emma. I really have appreciated your friendship over the last month.'

Emma unlinked their arms and reached inside her school bag for something. 'I've uh... I've actually got something for you.' she said, handing her a small money bag.

'What's this?'

'There's about ten pounds all in all. There's a five-pound note, and the rest is in coins. Think of it as your emergency fund in case you need to call me if you ever manage to sneak off.' Emma says, her cheeks blushing.

'I can't take this, Emma.' Evie protested.

'You must. Half of it is from my piggy bank, but the coins are from that missionary box that we were given at church months ago. I've been taking a few coins from it for weeks. I was going to save up for some new records, but I think your need is greater than mine. Doesn't the church say that charity begins at home?' Emma said with a big smile coming across her face.

Her hands shook as she slipped the small money bag into her pocket, holding back tears. 'I hope that I can repay you one day. I can't tell you how much I've appreciated your friendship since I've been in Bournemouth. You've given me hope, Emma, and I will be forever grateful for your kindness.'

Emma smiled and nodded, clutching her friend's shaking hand.

'Look, I've got to go, as Auntie Maureen will be waiting. I'll see you on Sunday. Thanks again.' She said, as she hugged her new friend as if her life depended on it.

They walked together... well, Emma walked, and Evie kind of waddled, as the baby seemed to have had a growth spurt recently and she found it hard to walk properly. They went through the corridor towards the double doors at the front of the school. They briefly hugged again, only pulling apart when they spotted one of the teachers tutting in their direction.

Evie walked out of the school for the final time and spotted Auntie Maureen's car almost immediately. She opened the passenger door and climbed in.

'Well, that's it now. You can concentrate on delivering a nice healthy baby for that lovely Catholic family who are going to raise your poor illegitimate child.' Auntie Maureen said spitefully.

'Thanks for that, Auntie Maureen. And how was your day?' Evie replied sarcastically as she buckled her seatbelt.

'Goodness knows how Felicity managed to raise such a rude, arrogant daughter. I blame your father's side of the family completely.' she hissed, driving out of the school at a respectable twenty miles per hour.

20

ED

Now

The rehearsals for the forthcoming tour have gone very well on the whole today. Mark's drumming is perfection as per usual, Jez's bass playing is as slick as ever and my vocals aren't too shabby, but I'm not overly happy with the backing singers, Cindy and Chyna, who have just joined us. They've apparently done loads of session work but I'm just not gelling with them musically. Cindy is the better singer; she can really belt out a tune. She's all big hair and has a very impressive cleavage to match, the daughter of a Jamaican reggae star who's worked with the likes of Sir Tom Jones and ABC whereas Chyna, who is originally from the Philippines, is apparently just there to look sexy, as she seems to spend most of her time pouting into her microphone, and I can hardly hear her vocals at all. They're great people, I just don't think they're a good fit with the band, but I fear we are stuck with them, as our manager, Toby Tucker, won't have a bad word said about them. There's a rumour that he's shagging one of them, or maybe even both, and that's fine if everyone's happy with that situation, but they're simply not fitting into the sound of The Mountaineers. Andy and Simon, the session musicians Toby has hired for the tour, however, are cracking, and they fit right in with us.

Toby walks back into the rehearsal room, clutching the smallest takeaway coffee cup I've ever seen, bought from one of those new hipster coffee shops that seem to have cropped up around the city. He sits down and turns to the backing singers.

'So, Cindy, your voice needs to blend with Ed's. Remember, it's not a competition to see who can sing the loudest. I want you two to work together. When you get it right, your voice can really complement Ed's. And, Chyna, I want you to bring all your sassiness to your performance. Don't forget to join in with your tambourine and keep your backing vocals light. Let's take it from the top.' says Toby. Maybe that's why I can hardly hear Chyna - I was right, she's purely here for sexiness and most likely can't hold a tune.

I'll certainly give it to the girls because after Toby's such explicit instructions, their voices start to sound as if they've always been on the more recent tracks. By the time we come to sing "Used to Be", Toby instructs the girls to hang back and just dance. "Used to Be" is always our last song, and I still get a buzz when the audience sing my words right back to me.

"With your blonde hair and ruby red lips, you were every schoolboy's dream,

    looking like a movie star staring out from a magazine.
    Oh, my head's in a state,
    why, oh, why did you make me wait?
    Let's be together forever,
    just you and me,
    no one else matters.
    They say we're too young to know (too young to know),

but this boy's dream eventually came true
because it was always you and only you.
The plan was to be together,
forever, forever.
My love for you will never fade,
our love was tailor-made.
Let's get back to how we used to be (how we used to be,
used to be).
Let's be together forever,
just you and me.
No one else matters.
They say we're too young to know (too young to know).
Our love was tailor-made,
why, oh, why did you have to leave?
We shoulda proved them wrong - it coulda just been you
and me.
Please come back to me,
let's get back to how we used to be... how we used to
be... used to be."

I wrote this song years ago, when Evie and I were together, but when she left, I revised the words slightly. Nothing like a broken heart to get the creative juices flowing.

'Loved it, guys. Girls, that was exactly what I wanted from you. Just brilliant.' Toby enthuses.

'It all seems to be pulling together.' I agree.

'I think that's enough for today. Get yourselves out of here.' Toby instructs.

'Anyone fancy a drink? My treat as a thank you for everyone working so hard today,' I enquire.

Toby makes his excuses, as does Cindy, but Chyna says she's up for a drink, as do Andy and Simon. Mark and Jez are always up for a drink. There's a pub just around the corner from the rehearsal room. I get the drinks in, and we're lucky enough to find some seats at the back of the pub. Andy and Simon take no time at all chatting to Chyna while I discreetly fill Mark and Jez in on my recent meet up with Virginia and explain about how her ex-husband sold the pool party photos to the press.

'I remember Ginny. She was a right laugh. Wasn't she going out with Jamie back in the day?' says Jez, leaning back in his chair.

'Yes, that's right.' I reply, taking a sip from my pint, remembering how Virginia and I betrayed both Jamie and Evie one fateful night. I've tried to cast that particular night out of my mind, as neither Jamie nor Evie deserved that.

'Her and Evie were as thick as thieves. Are they still in touch?' asks Mark, interrupting my thoughts.

I shake my head. 'Virginia never heard from Evie again. Same as me.'

'Ooh, that's a strange one. I thought you two were going to last the distance. It was odd the way she just kind of disappeared.' Mark continues.

'Yep. One day she was there, the next day she was gone. No note. Just lots of unanswered questions.' I scratch out small splinters of wood from under the table with my thumbnail, trying to keep myself in the present, afraid to face the reality of the only woman I've ever loved walking out of my life all over again. 'The only reason people have started talking about her again is because of "Used to Be". I know we've capitalised on the meaning of the song, and she has, somewhat unjustly, gained a notorious reputation from all of that, but people keep asking about our relationship, and quite frankly, I'm grateful, as it's kept us in the public eye, but I still want to find out what happened to her though.'

'Yeah, you're right. If it wasn't for the song, we'd still be playing small pubs and clubs. I've heard there are rumours that she was pregnant.' Mark observed.

'Yeah. Virginia thought that too. I don't know what to think right now. Anyway, enough about Evie. How about some more drinks?' I suggest, as I pat Mark on the back.

'Yeah, that would be great.' says Mark as Jez nods.

'I'll get another round in.' Jez offers, getting up from his seat and making his way to the crowded bar.

21

GENIE

Now

I wake up early, greeted by another beautifully sunny day. Gray's still fast asleep, so I tiptoe around him, not wanting to wake him, as I know that once he's awake, today will be a day of deep discussions, and we still have to tell the children about the existence of their older sister.

I go downstairs, and I'm pleasantly surprised to find that Gray's tidied up everything from the previous night, even remembering to put out the recycling. He really did stay up to tidy, it hadn't just been an excuse to avoid me. All I needed last night was to just go to bed and sleep. I was so exhausted from everything.

I make us both a cup of tea, take Gray's upstairs and leave it on his bedside table. He sleepily acknowledges it and closes his eyes once again. I decide to have my tea in the garden to enjoy the early morning solitude before everyone gets going with the day. The sunrays are just beginning to hit the patio, and I contentedly watch the birds greedily feeding from the bird table. It's a good half an hour before Gray joins me, his hair sticking up all over the place, wearing his old trackie bottoms and an ancient Metallica T-shirt.

'Good morning, Mrs McNamara. How are you on this fine and beautiful morning?'

'Not too bad. How about you?' I reply as Gray sits beside me at the garden table.

'I'm ok but I'm concerned about all the press attention that we're getting at work from the Netflix documentary. One of my sales guys messaged me this morning and said that he's had several amateur sleuths fishing for information about you by posing as potential clients to further their public profiles.'

'I'm sorry. I really am.' I reply, inwardly cursing the day Ed agreed to do that documentary.

'I didn't want to worry you but I wanted you to be aware.' Gray replies sympathetically.

'Oh God, it's all kicking off, isn't it?' I say, as I start to cry.

'Look, there's a temporary way out of this. I'm going to book some flights to Florida today as I think it would be good to get away and now that both kids have finished school, it's perfect timing. Think we could all do with a break. Jonesy said his villa is free any time over the next few months, didn't he?' Gray continues.

I nod, knowing I need to push myself by getting away from here, hoping it will help clear my mind. 'When shall we tell the children?' I ask tentatively. I mean about my secret, not the holiday, my mind still focused on last night.

'How about when the kids get back? Or shall we wait until we're away?' Gray picks at a thread from his tatty trackie bottoms.

'I favour today, although there will be an awful lot of questions to answer.' I say, wanting my secret to finally be out there, not wanting to hold on and dwell on the what ifs any longer.

'Today it is, then. I'm not going into the office today. I've decided to take a day's leave to spend with my beautiful wife.' says Gray with a big, reassuring smile.

'I'm ok. I don't need babysitting, you know.'

'I know you don't, but I would like to take you out to brunch before the kids get back with all their questions.' Gray sighs. 'To be honest, I've got some questions too.'

'I don't really know what else I can tell you.' I say somewhat defensively, looking away from him.

'Well, I just can't believe you haven't tried to find your baby for one.' Gray says. 'There are loads of different websites where you input all your information together with any known information about your child, and they do the rest. There have been loads of successful reunions.'

'Before I met you, I knew what I did was best for my baby at the time.' I say shaking my head in answer to his question. 'My parents told me that she went to a good family who couldn't have children. And then once Cassie came along, I didn't want to burst our little family bubble. I thought you might leave me for not being totally honest with you all these years. I mean, you might still leave me, now you know the truth, but it's a risk I had to take. I couldn't let you find out any other way.'

Gray shakes his head vigorously.

'I could never leave you, Genie. I love you too much for that. We have Cassie and Will together. We're a family who needs to stick together. I'm only sorry that you felt you couldn't confide in me sooner, but I do understand, I really do.' He reaches over the table to hold my hand for reassurance.

It feels good to have Gray by my side. I always feel safe with him. Telling him was a risk, but so far it seems to have paid off. But I feel guilty, so guilty about all the lies, all the half-truths I've told throughout our marriage, but dear Gray still just wants to help me, to try to fix me and put me back together again. I wonder if I would have been as strong if things were the other way around.

'Both children messaged while you were still asleep. Neither will be home before lunch. Let me freshen up and then you can tell me where you're taking me for brunch. I don't mind where, just make it somewhere quiet. I'll try to answer everything you want to know.' I say reluctantly, really feeling that I'm done talking for today. But it wouldn't be fair of me to shut down communication now, especially as Gray being Gray is being so incredibly reasonable.

'Leave it with me. The Bingham is nice and discreet. I could request outside seating.' Gray suggests.

'I'd better wear something decent if we're going to The Bingham.'

'You'll look gorgeous whatever you wear.'

I pop upstairs and pull out a couple of possible dresses from my wardrobe before changing my mind and settling on some pale blue linen trousers and a crisp white shirt. I loosely tie back my hair and apply some more lipstick and some bronzer to perk up my pale skin. I grab my bag and make my way into the garden.

Gray gasps. 'Wow, you look amazing.' he says, overexaggerating as usual.

'Thank you.' I roll my eyes but can't help but smile. 'You, however, look like you've just got out of bed.' I say, looking at the state of him.

'Good point,' Gray agrees. 'The table's all booked.'

'That's great. Now, go and shower. I'll lock up.' I instruct, shooing him upstairs.

I secure the patio doors and sit in the coolness of the sitting room, idly flicking through yesterday's paper while I wait for Gray. Within ten minutes, I hear him coming down the stairs.

'That was quick.' I say, closing the paper and putting it on the coffee table.

'I didn't want to leave my beautiful wife waiting too long, did I?"

"I guess not. Shall I go and find her for you?' I smirk.

'Oh, you'll do.' says Gray, laughing.

We lock the front door behind us and make our way to The Bingham for our brunch date. The sun is blazing hot as we start our walk to get there, and after just a few minutes, I long to be in the shade. Once we do reach The Bingham, thankfully, we're ushered to a nice shady table on the outside terrace, overlooking the River Thames.

We order a couple of salads with some bread and a couple of Aperol Spritzes.

'This is lovely. I should really take more time off work on days like this.' says Gray, looking out over the terrace at the perfect view of the river.

'It would be great to have you around more often, but I know how much the company means to you.'

As we wait to be served, I notice a woman from another outside table staring at us. It's probably my paranoia, always thinking that the press has caught up with me. My suspicions are confirmed as she appears to take a sneaky shot of us both.

'See that woman over there?' I whisper to Gray, indicating with a discreet tilt of my head in the woman's direction. 'She can't take her eyes off us and I'm convinced she's been taking photos of us.'

'Do you want me to have her thrown out?' Gray whispers back.

'No! Of course not. She might be totally innocent. Let's just be discreet with our conversation.' I reply, hoping to shut down any further questions that Gray may have for now. Our food and drinks arrive and as we eat, I'm just relieved that Gray has stopped cross-questioning me for now. I'm exhausted by talking, and I know that there will be so many more questions to answer once the children know the truth, most likely going over the exact same ones Gray has and is bound to ask. I think he senses my reluctance, because I can see in his eyes that he has so much to ask and yet none of what he wants to say is coming out of his mouth. I know the point of going out was to talk but I'm not going to make that move. Our brunch, despite the possible journalist, is a welcome distraction from everything that's going on.

Once we've finished eating and paid the bill, Gray and I decide to go for a walk along the riverside. We walk hand in hand, just enjoying being together.

'We certainly don't need to go abroad for hot weather, do we?' I observe, trying to steer the subject away from the baby before she's even mentioned, as Gray shakes his head.

Once we're back at home I sit back out in the garden with a sobering cup of tea as Gray checks on some work stuff.

As I drink my tea, I idly scroll through my phone. I've already been named by the influencer/TikToker Amira Malik as a possibility of being #thegirlinthesong so it won't be long before the truth is out there. My phone beeps with notification after notification as more and more people are alerted to Amira's most recent revelations. Gray returns from his office looking unusually flustered.

'You seen the latest?' Gray asks, holding out his phone.

I silently nod.

'Are the kids home yet?' he asks.

'Not yet, but Cassie's just messaged to say she'll be home in half an hour, and Will is just about to leave Tommy's.' I reply having just read their concerned messages on our family WhatsApp after the latest TikTok revelations. Things are starting to kick off again.

'This is too much for us to handle.' Gray says anxiously.

'I'm sorry.' I start to sob.

'Please don't cry. I'm just in the middle of confirming our flights with our work travel agents.' Gray says, rubbing my back.

'Please, let's just get away from here as soon as we can.' I reply.

'I'm on it.' Gray says, taking control.

'Thank you.' I whisper.

Within half an hour both children return home with so many questions about Ed that I feel that my head is going to explode. I placate them with promises of a further chat tonight when Gray has finished work and I busy myself, half-heartedly preparing dinner.

Gray eventually leaves his office.

'It's all sorted. We go tomorrow. Jonesy said we can have his villa for the next couple of weeks. We all need to put some distance between us and #thegirlinthesong hysteria. You can invite Maura out for the second week if she's free. I know how much you ladies enjoy the shopping outlets in Florida.' Gray says, trying to lighten the mood.

'You wouldn't mind?' I ask, turning towards his kind, handsome face to kiss him.

'Maura is family as far as I'm concerned. The children adore her, and she'd be doing me a favour. You know how much I hate clothes shopping.' he says, kissing me back.

'Right, well, I'd best call Maura and start packing.' I say as Gray returns to his office once again.

I grab my phone and send Maura a message about her joining us for the second week. She's probably at work and won't be able to answer her phone.

I go upstairs and start looking through my wardrobe to see what I can pack. I sort out a few sundresses, some shorts, vest tops, a couple of swimsuits, underwear and sandals and then do the same with Gray's clothes. I will leave the children's until later once they know we're going away. Will has grown so much over the last few months, and I don't have a clue as to what clothes still fit and Cassie changes her mind so often as to what she likes wearing that it would be a thankless task.

I call the children. 'Once your dad has finished on the phone, we need to have a bit of a chat. We've got some news.'

'Oh ok, sure. When's dinner? I'm starving.' says Will, ruled by his stomach as always. I roll my eyes. Cassie is quiet and sits in the living room, furiously tapping away at her phone. I'm concerned that she's brooding.

Will goes upstairs to his room, and within minutes, I can hear his booming voice talking to his friends on the Xbox. Children today seem obsessed with technology, whereas in my day our obsession was music. How times change.

Gray finally emerges from his office with a big grin on his face.

'You look very pleased with yourself.'

'I am. Gerry is all up to speed, I've got all the codes for the villa, and I've organised car hire.' Gray replies.

'We'd better tell the kids, then, as they'll need to pack. I'll call them.' I say.

Both children eventually appear, phones in hand, and we all sit around the kitchen table.

'I've booked tickets for Florida. We go tomorrow afternoon.' Gray announces.

'Yes.' says Will, punching the air. 'Excellent. I can't wait to tell Tommy.'

'Cassie? What do you think?' I ask, noting her silence.

'Sure. It will be great.' she replies flatly.

'You could sound a bit more excited, Cassie. It's just what we need as a family.' scolds Gray.

'Sorry, Dad. Think I'm just a bit tired after last night. I'll go and start packing.' she replies with a forced smile.

'Sure, darling. Off you go. Just let me know if you need any help.' I add, concerned that Cassie doesn't seem her normal self. I'm kind of hoping she'll accept my open invitation to help her pack at some point so I can speak to her about what's going on inside that mind of hers.

Cassie and Will disappear upstairs to supposedly start packing, whilst Gray complains about the amount of clothes that I've packed.

'Surely no one needs that many shoes. Or indeed that much underwear.' he says, looking in disbelief at my attempt of packing, even though I've pretty much packed the bare minimum. 'There is a washing machine, you know.' he adds.

'Well, you might be able to survive on a small amount of pants, but I, however, like to have some sort of choice with my underwear selection.' I reply as Gray grabs hold of me and pulls me close.

'You know I'm only teasing you, Genie. You take whatever you like, darling. But don't forget that you and Maura will get to do some fairly serious shopping once we're there.'

I nod, purposely adding a couple more sets of underwear. Tomorrow can't come soon enough, but once we're away, I'll have to reveal my past self to my children. I only hope they'll understand.

22

ED

Now

With the recent revelations that Evie was possibly pregnant when she left has increased the interest in the band and ticket sales for most dates on our Reunion Tour are almost sold out. Amira Malik is also now convinced that Genie McNamara from Richmond is Evie Del Rio and to be honest I guess she could be. Unfortunately, there aren't too many up-to-date photos of Genie McNamara apart from a profile photo on a very old Instagram account that I suppose could be Evie but Evie/Genie hasn't said a word as yet. There have been no interviews to the press. I think fondly back to being in our first band The Propellers with Mark and Jez and all the attention we used to get from the girls. Being in a band holds some sort of fascination to people. Mark and Jez seemed to swap girlfriends every few weeks and there was never any shortage of willing volunteers. Jez eventually settled down with Poppy, a girl he had known since primary school. But the one real consistency was Evie and me. We were the power couple of our group. Girls would always try and chat me up, but I only ever had eyes for Evie.

The last time I saw Evie, we had a great day hanging out at Mark's house, me jumping in and out of the pool. I remember the day quite well, as Evie had rowed with her Mum yet again and had just run out of the house to come and join us. If only I'd known at the time that that was to be my last day with Evie, I would have paid her more attention. Unfortunately, us lads were more concerned with showing off to each other by divebombing into the pool. I remember kissing her goodbye and offering to walk her home, which she refused as I was never in Mrs Del Rio's good books, and Evie was anxious to get back.

The photos Virginia showed me are the last ones of us all together, but I'm still not sold on Virginia's hunch that Evie was pregnant when she left.

I've decided I'm going to drive to the gym, as the car needs a run. I've been so busy recently that I haven't done much driving, and my leased Mercedes has been gathering dust in the communal garage. I'm lucky that we have tight security here. Sid our security guard, is a right character: an ex-policeman who can sniff out a wrong-un a mile off. He always has time for a chat and is constantly ready to dish out some advice, whether you ask for it or not. He has his finger on the pulse, and if he likes you, you're sorted. He got rid of a lot of tabloid photographers who were hassling me when the press found out where I live.

'Good afternoon, Mr Nash.' Sid calls out from the other side of the garage, where he's using his litter picker to rid the garage of any bits of rubbish that have dared to take up residence.

'Hi, Sid. Please call me Ed. Mr Nash is reserved for my dad.' I joke. He often calls me Mr Nash despite my persistence to get him to only use my first name. It's like he needs fresh permission every so often to use my first name.

'Of course, Ed. How's life treating you? You're not

having any trouble with the press at the moment, are you?' he enquires.

'They seem to have given up turning up here since you got rid of them the last time, but the interest of social media has intensified since that Netflix interview.' I reply. 'I've been so busy recently that I've been neglecting my car, so I thought I'd give it a run. I'll catch you later, Sid.' I say, climbing into my car. I drive up the ramp from the car park, giving him a wave as I leave. I know that if I don't leave now, Sid, who likes a chat, would have me there for at least another fifteen minutes.

It's good to be behind the wheel once again, and as the weather's still warm, I decide to have a slow drive through Richmond Park. What's the point of having a convertible if you don't have the roof down now and again? I love Richmond Park. There's a sense of freedom when you are here, whether you are jogging, walking, cycling or driving. I wonder if 'my Evie' is Genie McNamara from Richmond who TikTok seem to be obsessed with? Weird to think that if Genie McNamara is Evie then we might even have passed each other in the street as we live just miles from each other. I'd love to have just half an hour with Evie to chat to her; find out about how life has treated her, to see if we do have a child together. Women have tended to come and go in my life. No one has ever put up with me for more than a couple of months. It's always the drinking, the drug taking and the inability to keep it in my pants, so who can blame them really? What have I achieved really? Not a lot. I've written a bunch of songs that have only become popular because of a TV show, I've drank too much, taken far too many drugs and let people down along the way. Not much of a catch really. Why on earth would Evie be interested in me now?

The drive around the park has certainly given me some headspace, although I think I sometimes think far too deeply about everything. Maybe that's what helps me write my lyrics. I find it easier to say what I feel through my music.

I arrive at the gym and park up. I keep my sunglasses on as I walk through reception, as all the receptionists know who I am and I'm beginning to think one of them leaked my home address to the press. I mean, I can't prove it; it's just a hunch.

I really bust it out in the gym. I hit the running machines, do some weights and spend time in the outdoor jacuzzi and sauna afterwards. Once I'm done working out and relaxing, I go to the changing rooms, where I get showered and then get dressed.

I grab a coffee from the café and sit outside in the recently remodelled and landscaped gardens. I scroll through my social media accounts. There's a link to a story on one of the tabloid sites that catches my eye: "Is this Ed 'Nasher' Nash's Evie Del Rio, the inspiration behind the hit song "Used to Be" by The Mountaineers?

There's an article, if you can call it that, saying that Genie McNamara and family were spotted at Heathrow Airport, jetting off somewhere nice and hot to escape #the-girlinthesong media storm.

I press on the link and find a slightly blurred photo of Genie McNamara, her husband and her two kids arriving at Heathrow Airport. It doesn't even say where they are going. I take a further look at her children, although their faces have been blurred by the press as they seem quite young, so there's no possibility that either of the children could be mine. If Evie had had a child all those years ago, they would be in their early thirties which seems mad seeing I'm just approaching fifty. I google Genie McNamara to see what else is out there and find photos of Genie and her family coming and going in Richmond. Intrusive photos, where the family are caught off guard and I momentarily feel bad that Genie McNamara's family are experiencing this amount of scrutiny, but at the same time, I am hopeful that in time all this information will help me find Evie.

I finish up my coffee and pop my phone in my back pocket of my jeans and leave the gym. The weather is still warm and I put the roof down again on my car, enjoying the early evening breeze and the sun on my face, drive straight in to the underground car park back at the flat and take the lift upstairs and sit on the balcony and continue googling Genie McNamara but there's not much written about her, apart from what I've seen already.

23

EVIE

Then

Evie knew she had to get away from Bournemouth. She just couldn't stand it any longer living at Auntie Maureen's house with her and her mother. They were driving her mad. They had already enrolled her at the local college for a January start to do a secretarial course and were encouraging her to retake her A Level History to get a better grade. Thankfully with the birthday money that her dad had secretly given her together with the money from Emma and her emergency fund which she had managed somehow to hide from her mother, she now had enough to plot her escape. Brighton was somewhere that Emma had suggested, and it wasn't too far away, she decided that travelling by coach would be her cheapest option. She felt that it would be too risky to try and hitchhike as a girl on her own. She'd had a bag packed for ages with just the essentials which she'd hidden at the back of her wardrobe. She pretended to be ill, so her mother had to do her shift at the church, and she did a runner when Auntie Maureen went to the toilet. She might just have slipped a laxative or two into her tea, so she spent ages in the toilet. She left a brief note, saying that she couldn't take living in Bournemouth anymore and not to look for her.

Evie ran as fast as she could out of Auntie Maureen's soulless cul-de-sac, her small hessian rucksack digging into her shoulders through her thin denim jacket. She reached the bus station and paid for a one-way ticket to Brighton which was due to leave in twenty minutes and used the time to buy herself an overpriced sandwich and a drink from the little kiosk close by. She located a phone box and dialed Emma's telephone number carefully. Thankfully she answered after a couple of double rings.

'Hi! It's me! I just wanted to say that I've only gone and done it. I slipped a couple of laxatives into Auntie Maureen's tea and Mother is at the Church doing my shift because I pretended that I was ill. The plan worked!' she gushed with excitement.

'Well done! I'm so pleased that you got away. How long before your bus leaves?' Emma asked anxiously.

'Just over ten minutes. I don't think Auntie Maureen is going to leave the bathroom anytime soon to try and stop me!' she laughed.

'Listen, take care of yourself. Don't tell me where you end up staying as my parents are bound to get it out of me and will definitely tell your mother. Good luck! I hope we get to meet up again one day.' Emma said, her voice slightly breaking, as she forced herself not to cry at the thought of her friend finally leaving for good.

'Thanks Emma, for everything. You've been such a good friend to me. I really appreciate all the help that you've given me in planning my escape.' she replied.

'You're welcome. I still think you are so brave Evie. Good luck with Brighton.' said Emma starting to choke up.

'Bye Emma. Take care and please do look out for my

baby on the off chance she ever appears at church with her new parents.' she asked, wiping the tears away from her eyes.

'Of course I will. Bye Evie. Safe journey.'

'Thanks Emma. I'm sure our paths will cross again.' she replied.

She placed the phone back on its' cradle and walked towards the coach and made her way to her seat. Thankfully she had a seat near the window and just up until the last minute it looked like she was going to be lucky and get the whole seat to herself when a young woman and her baby clambered on board. She managed with some help from a couple of young men to accommodate her small rucksack on the shelf above and then proceeded to rock the baby to sleep who was swaddled in a large, tie-dyed sheet which was wrapped around her waist.

'Sorry about being so last minute but I had to change his nappy. Didn't want to stink out the coach!' she apologised to Evie with a smile.

'Oh, don't worry. I was half asleep anyway.' Evie replied, horrified to be so up close and personal to a baby so similar in age to 'Milly'.

'Hope you managed to catch up on your beauty sleep as little Rex hardly ever sleeps on coaches.' she continued. 'I'm Margie by the way.'

'Err. Hi Margie. I'm err Genie.' She replied, not wanting to reveal her real name.

'Nice to meet you, Genie!' Margie said sticking her hand out to shake hers. Evie returned the handshake, hoping to God that Margie had washed her hands after changing Baby Rex's nappy earlier.

Margie very deftly managed to not only breastfeed Rex but also read Pet Sematary by Stephen King at the same time. She could never have coped like Margie was, Evie thought. Margie seemed like a natural and she must have only been a couple of years older than her. Baby Rex contentedly slept after his feed, all the way to the coach terminal in Brighton.

'I can't believe he slept all the way!' Margie exclaimed. 'It must be your calming influence. You'll be good once you have your own baby. But don't make my mistake and have a baby too young. Live your life first that's my advice but saying that I wouldn't swap him for the world! Would I? My little chubby chops?' Margie continued talking in that high-pitched voice that all new mothers seem to talk to their babies with.

'He's gorgeous.' Evie replied. 'You're very lucky to have him and he's so lucky to have a mum like you.' she added, desperately trying not to cry, thinking about her own baby that she had let her mother give away.

'Ahh thanks darling. Are you on your way home or just visiting?' asked Margie.

'Oh, um I'm moving here to work.' she stammered.

'Ooh what do you do?' Margie asked.

'Anything that pays me!' she laughed nervously.

'Do you mind cleaning?' Margie continued.

'No. I'll consider anything that pays!'

'I saw a note in the window of one of the local pubs the other day. They're looking for a cleaner. It's called The Hidden Snicket. It's quite near The Lanes.'

'Thanks. I'll check it out.'

The coach parked up and Evie helped Margie retrieve her rucksack from the luggage rack as she secured Baby Rex in his swaddling which she expertly secured around her waist.

'Thanks for your help. If you ever fancy a free portion of chips, I work at the little fish and chips kiosk at the start of the pier on Sundays as that's the day that my mum has Rex. It's nice to earn a little bit of money and it gets me out of the house!' Margie explained.

'I might take you up on your kind offer. Thanks.' Evie replied, handing Margie her battered rucksack.

'Thanks doll. I'll look out for you. You should definitely check out that job. I think you get your meals and accommodation thrown in too.' Margie said.

'It sounds better by the minute.' Evie said with a smile.

She waved goodbye to Margie and Baby Rex and asked the bus driver for directions to The Hidden Snicket. After the bus driver had said cross the road here and take a series of turn lefts and turn rights, she was so confused she decided to just take a few minutes to enjoy the sight of the sea and the magnificent pier. She breathed in the fresh sea air and she just knew that she'd made the right decision to leave. She noticed the fish and chips kiosk where Margie worked and made a mental note to drop by to see her on a Sunday. At least she now knew one friendly face in Brighton.

After what seemed an eternity, she managed to locate the pub that Margie had mentioned. It was a small little bar just off The Lanes, blink and you'd miss it. It was very quirky with a selection of gothic candles on the tables with two huge black chandeliers that hung from the ceiling and just as Margie had mentioned there was a small card in the window advertising the cleaning job. Evie pushed the heavy wooden door open and walked up to the bar to be greeted by a curly red-haired woman.

'Can I help you darling? You look a bit too young to be served.' the red-haired woman said with a broad, friendly smile.

'Oh hi. I don't want a drink. I'm almost eighteen, but I am interested in the cleaning job.' Evie said, cursing herself that she had revealed her real age.

'Do you have any cleaning experience?' the red-haired woman asked.

'Umm well I always used to help my mother clean our

house and I used to help clean at our local church.' Evie bluffed, although there was certainly an element of truth there.

'That all sounds good. You know that the job comes with accommodation above the pub, basically so you can start early in the morning before I have to deal with the deliveries and paperwork and then we open at 11:00a.m.' she continued.

'It all sounds great. I'm a hard worker and a quick learner.' Evie eagerly replied.

'Well, you sound perfect, but I don't even know your name! I'm Maura by the way.'

'I'm Genie. Great to meet you, Maura.'

'When can you start Genie?'

'Now!' Evie replied somewhat over enthusiastically.

'Great! Pop upstairs and see the room. It's small but you've got your own sink. You'll only have to share a bathroom with me as my last live in barman just went back to Australia.'

Maura called through to the back of the pub and a skinny young guy with a mohican and assorted piercings appeared.

'Dom. Be a love and keep an eye on the bar while I show our new cleaning lady to her room.'

'Sure Maura. Do you mind if I change the music?' he asked, smiling which showed off a couple of gold teeth.

'Of course you can my love. Nothing too hard core though. I don't think my head can take it! It was a bit of a late one last night!' she said with a smile and a wink.

Maura lifted the hatch at the end of the bar, and she led Evie up a narrow wooden staircase.

'You're right up at the top I'm afraid.' Maura revealed as she continued walking up the stairs.

'No problem.' Evie replied, following behind.

Finally, they reached the top floor, and Maura opened the door to a bright, pretty little room with a single bed, a bedside table, small wardrobe and as she'd mentioned a tiny porcelain sink. The brightness of the room was such a contrast to the darkness of the bar downstairs.

'It's perfect!' Evie exclaimed, seriously impressed that this perfect little space was all hers.

'Well, the job's yours if you want it.' Maura said. 'I usually ask for references, but I have a good feeling about you Genie.'

'Thank you, Maura. I won't let you down.' Evie replied with a big smile of absolute relief.

'I'll let you get settled. There's a set of fresh linen in the wardrobe and a couple of towels. Start in the morning darling. I'll get you an overall from my stock for you. I reckon you're a small.' Maura said returning her smile. 'When you're sorted, pop down and meet the rest of the gang and I'll get Rudi our chef to make you some dinner. I nearly forgot, here's a key to your room, just so you feel safe, and the larger key is for the front door.' Maura said kindly, closing the door.

Evie couldn't believe her luck ending up here. If she hadn't met Margie on the coach, then she would never have heard about the job. Maura seemed lovely and amazingly she hadn't asked for any references. When Evie had left Auntie Maureen's she hadn't ever really thought much more beyond getting away from Bournemouth, but here she was just hours later with a job and somewhere to live. She looked inside the wardrobe and found the freshly washed and ironed bedsheets and made up her bed, plumping up the two pillows. She looked out of the sash window at the darkening sky and finally she felt free.

After emptying her small rucksack and hanging the small amount of clothes that she'd brought with her, she made her way back downstairs where Maura was pouring a pint behind the bar.

'Hi Genie. Sit yourself down and have a look at this menu, choose what you want. I'll get Rudi to cook it for you.' Maura said generously.

She poured over the menu before settling on a toasted cheese and ham sandwich with some chips which probably wasn't the wisest of choices as it reminded her of being with Ed and enjoying toasties made with the Breville machine on one of their stolen afternoons together. She wondered how he was, did he miss her, or had he simply just moved on – maybe he was now dating someone new. She couldn't blame him, if he was. If Ed had disappeared on her, would she have waited for him. Probably not. Although she missed her old life in London, it was far better to start again in Brighton. The thought of having to tell Ed that she'd had their baby and had been forced to give her away was a conversation that only brought her shame.

'Pop yourself into the kitchen and introduce yourself to Rudi and tell him what you want while I work the bar. I'll come and join you when I get a quiet moment.' said Maura, interrupting Evie's thoughts of her ghosts from the past.

Evie went to track down Rudi in the kitchen and found a surprisingly very young, blonde guy prepping the food for the night ahead.

'Rudi?' She called out.

'Yes. Hello I am Rudi. How can I help you? he replied in an accent she couldn't quite put my finger on.

'I'm Genie. I'm the new cleaner. Maura said to come and see you.'

'You want food, yes?' Rudi asked.

'That would lovely. Thank you, Rudi. Could I have a cheese and ham toastie with some chips please?'

'Yes of course. You leave my kitchen and sit down, and I bring you food. Thank you.' He instructed somewhat officiously but Evie realised that there was probably something lost in translation along the way.

Evie returned to the bar area and sat down at a small table tucked away in the corner, taking in her new surroundings. The bar wasn't that big, but it had a long counter and then a series of small tables with either two or four chairs which were more suitable if you were eating. The black chandeliers that Evie had noticed earlier shone brightly and each little table had a lit white church candle placed in an old wine bottle. After about ten minutes, Rudi emerged from the kitchen with an enormous, toasted sandwich for her with a huge portion of chunky chips, complete with sauces.

'You eat now Miss Genie.' Rudi said, retreating almost immediately back to his kitchen.

'Thank you, Rudi.' she called out to him.

Evie must have polished off her food in about five minutes flat as she hadn't eaten since her expensive sandwich that she'd bought at the coach station.

'You look like you needed that!' remarked Maura who joined Evie at the table.

'Wow! Rudi's a good cook. That was amazing.' Evie gushed.

'He's great, isn't he? Maura smiled. 'He's come over from Germany to practice his cooking. He'd like to open his own restaurant one day. He's also perfecting his English too.'

'I think he'll be very successful. That toastie was heavenly!' Evie gushed.

'I'll be sure to let him know.' Maura said with her big warm smile. 'Do you fancy a cold drink or maybe a tea?'

'Just a coke please.'

'Dom! Be a darling and fix Genie a coke, would you?'

Dom was over within a couple of minutes and placed a tall glass of coke loaded up with ice in front of Evie.

'Thanks Dom.' Maura and Evie said in unison, which made them both collapse into a fit of giggles.

'What a nice polite girl you are Genie. I think you'll fit in just perfectly here, don't you think Dom?' Maura said.

'She will Maura. You always manage to find the right people to work here.' Dom agreed.

'I think they have a way of finding me.' Maura said with another big smile.

24

GENIE

Now

It's such a relief to get away from London and Jonesy's villa is the perfect relaxing hideaway. I keep going over and over how I'll break the news to the children that somewhere out there they have an older sister. I just can't tell how they're going to react. Cassie seems so withdrawn since she got back from Mel's but, wrapped up in my own drama, I've neglected to really talk to her about what's wrong. Cassie and Will have already had a bust-up over Will splashing Cassie with water from the pool. Hopefully, they'll settle down. Everyone's probably tired and jetlagged, so things will seem better in the morning, after we've all had a good night's sleep.

It's 10:30 p.m. The children have retreated to their rooms, so Gray and I are enjoying a glass of wine outside, looking out over the glistening pool, listening to the comforting sound of the mini waterfall flowing from the jacuzzi, into the pool.

'Fancy a dip?' Gray asks suggestively, moving his chair closer to mine.

'Are you sure that's all you're after?' I reply with a tired smile.

'Well, at my age, I'll take anything I'm offered.' Gray winks.

'Gray! Don't forget the kids are here, you know.'

'Come on, Genie. We're on holiday…' Gray says, kissing my neck gently but passionately.

'I'm not sure where my swimsuit is.' I protest weakly. I know I'm making excuses but all I want to do is have a few glasses of wine and then go to bed.

'Who needs a swimsuit?' Gray pulls back slightly and shrugs, starting to read my mood.

'I do. I'm not going skinny dipping, so you can get that idea out of your head.' I mean for it to sound like a gentle rejection, but it comes out harsh.

'Spoilsport. Don't worry, we've got two weeks.' Gray says, finally giving up on the idea of skinny dipping but only for tonight.

Gray pours us another couple of glasses of wine as we sit, enjoying the water on our tired feet. When the wine's all finished, we stay outside, taking advantage of the warm night air and then dry our feet on a couple of towels and make our way inside.

Gray checks the locks, sets the house alarm and looks in on the kids - an old habit that seems hard to break - before he gets ready for bed in our ensuite bathroom. We each have our own vanity basin, so I have plenty of room for all my pots and potions. Within a couple of minutes, Gray has undressed and brushed his teeth. By the time I've taken off my makeup and cleaned my teeth, Gray's already fast asleep, letting out a very light but equally annoying snore.

I climb into bed beside him, switch off the bedside light and fail miserably trying to find the curve of his legs, Gray usually finding the curve of mine, but this bed is so big that there is such a huge amount of space between us it's an impossible task. I toss and turn for what seems hours, but when I check the time, I've only been in bed for about half an hour. Thankfully, Gray's in such a deep sleep and I'm physically so far away from him that my constant tossing and turning doesn't seem to trouble him.

'Good morning.' I open my eyes to a very cheery and very awake Gray, cup of tea in hand.

'Good morning.' I say groggily, sitting up in bed, propped up by several plump pillows. I try to wake myself up, feeling like I've not slept at all. Taking the tea from him, I glance at the time. My eyes widen, and if I'd taken a sip of tea, I probably would have spat it out. 'Gray, it's only 6 a.m. What on earth are you doing up?' I pause. 'What on earth are you doing waking me up?'

'Well, I'm obviously still working on London time. Sorry, I just thought I'd treat you to a cup of tea, for a change.' Gray genuinely looks like a wounded puppy.

'It took me ages to get to sleep. I had to listen to you snoring for ages.' I grumpily reply.

'Ok. Point taken. I'll take myself back downstairs and let you sleep.' he says, kissing me gently on the top of my head.

I drink my tea and then snuggle back under the covers. I manage about another hour of sleep and then decide to join Gray downstairs. I'm still tired but I'm certainly not going to get any more sleep this morning, what with Gray crashing and moving about downstairs. Our bedroom is directly above the kitchen, which is just so where he happens to be. Incredibly, the kids are still managing to sleep through all the noise.

I slip on my kimono-style dressing gown over my nightdress, complete with a pair of flipflops, and walk downstairs. Gray, bless him, is trying to cook poached eggs and bacon. I've not seen such a mess in a kitchen before though. Well, not since he last "cooked" a breakfast, which was for my last birthday. I'm dreading the washing-up and cleaning.

'I thought I would cook you some breakfast.' he says,

looking at me with a big smile. He adds, somewhat sheepishly, 'Sorry. As per usual, I've made a bit of a mess.'

How could I be cross with him? He's always trying so hard to do nice things for me. Although, to be honest, looking at the mess, I would have been grateful for just another cup of tea. I could have cooked and cleaned, and it would have probably taken me less time than this will take to clean.

'It looks wonderful. Thank you. Is it warm enough to eat outside, do you think?'

'You go and check, let me know, and I'll bring you your breakfast in a minute.'

I slide open the patio doors. It is warm enough to sit outside, although the sun hasn't quite come over the pool yet. The villa overlooks a tranquil lake where, if you're lucky enough, you can see different species of birds swooping down to try and find fish. I call out to Gray to bring the breakfast outside. He's managed to find a tray and is carefully trying to balance poached eggs on toast with a couple of glasses of orange juice. I close the door behind Gray, and we tuck into our breakfast.

'Sorry, the eggs aren't really up to your usual standards, but I am trying.' Gray says.

My heart aches with love that after what he's recently found out about me, he somehow feels he's the one who needs to make an effort. How did I get so lucky?

'They taste all the nicer because you cooked them.' And they really do. The love put into this breakfast really changes the whole appeal.

'Really? You're not just saying that to not hurt my feelings?'

'Really. It's all just perfect. Thank you.' I lean over to plant a kiss on his cheek, but he turns his head, so gets a gentle peck on the lips instead.

'Gray!' I begin as he artfully kisses me again just as Cassie comes outside to join us.

'O-M-G, you two, get a room.' she shouts, shielding her eyes, pretending to be embarrassed.

'You should be happy that your parents still fancy each other.' says Gray.

'Ok, Dad, just stop. I really don't want to hear any more.'

As if on a Cassie rescue attempt, Will joins us, rubbing his eyes whilst looking at our empty plates. 'Have you had breakfast already without me?' he says indignantly.

I nod. 'Your dad treated me.'

'Nice. Is there anymore, Dad?' Will looks at Gray expectantly.

'Sit yourself down and I'll cook you the same. How about you, Cassie?'

'Don't bother. I'll help myself to some yoghurt. I want to look good in my bikini.' Cassie replies curtly.

'You're on holiday, for God's sake. Have something a bit more substantial.' Gray says encouragingly. 'Plus, who you trying to impress? Me? Your mum? Will? Because I don't see anyone else here.'

'Oh, go on, then.' she relents. Finally, there's a smile from her.

Gray causes yet more havoc in the kitchen as he cooks for the children whilst I discreetly try to tidy up after him. We then all sit outside, happily watching as the sun finally comes over the pool. It's not long before Will is splashing around in the pool again. Cassie sits on a sun lounger, shades on, busily messaging Mel whilst Gray and I sunbathe. I sent Maura a message last night just so she knows we've arrived safely. She messaged to confirm she's able to join us, she just needs to sort out a cattery for her beloved cats and book her flight. I also left a voicemail for my parents to let them know we decided to go away. It was more for my dad's benefit, as I know he'll now pop over to water the garden and take in the post. Mother probably won't approve of us going away at such short notice, but she no longer controls my life.

I half-heartedly pick up a novel that I've been "reading" for months but failing to make any headway with. No fault of the book itself, I've just been too on edge since Ed and his music re-entered my life and turned it upside down. I don't blame him for exploiting our teenage relationship to further his music career. By the sound of things, he's drifted for pretty much most of his life up until recently, and he probably just needs the money. When I had to give Milly away, I shelved any feelings I had for Ed, as it was just easier that way.

As I was quite weak after having Milly, my mother used that as an excuse to keep me at home. I wasn't allowed anywhere by myself. To be honest, it was worse than when she didn't allow me out after Ginny's party. At least then I could see my friends at school. Stuck in Bournemouth, I was like a prisoner, as I didn't know anyone there except my mother and my aunt. Dad was still working in London, and as they'd sold the family home in Barnes, he was renting a bedsit close to where he worked, coming down to see us in Bournemouth every other weekend. I would have loved to have spent more time with Emma, but friendships weren't allowed.

Nothing I ever did was good enough for Mother. My exam results weren't as good as I'd hoped for after all the upheaval. So, there I was, stuck in an unfamiliar area, penniless, alone and locked up with two malicious middle-aged women.

'Fancy a drink?' Gray asks, interrupting my teenage memories.

I nod and smile. 'Just a diet coke please.'

Gray grabs a beer and my diet coke from the fridge and goes in the pool. I follow and join him, undoing my sarong.

'This is just what we needed, isn't it?' says Gray, moving closer to me in the water.

"Yes, it's perfect. Thank you. Although I think Cassie is very quiet, don't you?' I ask, wanting reassurance that Gray too has realised things with Cassie aren't quite right.

'Oh, she's probably just a bit jetlagged. You know it takes a while to acclimatize and what with the time difference and the fact she probably didn't get much sleep at Mel's the other night. She must be just feeling a bit off.'

'Yeah, maybe. But call it a mother's intuition - I don't think she's her normal self. And we're just about to drop a bombshell on them.' I continue, refusing to be placated by Gray.

'Is tonight the night?' Gray whispers.

I nod. 'I'm so scared about what they're going to say though.'

'It'll be ok. They're good kids. I'm sure they'll understand.' Gray says, always the optimist.

'I really hope so.'

'We've brought them up well. I'm sure there'll be a lot of questions, but we'll get through it.'

'You think?' I say, desperately wanting to believe him.

'Positive.' he replies, leaning over to kiss me. 'You taste of sun cream.' He laughs.

'And you taste of beer.' I laugh back at him.

'What do you expect? I'm on my holidays.'

When Gray's away from the stresses of work, he's just like a big kid. I can see so much of Gray in Will. They're both so refreshingly uncomplicated and full of fun, whereas I fear that Cassie has inherited all my worries and anxieties. Time will tell how they will both cope with my latest bombshell.

25

ED

Now

The photos of the supposed adult Evie Del Rio (aka Genie McNamara) are all over the press and social media. I spend far too long doomscrolling #thegirlinthesong hashtag on my iPad, desperately looking for further stories or photos of Evie when I'm not at the gym or rehearsing. I'm not getting any further to finding out the truth. Each article is full of supposition, each theory and story wilder and more absurd than the last.

I run my hand through my hair, reminding me that I need to get my hair cut soon. I can't get away with leaving it too long anymore as it just looks aging and despite my lifestyle, I like to pride myself that I look younger than I am without any surgical tweaks. Only last week there was a brutal article in The Daily Mail comparing members of the public who were the same age as certain celebrities. There was one poor bloke called Trevor, a postman from the East End who was the same age as me who didn't come off too well compared to me and they'd obviously chosen the worst possible photo of Trevor. Our photos were side to side, pointing out what

Trevor needed to do to look younger. Trevor had a florid complexion and stringy, long hair slicked back in a greasy ponytail. They had listed a handful of 'tweakments' that would benefit Trevor. Who bloody commissioned such banal rubbish in our press I thought, but the public lapped it up in their droves.

I abandon my iPad and make myself a coffee and open the patio doors from the sitting room that leads on to the balcony, taking in the breathtaking views of the river. I have a lot to be thankful I thought. And that's when it came to me, I would start doing a few TikTok posts myself and then I would have total control over what I posted rather than all these blatant lies and inaccurate rubbish that social media continually churned out. Toby wouldn't mind. Any publicity was good publicity in his eyes.

I grab my phone and start talking to the camera. The first couple of videos are complete nonsense, by the third one I'm on a roll. I talk about the tour on how we were all looking forward to being back on the road again to reconnect with our fans. I give an idea of what our British audiences can look forward to from our gigs and hint about the possibility of some surprise guests. We haven't even sorted out all our support acts, but it is some sort of content, nevertheless. I post the first video on TikTok, and the likes and comments start flooding in.

It is now time to address #thegirlinthesong furore which had all started from my appearance on the Netflix documentary.

'As you are all aware since appearing on Musical Muses: The Girl in the Song documentary on Netlix, I have been tirelessly searching for my ex-girlfriend Evie Del Rio. Primarily I initially wanted to find her was for us to possibly reconnect but also to find out why she left without saying goodbye to me and her other close friends. Now after so much speculation

and seeing old photos that have recently resurfaced there is a third reason why I need to find Evie and that is to see if the rumours are true about her leaving because she was pregnant. I need to know the real truth; whatever it may be.

I finish up the video by thanking all our fans for their interest in our music and forthcoming reunion tour before speaking directly into the camera as if I was talking to Evie.

Please Evie, if you happen to see this video, please get in touch. I'm here if you want to talk.

Tomorrow I'll be doing a run through of all the songs on our debut album Past Times and the meanings behind them. Until then, thanks for watching.

I upload the video and post it, remembering to use #the-girlinthesong. I doubted Evie would ever see my ramblings. But it was worth a shot. Minutes later my post is full of comments. Most of them complimentary.

26

GENIE

Now

As we got a taxi to the villa the night before, Gray needs to go and pick up our hire car and decides to take Will who has been trying to persuade Gray all morning to hire a Mustang. Both Cassie and I have put them both straight on that, concerned about our hair as they would bound to want the roof down, despite the soaring heat!

They are back before we can even think about doing anything more than sunbathing.

'We're back. And we've got Dunkin' Donuts.' Will shouts.

That's enough to get Cassie moving, and she happily helps herself to a jam-filled doughnut, all thoughts of dieting thankfully forgotten. She even laughs as jam from her doughnut explodes all over her cover up. Gray and I grate-fully drink our first proper American coffee of the holiday and share a glazed doughnut whilst Will proceeds to eat three in a row. I don't know where that boy puts his food because he's as slim as a rake. For the remainder of the afternoon, we all just laze in and around the pool, enjoying relaxing and generally doing nothing. I'm reading, Cassie's sunbathing and appears to be asleep while Will bounces from pool to spa before eating yet another doughnut.

'What does everyone fancy for dinner tonight?' Gray asks.

'Can we go to that new steakhouse near the big Walmart that Uncle Jonesy recommended? It sounds amazing.' Will replies.

'Yeah, I don't see why not. I'll call ahead and book a table.' Gray says before anyone has a chance to disagree.

Cassie and I go off to get ready for dinner, and after Will and Gray have a last swim, and then Gray makes the call to the restaurant before they both hit the showers.

As Gray comes out of the shower and wraps his towel around his waist, I'm putting the final touches to my makeup at the dressing table.

'You look amazing.' Gray says, kissing the back of my neck. 'Are you starting to relax?'

'A little, I guess, but I don't want to wait too much longer to speak to the children. Perhaps after dinner when we get back to the villa?' There's a slight shake to my hand as I try to apply my mascara.

'It sounds as good a time as any.' he says, giving my free hand a squeeze.

It doesn't take Gray or Will long to get ready, although we still have to wait for Cassie to dry her hair.

'Come on, Cassie. I'm starving. No one's going to be looking at you anyway.' Will says, deliberately antagonising his older sister, his shoes already on to leave.

A screech of annoyance sounds from Cassie's room. 'Shut up, Will. No one's going to be looking at you, you mean. I bet you haven't even done your hair.'

'I just rely on my naturally good looks…'

'Enough, you two, Gray interjects before the pair launch

into a full-on argument. 'Let's get in the car before we lose our table at the restaurant.'

The car's great, with plenty of room for all of us, and the children even manage to be civil to each other on the short ride to the restaurant. We announce ourselves to the cheery girl on the front desk, who gives us a buzzer. We go outside to join the rest of the fellow would-be diners. Within five minutes, our buzzer is vibrating. In less than a minute, we're sitting in a comfy air-conditioned booth, perusing a menu of incredible steaks and burgers.

Will goes for a T-bone steak and chips, Gray has a New York strip and Cassie and I both go for fillet. All the steaks come with salad and either a baked potato or chips. By the end of the meal, we can hardly move, except for Will, who's already eyeing up the dessert menu. Will orders some traditional Key lime pie, but Gray and I just have a coffee. We're going to need our wits about us later. Gray settles the check - as the Americans like to call it - and we make our way back to the villa, stopping briefly at the pharmacy to stock up on some additional sunscreen and a few other bits and pieces that we need. The plan is to go to the big supermarket over the next few days.

Once back at the villa, we all rush to get changed and just let our food go down, except for Will, who's in the games room, shooting some basketball hoops. That boy has such an appetite, but I guess he does burn it off, as he can never stand still. As Gray and I get changed, we discreetly discuss how to broach the subject of Milly.

'I don't think I can do it.' I croak. 'I feel sick.'

'You'll be ok. I promise.' Gray replies.

I lean forward and grip the dressing table, looking at Gray through the mirror. 'You'll back me up, won't you?'

'I've always had your back, and I always will, whatever happens.' he says, planting a kiss on the top of my head, desperately trying to reassure me that everything will be ok. I just hope that he's right.

I take my time changing into a pair of joggers and a T-shirt, hanging up my dress, brushing my hair again and checking my makeup, doing absolutely everything I can to keep my secret from the children for that little bit longer. Even though I feel like a trembling wreck inside, at least I look ok outwardly.

Gray calls the children through to the living room area, telling them we need to talk to them about something important. My stomach is in knots, my delicious steak meal threatening to come right back up again. This is really it.

I join Gray in the sitting area, walking in a much more confident manner than I really feel. I take a seat next to Gray, taking hold of his hand for absolute reassurance that we are in this together.

Gray calls the children again, and Cassie eventually emerges from her bedroom, Will finally walking away from the basketball hoops to plonk himself next to his sister.

'You both look like someone's died.' Will observes.

'Oh my God. Did something happen to Granny or Grandad?' asks Cassie, her face full of concern.

Gray shakes his head. 'They are both absolutely fine, but we do have something very important to tell you.'

'You're not getting a divorce, are you?' shrieks Cassie.

'No, of course not. Your mum and I are just fine.'

'You're very quiet, Mum. What's up?' Will asks, much calmer than his sister. They both look at me expectantly.

'Mhmm.' I manage, a solitary tear rolling down my cheek. I don't trust myself to speak properly right now without breaking down. My throat has closed up, and although I know the words are there, I physically cannot speak.

Both children look over at me, waiting for me to say something. Gray gives me a reassuring nudge.

'I've been struggling with things that happened to me when I was almost eighteen. But before I fully explain everything, I want you to know that I absolutely adore and love both of you so, so much and would do anything for you. I only wish my parents had given me the same consideration.'

Cassie moves to sit next to me and strokes my hand softly, willing me on to continue.

'When I was in sixth form, I started going out with my first boyfriend. At first, everything was great. It was new and exciting. Stupidly, we both, and all our friends, started regularly drinking, and I hate to admit that we used to smoke a bit of weed too.' I confess.

Both Will and Cassie's faces are in total shock, as they know my stance about any type of smoking. You really don't want to hear about your mother's youthful misdemeanours at their ages, but they need to hear the truth from me.

'I know this is hard for you to hear, but I want to be totally honest with you both, and I want to be the one who tells you the whole truth. I don't want you getting incorrect information from the tabloids or TikTok.'

Both silently nod.

'We started sleeping together not long after we got together, and it's not something that I'm proud of. I now know with the benefit of hindsight that we were far too young. My parents tried to split us up, and they grounded me several times, but I still managed to meet up with him and my friends when Mother was doing her voluntary work and when Dad was at work.

'It wasn't until early April that my mother realised things weren't quite right with me. She caught sight of me coming out of the bathroom one evening and noticed that I'd put quite a bit of weight on. She got a bee in her bonnet that I was pregnant, asking me time and time again if I was. I didn't have a clue if I was or not, but the more she shouted at me, the more things suddenly started making sense. Dad arranged for me to have an appointment with a private doctor.' I pause and swallow. 'They confirmed that I was over three months pregnant.'

They still both look stunned, neither in any rush to respond, but I need to continue and explain everything.

'It's hard for me to find the right words to explain everything. My mother, as you know, is very religious, and she was absolutely horrified to find out that I was pregnant, so she took me to stay with her sister, my Auntie Maureen, in Bournemouth to continue the pregnancy in private. Dad stayed in London because of work. He also had to organise the sale of our house, as my parents didn't want anyone to find out about my pregnancy. He would come and visit us every other weekend, and those were the times that I lived for. I wasn't allowed to contact my boyfriend or any of my friends. We basically just upped and left, never to be heard of again.'

'What happened to the baby, Mum?' asks Cassie, her voice almost a whisper.

'My mother's plan was for me to do my exams, have the baby and then have it adopted. I had no choice in the matter. Mother didn't want any shame brought upon the family. I took my exams at the local sixth form and tried to forget about my old life in London. I started to bleed at thirty-seven weeks, so they rushed me to hospital, where they realised the baby had decided to come early. She was born safely, although a little small. Milly, or at least that's what I would have called her. Mother and Auntie Maureen had been in touch with a local Catholic adoption agency who had lots of worthy childless couples only too willing to adopt a new baby. To be honest, I was so out of it I hardly even remember seeing her properly. And then she was gone.'

'We've got a sister, and you never even told us?' says Cassie, removing her hand from mine, rage starting to overtake her. I nod, concerned by her reaction.

'I'm sorry. I really am, Cassie.' I don't know what else I can say. There are no words that can change this situation or make things any better.

'Where is she now?' Will asks gently.

I shrug sadly. 'I don't know. Hopefully, she's had a good life with her adoptive family.'

'How long have you known, Dad?' Cassie hisses at Gray. I've never seen her this angry, or hostile, ever, and it's all my fault.

'A couple of days.' Gray replies calmly, understanding of her reaction, ignoring the way in which she's talking to him. 'It's taken Mum a long time to come to terms with everything that happened to her.'

'Didn't you ever try to find each other like they do on the telly?' Will asks thoughtfully. I feel relieved that at least one of my children is showing understanding and acceptance. I don't know if I could handle double the negativity.

'I couldn't do that without telling your dad first. And... the longer time went on, the more I panicked that he'd leave if he found out.'

'I completely support your mum, and this doesn't change how I feel about her. I'm only sorry that she didn't feel she could tell me earlier so that we might have perhaps been able to find Milly.' says Gray loyally, once again showing me that I was wrong to hold secrets from him. Every time he shows he's here for me, I feel so lucky to have him. And then I have to swallow down a lump of guilt.

'I still can't believe you kept Milly a secret for all those years. How could you keep lying to us all for so long? It's like we don't even know you anymore. How can we ever believe a single word that comes out of your mouth?' Cassie shouts, pointing accusingly at me.

I feel physically sick. I want to make things right but whatever I say to Cassie now is just not good enough. The damage has been done. 'I'm sorry.' I whisper. I just want to hold Cassie, with all her hurt, and tell her everything will be ok, but she's looking at me like I'm a stranger.

'I just shelved the idea that I'd even had a baby, but there was always a void in my life until you came along, Cassie.' I continue, hoping she can see how much she means to me, that she *can* still trust me and the last thing I ever wanted to do was hurt her.

'I couldn't get pregnant for years and then you came along, and we were so happy, and everything was just perfect and not long after we had Will. There's also a reason I've chosen to tell you all about Milly now which I will explain.'

'Don't bother Mum. I think I've worked it out. You're #thegirlinthesong that Ed Nash has been banging on about, aren't you? You're Evie Del Rio. TikTok has been awash with rumours ever since that Netflix documentary was released.' Cassie says, almost triumphantly.

'Umm. Yes, I am. I'd hoped that you wouldn't work it out.' I reply quietly.

'It's because Grandad sometimes calls you Evie and you have to admit that Del Rio is quite an unusual surname.' Cassie continues. 'You don't have to be a genius to work it out.' She looks at me with almost a kind of loathing burning from her eyes. This is not the sort of reaction I'd expected from Cassie, and it unnerves me.

'I just want to forget that part of my life and concentrate on my family…' I begin.

'But Milly is part of your family… of our family. What sort of mother doesn't want to find her firstborn child? Do you know, I actually feel sorry for Ed Nash. Poor bloke deserves to know that he has a daughter. You're a disgrace, a complete liar and a poor excuse of a mother!' Cassie rages, her spittle lands on my cheek. I'm silent. My heart literally aches for the pain that I've caused my family.

'Cassie, how dare you speak to your mum like that. Apologise immediately.' Gray shouts as he stands in front of me, as if I'm some vulnerable object he needs to protect. But I don't need protecting. Cassie does. This is all my own fault. How can I be angry at her words when I caused this mess? What right do I have to fight against her or stand up for myself?

'No. She acts all high and mighty, when the truth is, she did all the things she's always told us not to do. She's a hypocrite.' she screams, pointing at me, accusingly.

'Cassie…' Gray begins.

'It's fine, Gray. I know I'm a hypocrite.' I put my hands on his arms, gently moving him to the side. 'I wanted you two to learn from my mistakes.' I say, eyes darting between Cassie and Will. 'I've always tried to protect you both and help you from making wrong decisions. You both know that I have a very odd relationship with Grandma, and I have always tried so hard, not to be like her. I'd like to feel you could both come to me for help, whatever the situation. I'm sorry I've disappointed you, Cassie, but all I know is that I love you both so much, and whatever you think of me, that will never change.'

'You seriously think you're any better than Grandma after lying to your children and your husband for years?' Cassie marches off to her room, slamming the door. My insides tighten. She might as well have slammed my heart in the door as she left. Cassie's known for her emotions. That's what makes her so empathetic and caring. That's what also makes her hurt harder though. I could have handled just a "I hate you" because she would never have meant it. Once Cassie calms down, she always ends up swept up in guilt. I've often held her like a little child in my arms after an emotional outburst. But being compared to *her*—my mum—with the image of her I've had my whole life… that somehow hurts more.

'I'm sorry, Mum, about everything that has happened to you. I'm trying to understand everything, I really am, but wow, that's amazing to think we've got an older sister. Don't worry about Cassie. She'll come around eventually. She's been such a moody cow since we left London.' says Will, giving me a hug. I wasn't the only one who noticed her mood change, then.

'Thanks, Will. And if there's anything you want to ask me about what I've told you, I'll try and be as honest and open as I can. I love you.' I say, giving my six-foot son a big hug back as he lays his chin on the top of my head.

'I love you too, Mum. I'll try to talk to Cassie.' he says, leaving the room.

'Genie, I'm so sorry Cassie spoke to you like that. It was unforgivable what she said to you, but goodness, how amazing is Will? So accepting and so mature. I was sure it was going to be the other way round.' Gray places an ever-protective arm around me.

'It's fine. I think Cassie is struggling in general, and this revelation is not what she expected, although she worked out that I'm #thegirlinthesong all on her own, well, with a little bit of help from TikTok. I think she's in shock. Also, to find out you have a grown-up sister is quite a lot to digest.'

'You're too understanding. She should never have spoken to you like that. I'll be having words with her later.' Gray says, shaking his head in disbelief.

'Please, Gray, leave her. I think she'll talk to me in her own time, perhaps one-on-one?' I bite my bottom lip, dread entering my mind. 'My only fear is that she talks to my mother.'

'You don't think she would, do you?' Gray replies, his brow furrowed by the harsh reality of the potential consequences of my revelation. Neither of us thought much further ahead than just telling the children.

'Well, she's always been the apple of my mother's eye. A legitimate granddaughter she can be proud of, whose parents are actually married.' I mutter.

'Let's hope Felicity doesn't get involved. Hopefully, Tony can smooth things over.' Gray adds.

'Dear old Dad. He's had a lifetime of smoothing things over between us.' I say wearily.

The children spend most of the rest of the evening in their rooms while Gray and I share a bottle of wine outside, enjoying the peace and stillness of another hot and humid night. We've just finished our first glass when Will comes out to see us.

'How's Cassie?' I immediately ask.

'Sulking. She can't even speak to Mel because of the time difference.' he says with a smug smile. I've been so wrapped up in Cassie not telling Mum that Mel didn't even enter my head.

'Neither of you must speak to anyone outside of the family about what Mum has told you.' Gray warns, speaking quickly and sternly. 'We are trying to decide together what the next steps are.'

'Don't worry about me, but you'd better speak to Cassie, as she's bound to tell Mel. They tell each other absolutely everything.'

Gray sighs. 'He's right, Genie. I'll go and have a chat with her. You stay here, relax and have another glass of wine.' Gray holds Will's arm gently as he passes and says softly, 'You'll keep Mum company, won't you, Will?'

'Yeah, sure. Can I have a beer, Dad?' Will asks, taking advantage of the understanding child versus the angry child situation.

'Go on, then. But just the one, and don't think you're going to have one every night.'

Gray leaves to talk to Cassie whilst Will goes off to get his beer. I'm left alone with my thoughts, wondering if things with Cassie will ever be the same.

27

ED

Now

We're knee deep in rehearsal mode for our reunion tour, when I realise that after the success of my recent TikTok videos I should maintain the momentum and post some more. So, I take a few short videos of our rehearsals ready to post later. I can make up the narrative at home. I'm planning on driving home straight after rehearsals as I've got a gym session planned for later, so they'll be no diversions via the pub tonight.

Toby is fired up by the success of our rehearsals and I must agree that we are sounding good. Later, both Mark and Jez accept my offer of a lift home and afterwards, I drive straight to the gym having remembered to pack my gym kit earlier this morning. Buoyed up by the success of the rehearsals earlier in the day, I focus on my cardio with sessions on both the running machine and the bike. I do a few stretches, shower, pick up a chicken salad from the gym café and drive home.

As I eat my salad, I for once relish the silence in my flat and start to write something in my head as I post a couple of snippets from the earlier videos. I then decide to just shoot the breeze and start talking into the camera about my day in one of them and then I decide to talk quite candidly about still hoping that Evie might reach out. I like taking back the control of the narrative of my life, it feels quite empowering and maybe, just maybe Evie might see my video and reach out. The clips of the band have the desired effect and are being reposted rapidly and once I post the one where I reach out to Evie personally, #thegirlinthesong is back trending again on all social media channels. Feeling inspired I grab my guitar and start putting down some chords to go with lyrics that have been in my head for a while, and it sounds good. I'll play it to Mark and Jez at the next rehearsal to see what they think. Creatively and professionally, I feel I'm at the top of my game, but personally there's a drought, apart from my few good friends who I can always rely on. My relationship with my parents is strained although I think Dad would keep in touch more often if Mum wasn't so fixated on Paul and the way he coerced me to leave home not long after Evie left. Looking back, I guess she did have a cause for concern as he is responsible for encouraging me to drink heavily and take drugs. Paul didn't turn out to be the great guy that I originally thought but I'm keeping my distance from him now as much as I can and keep contact with him to a bare minimum.

28

GENIE

Now

I wake up early. It's a mixture of jetlag and coming to terms with the bombshell that I've just dropped on the children. Thankfully Gray as per usual seems to be coping ok, in fact he seems more concerned about me and how I'm coping but then that's Gray all over. He's been caring for me and trying to fix me since we met. Cassie's reaction has been the biggest shock to me, she can barely look at me, let alone hold a conversation or maintain eye contact. Will, just like Gray is far more accepting of my former life.

I know I seem like a hypocrite as I have always encouraged the children to be honest, not to smoke, keep drinking to a minimum and not be tempted by having sex too soon. It's been like my mantra. And now they know why. Unlike my friends, I was the one who got caught out. And my mistakes are now out there for everyone to know about – although they haven't quite worked out exactly who I am, but I'm sure it won't take long for TikTok to find me. My past is finally catching up with me.

I slip out of bed, leaving Gray fast asleep. I'm relieved no one else is up and awake. I put on a pot of coffee and scroll through my phone while I wait. I'm greeted with a blurry photo of us all when we first arrived at Heathrow Airport, entitled "Is this Ed Nash's #thegirlinthesong?" Thank God we're away currently; it's good to put over four thousand miles between us and the ever-continuing media storm all started by Ed and his desire to find out why I left. There's also another piece about Ed, picturing him with Jez and Mark coming out of a rehearsal room in Soho. I'd recognise them both anywhere. Life must have been kind to them as they have both aged well. My stomach does a little flip as I study the photo in more detail. I always thought that any feelings I ever had for Ed had disappeared, but the photo is so natural, all of them caught off guard and I remember fondly the boy who was my very first love. Like both Jez and Mark, Ed's hair is now shorter, I remember his vivid and mesmerizing blue eyes that were once so familiar to me, covered up with obligatory rockstar sunglasses. I feel a flush rise from my chest to my neck and face and finally to the tips of my ears, despite the refreshing and cool aircon. I feel guilty to have my deepest, darkest thoughts of Ed suddenly resurfacing after a lifetime of denial. I've never even looked at another man in that way since being with Gray. He's my soulmate, my rock, my Mr Dependable who rescued me all those years ago. He deserves so much more. Of course, Ed will always hold a special place in my heart – he was my first boyfriend, my first love – but it wasn't real. Even if I hadn't got pregnant and been made to leave London, we probably wouldn't have lasted. First love rarely lasts. Meeting Gray turned my life around, and I will be eternally grateful for that.

My thoughts are interrupted, and I jump as Gray places his hands around my waist, kissing my neck.

'You ok, Genie?' He says and I'm convinced he can feel the heat from my face.

'Yeah. Just woke up early and fancied a coffee.' I reply, feeling guilty for my earlier thoughts of my past.

'Sounds lovely.' Gray replies, as he reaches up and takes another cup out of the cupboard. I pour out our coffees and we go and sit outside companionably in silence waiting for the sun to come over the pool.

It's not too long before we are joined by Cassie, who has made herself a cup of green tea. She takes a seat next to Gray.

'How are you feeling after last night?' Gray asks, reaching out to try and hold Cassie's hand, but she snatches it away.

'Disappointed.' She replies, deliberately using the hack-neyed expression that most parents tend to use when discussing their children's behaviour.

'It's an awful lot to take in – it has been for all of us but surely you can understand how difficult and upsetting all of this is for your mum? Remember Cassie, we're a family, and we need to stick together and support each other.' Gray says, touching my hand, reassuring me as always that he's got my back. He looks exhausted.

'But part of our family is missing, and Ed has been denied ever knowing his only child.' Cassie responds.

'How come you're team Ed?' Gray asks, a sarcastic note in his voice.

'Well, I think he has the right to know he has a daughter. He hasn't got any other kids. And Milly has the right to know who her real parents are.'

'Milly probably had a great life, with loving parents. She might even have some siblings too.' Gray says, trying as always to justify my actions.

'Probably isn't good enough. Will and I are her siblings. What if she's had an awful life? She might even have some children of her own. Oh my God, I could be an auntie!' Cassie says, dramatically flicking her hair back, resorting to being a typical teenager and making the situation all about her.

'Ok, ok, Cassie. Let's not get too carried away. It's up to Mum as to what she wants to do, and I want you to apologise for the way you spoke to her last night.' Gray says sternly, taking a big sip of his coffee.

'I don't see why I should have to apologise to her. She should be the one apologising to us for lying for years. Don't you think your marriage has been one complete lie?' Cassie asks, entering dangerous territory, almost forgetting I'm sitting right here, listening to every word that comes out of her mouth.

'Your mum had her reasons for not telling us the truth.' Gray says calmly. 'I think she's been in denial since she had to give her baby away. I couldn't have asked for a better wife or mother for you two. Show your mum some respect and some compassion, please, Cassie. I'm quite taken aback by your reaction, to be honest. Apologise to your Mum immediately.' Gray bites back.

'It's just a lot to take in. Our lives have been turned upside down since Mum's revelation and I think I've messed up my exams as well.' She blurts out.

'It's ok, Cassie. I know yesterday was such an overload of information and I'm sorry you've been so stressed about your exams, but it's not the end of the world if you haven't got the grades you hoped for. You can always do some retakes in November or the following year.' I interject. 'Don't get stressed until you know what you're dealing with.' Gray says calmly to Cassie, placing a protective arm around her.

'I just don't want to disappoint you both, as I know you've spent a lot of money on my education, but I think I just took my eye off the ball a bit and I didn't study hard enough.' She confides to us both.

'I'm sorry, we didn't realise you were struggling.' Gray

says, shaking his head. 'But please don't worry about the money we've spent. My parents left me their house, which, although it wasn't a huge house, when I sold it, I decided to put the money into an account that was just for your education. I wanted you two to have the opportunities I didn't.'

'You've done alright for yourself, Dad. You're a partner in your advertising firm.'

'I've done ok, but I might have done better if I hadn't gone to the local comp. It was pretty rough at my school. If you were remotely academic, you got picked on, so I played it down,' Gray explains.

'I'm sorry if you feel we have been hard on you about your studying. As you now know, I didn't do particularly well in my exams because of my situation and I guess I just wanted you to have the chances that I didn't.' I try to reassure her.

'How about I cook us all some breakfast? Gray says, trying to lighten the mood. 'Or do you fancy going out?'

'Let's have breakfast here, and maybe we could go out for some lunch?' Cassie suggests, happy to change the topic of conversation.

'Sounds like a plan.' Gray agrees.

He whistles away as he prepares breakfast. We can always depend on Gray to diffuse the situation. I sit with Cassie in silence, I know I haven't been there for her recently and I realise that I have been caught up in the total chaos of my own life and I have forgotten that I also need to protect and nurture my children.

Gray soon joins us again outside with three perfectly cooked breakfasts, precariously balanced on a tray that he's found in the kitchen.

I notice Cassie taking a furtive glance at me as I run my hand through my messy hair. I must look like a wreck as I tossed and turned all night. She stops eating.

'Mum, I'm just upset that you didn't tell us sooner about Milly, and I don't like the fact you haven't tried to find her.' She says quickly, not wanting either of us to stop the flow of her words.

I lean forward and sigh. 'I think about her every day. Mother said she was better off without me, so that's what I started to believe. The longer I didn't say anything, the harder it became to say anything at all. Even Auntie Maura has no idea. She's due to come out to see us next week, so I'm going to tell her then.' I reply, my eyes clouding over as I struggle hard not to cry. Cassie looks like she wants to reach out for my hand, but she clearly changes her mind and carries on eating her breakfast.

'Cassie, do you want to see if Will is ever going to join us?' Gray asks, breaking the tension in the air.

'Sure.' She agrees, only too happy to get away from any more awkward discussions as she runs away upstairs. We hear Cassie's loud strident tones as she tries to wake up her brother.

'Wakey, wakey.' she shouts.

Will arrives downstairs, dressed in last night's shorts and T-shirt. He reaches over to kiss me.

'We've just had a cooked breakfast. But I'm sure Dad will cook for you as well. Oh, and Auntie Maura's coming out next week for the big reveal mark two.' Cassie says, somewhat spitefully, bringing her brother up to date.

'That'll be a right laugh with Auntie Maura here, and I'm sure she'll take the news ok. You should go easy on Mum, yeah? It must have been hard for her. It's like you getting pregnant now and Mum and Dad making you give the baby away. But you'd obviously have to find a boyfriend first.' he adds with a grin.

'Shut up, Will. You never take anything seriously, do you?' she snaps, crossing her arms.

'I do. You've got to learn how to chill out a bit, Cass.'

'Enough you two.' Gray scolds, but I'm enjoying their bickering as it's almost like we're back to normal. Obviously, things have changed and we can never go back to the way things were.

'Morning. Any chance of one of your fry ups? Cassie told me that you'd already cooked.' Will asks cheekily.

'I guess I have to play fair.' Gray replies as he goes inside to start the next breakfast shift, leaving me with both children. I feel nervous and hesitant as I bite my nails, not having had either the time or inclination to have a pre-holiday manicure. Will chats away to me quite effortlessly.

'You alright?' he asks, giving me a reassuring hug.

'I'm getting there.' I reply, smiling weakly. 'If there's anything either of you want to ask me, then please do.'

Cassie looks thoughtful, as if she has a thousand questions to ask me but remains resolutely quiet.

'I just wanted to thank you for telling us about everything. It can't have been easy for you, Mum.' Will says.

'Thanks, love. I really appreciate that.'

We spend the next ten minutes trying to make small talk, fake marvelling about the birds swooping for fish in the lake behind the pool. Thankfully, Gray saves the day by coming out with Will's fry up, so none of us feel obliged to say anymore. Will literally demolishes his breakfast in about five minutes, complete with a huge glass of orange juice.

'What does everyone fancy doing today?' asks Gray.

'I'd like to go kayaking. It doesn't have to be today though. There was a big feature about some lake close to here on one of those travel programmes recently where you can go jet skiing and kayaking. It looks awesome.' Will says enthusiastically.

'Sounds like a definite plan for another day. We could

look them up online and book something for later in the week.' Gray agrees.

'Brilliant.'

Cassie glares at her brother as he seems to have woken up in such a positive mood, compared to the look on Cassie's sullen face.

'I guess it's another pool day. I'm good with that.' Will further enthuses, as Cassie looks over with one of her 'resting bitch faces' as Will always calls them.

'That's fine.' Gray says. 'Although I do need to pop to the supermarket to pick up some extra food. I don't mind going on my own.'

'I'll help.' Cassie swiftly offers, clearly horrified by being left alone with me and seeing right through her dad's plan of the three of us playing happy families.

'Oh ok, Cassie. That would be great. Genie, can you put a list together of what we actually need? You know I'll only bring back bacon, eggs, beer and wine otherwise.' Gray says, laughing at his own joke, sensing the tension.

'Sure. Give me a few minutes.' I say, as I go inside to make a list, leaving the three of them outside but I still manage to overhear their conversation.

'I thought you might have liked to spend some time with your mum.' Gray says to Cassie, frowning.

'Oh, I just fancied getting out of the villa, that's all.' she lies. 'Will went with you to choose the car, so I just thought it was my turn to have a trip out. It'll be quicker if I come with you. You take ages shopping, as you always get side-tracked by the wine aisle.' Before Gray can say anything more, to maybe try and sway Cassie to stay here instead, she adds, 'I'm just going to put something more suitable on for shopping.'

She returns shortly, wearing a pair of khaki shorts with a

white vest, flipflops and sunglasses which complete her shopping outfit.

Gray waits for her, as I message him my lengthy shopping list.

'Bye, you two. Have fun.' says Gray, waving.

'Mum's going to film me doing backflips into the pool for Snap.' Will replies like an overexcited puppy.

Gray and Cassie are away for ages, but being with Will is just effortless and I find myself belly laughing at Will's efforts of backflipping into the pool while I try to film him. I'm absolutely soaked through, but I don't mind at all. I haven't had this much fun in ages.

'You two look like you've been having too much fun without us.' Gray jokes on their return.

'We've got doughnuts and drinks.' Cassie says, sitting down at the table, helping herself to yet another sugary doughnut, washed down with an iced smoothie.

'Pass us one, Cass.' says Will, pointing at the doughnuts.

'No eating in the pool, Will. You know the rules. Come out if you want to eat.' I remind him.

Drinks and doughnuts finished, we all chill around the pool while Gray does a bit of research about kayaking.

29

ED

Now

I'm awake early again, so I decide to get another work out in before our rehearsal. As I drive through the barrier, true to form, Sid is tidying up the front of the flats, picking up a bit of litter that has dared to find itself in our communal flowerbeds. I put my window down.

'Morning! Another hot day ahead.' he calls out to me as I approach the ramp to the underground car park.

Despite the early hour, the gym is busy, but I manage to do a run and my weights routine and then drive back home and park up, deciding to race up the communal stairs. I bump into one of the Australian girls getting ready for another epic exercise session. We nod at each other as I run past, up all ten flights of stairs without stopping. I feel physically sick by the time I get inside the flat. I bet that Australian girl wouldn't have been out of breath but, hey, that's the difference between being in your twenties and being almost fifty and I have just been to the gym.

I shower and get ready, then grab another coffee and make myself some porridge to give me some energy for the forthcoming day. I call Mark to see if he wants a lift to the rehearsal room, which he gratefully accepts, as he's worn out from doing the school run. It's tricky juggling responsibilities for all his children. He has the twins Misty and Alanis with his first wife Marsha and another daughter, Marnie with his ex-girlfriend Frida and finally there is Baby Luna who still doesn't let anyone sleep through the night who he has with his second wife Rosita. It's exhausting but he just about manages to keep everyone happy.

Mark lives in Richmond, so it doesn't take too long to get to him. I've never seen a man so grateful for the offer of a lift.

'Alright, mate?' I ask as he climbs into my car.

'Yeah, just knackered from last night. I'll get my head down for forty winks and then I'll be as right as rain.'

Mark nods off with ease, and I concentrate on navigating my way to the studio, listening to Radio X London, who seem to be really championing our latest single "No More Tears" even though most of their listeners are certainly not in our age demographic. I still get such a buzz whenever our music is played on the radio. The journey to the West End is uneventful, and I manage to do it within forty-five minutes. I park in the studio car park and give Mark a nudge. We make our way to the rehearsal room. Cindy and Chyna are already here, but Andy and Simon are still to make an appearance, as is Jez. He only lives just off Chiswick High Road, so I don't think he'll be too long. Amazingly, Toby isn't here yet. I'm convinced he's shacked up with Cindy, but she's denying all knowledge of why he isn't here. Jez is the next one to arrive.

Toby's assistant Fifi comes through from her temporary office, informing us that Toby will be delayed by about half an hour due to having to go to an emergency dental appointment, and we are to set up and start practicing. We're already in the rehearsal room setting up when Andy and Simon arrive.

'You're lucky Toby's had to go to an emergency dental appointment. He doesn't tolerate people being late.' Cindy warns them.

'Since when are you the boss?' Andy asks under his breath.

'Sorry, did you say something, Andy?' Cindy fakes a toothy grin, knowing damn well what he just said.

'I said, let's get started. Show Toby what we can do.' he lies.

Everyone's in position, and we start off with some of the newer material. Cindy and Chyna's backing vocals work well on most of the numbers. Despite Mark's lack of sleep and his busy morning, he's on fire behind the drums. Simon's guitar playing complements Jez's now legendary bass playing, and by adding in Andy's keyboards on certain numbers, we are sounding very together. My voice seems to be holding up as I scream out some of the more shouty, rocky vocals and then I manage to reign it in on some of the slower, gentler songs.

'I'd like to practice 'Used to Be' once more, please.' I announce. 'Girls, you hang back on the backing vocals, but if you can do that dance routine you did last time, that would be great.'

Everyone gets into place and does their thing. It's all sounding slick and polished. Toby returns just as Mark's drumming signals the end of the song and lets out a loud whistle and gives us a round of applause.

'I can hardly speak because of the injection they've just given me at the dentist but that was spot on. Just brilliant.' he slurs.

It was definitely the right move to just have the one set of vocals on "Used to Be". Although Toby's happy with our progress, he's a hard task master and has us go over some of the songs repeatedly. By mid-afternoon, we've all had enough, so we take a break, and Toby gets Fifi to order in some food for us. I keep it healthy - just a salad and a bit of sushi - as I know Toby will be watching my calorie intake until the tour.

After our break, we don't finish rehearsals until nearly ten-thirty. We're all getting ready to go when Toby pulls me aside.

'I see from the recent press that congratulations might be in order, if the tabloids are anything to go by.' Toby says with a big grin on his face, rubbing his chin and his ridiculous excuse for a beard.

'What do you mean?' I say, shrugging, car keys in my hand.

'That your missing Evie Del Rio may have had your baby and that's why she disappeared, well according to the mighty TikTok.' Toby says incredulously, almost rubbing his hands together with glee over the prospect of some more free publicity for the tour.

'It's all hearsay Toby. I still haven't been able to find Evie.' I reply, sadly.

'I'm sorry about that but on the plus side of things, it's all great press for the tour though. Your youthful exploits with Evie Del Rio have really helped with selling this tour, you know.' Toby says with a cunning smile.

In the back of my mind, I keep going over what if Virginia was right all along and Evie simply left because she really was pregnant. Every time Evie is mentioned, the thought resurfaces. I need to know one way or another.

'Good stuff, Ed. I'll see you in a couple of days but do keep your fitness regime up. I'll get the personal trainer sorted for you next month so you're in top shape for the tour. Now, get yourself out of here.' Toby instructs as he clocks

Cindy waiting for him. They're definitely shagging. She's so his type.

I walk out to the reception area, where Mark and Jez are both waiting for me.

'Any chance you could drop me off on your way home?' Jez asks.

'Sure, mate. Come on, you two. Let's get you home. Poor old Mark's got the bloody school run again in the morning, so he could do with getting his head down.'

Mark opts for going in the back of my car so he can try to sleep, and it gives me the opportunity to catch up with Jez. The chat is easy, as we've known each other since our school days. We chat about our respective health kicks in readiness for the upcoming tour.

'No nice new woman to tell me about?' I probe. It's about time Jez had a new girlfriend. He's such a decent bloke, and I know he could show someone the world.

'Nah, I'm giving them a miss. I haven't got the energy for it all. I quite like the look of Cindy, but I think she's shagging Toby, so I'm certainly not going anywhere he's been.' He laughs. We're making good progress through the traffic despite the initial bottle neck around the streets of Soho.

'Yeah, I picked up on that too. Has Chyna said anything about it?'

'Chyna doesn't even give me the time of day. I think she's got her eye on Andy. I don't know what she sees in him.' he ponders, shaking his head.

'He's just one of those guys with the gift of the gab, isn't he?'

"Yeah, I guess so.' muses Jez.

'Have you been seeing anyone recently?' Jez asks. I shake my head.

'You still hung up on Evie and the whole pregnancy theory on TikTok?'

'Since when have you been interested on TikTok?' I joke, elbowing him.

'I like to keep up to date with what's going on.' Jez replies seriously.

'You know I met up recently with Ginny Weathers or Virginia Baker as she now likes to be known as. She was the one that first planted the idea in my head that Evie was pregnant and that's probably why she left. It was her photos that got leaked to the press.' I explain.

'Ginny sold you out?' Jez asks incredulously.

'No. Not Virginia. It was her ex-husband. He took copies of the photos after their daughter had mentioned that I'd been over.' I reply, really hoping that I haven't been hoodwinked by Virginia and that she has told me the truth.

'Well, it explains a lot I guess as to why Evie left. I wonder if she had the baby? You could be a dad, which is incredible!' Jez replies.

'I know. I've always wanted a family of my own, but I've never really been in that situation where children were on the cards, you know?' I say, lost deep in my own thoughts.

'I understand. I'm the same. I feel I've missed out. And you're not the guy the press always go on about. If they knew you, like me and Mark know you, they'd realise you're one of the good guys.' says Jez, who, despite looking like a Hells Angel, although his hair is shorter now, is one of the most sensitive people I know. He married very young to his first proper girlfriend Poppy, a real hippy chick with the palest skin you had ever seen, bright green eyes and red hair. They first met at primary school and then reconnected as teenagers, but she tragically drowned after a midnight swim on their honeymoon in Thailand.

They'd enjoyed the most blissful couple of weeks just being together - swimming, snorkelling, sampling exquisite Thai cuisine, rock climbing and hiking - but on the very last night, they went to a Full Moon Party and shared a Magic Mushroom shake. They apparently both felt very chilled at first, but as Jez was so out of it, he lay on the sand while Poppy danced her way to where the waves gently lapped the shoreline, paddling in the sea just up to her ankles. She called out to Jez to come and join her, as she wanted him to experience the beauty of the moon's reflection on the water.

By the time Jez managed to join Poppy, the water was almost up to her shoulders. Jez just couldn't seem to keep up with her, and the more he tried to, the more she seemed to be just that little bit out of reach. The last sighting Jez had of Poppy was her mouthing "I love you" as the waves finally took her.

They never recovered her body, and rumours of their extreme drug abuse and sex-fuelled orgies plagued Jez for years. There were even rumours that Jez had persuaded Poppy to take her own life so he could cash in on her life insurance. None of it's true, of course, but it made Jez a changed man. For a while, he joined a Buddhist retreat, where he tried to learn how to deal with his grief. Two years after Poppy died, he finally returned to London after travelling throughout Southeast Asia, which had always been his and Poppy's plan. He was older, wiser, didn't do drugs anymore and was ready to make music again, much to my and Mark's delight.

We reach Chiswick High Road, and Mark wakes up just as Jez reaches his front door after leaving the car.

'Do you want to join me in the front, Mark?'

'Yeah, I need to wake up a bit, as I'll be looking after Luna when I get in. Rosita is exhausted.' Mark decides to clamber into the front between the two front seats, over the handbrake. He collapses into the passenger seat and runs his hand through his hair. Not the easiest way to get into the front seat, but I guess lack of sleep can do that to you.

'You look pretty done in yourself. Have you thought about getting someone in to help you with Luna?'

'I would pay for a maternity nurse just like that' - he snaps his fingers – 'I tell you, but because it's Rosita's first baby, she wants us to do it all ourselves. There's no one giving out prizes for driving yourself into the ground.' he mutters. He looks out the window and turns silent, seemingly to focus on staying awake for the rest of the car journey.

We reach Mark's, and he waves to me as he walks up the drive. I eventually arrive home tired but still on a high from rehearsals. They went much better than I thought, and with a few tweaks, the British public are going to be in for a treat come October time.

30

GENIE

Now

It's Gray's turn to get up early and despite another late night, I'm awake early again too. Gray leaves me in bed to sleep but I hear him putting the coffee machine on. I watch him from the bedroom window as he sits outside to watch the sunrise and I notice that he appears to be catching up on some work, as he has his work phone with him. He promised me that he wouldn't work on this holiday but who am I to lay down the rules, when I've been keeping a secret from him for our entire married life.

The sunrise looks beautiful and was clearly worth getting up early for. As Gray finishes off his coffee he dangles his feet in the cool water of the pool, enjoying the silence. I take a last look at him and return to bed, exhausted by another bad night and drift off to sleep.

I doze for about half an hour before I hear Cassie's voice from outside. I walk downstairs and pour myself a coffee and listen surreptitiously in on their conversation.

'Morning, Dad, you're up early. Are you still suffering from jetlag?' She stands in the doorway and unties the hair tie from her hair, letting her hair flow, a kink in it where the hair tie was.

'Perhaps, but I just really think I'm learning to enjoy the silence that comes with early mornings.' he replies, still staring at the beautiful sky.

'How about I make you some breakfast for a change?' Cassie suggests, joining her dad on the side of the pool. She's got a genuine smile on her face, and she seems calm.

'That would be amazing. Maybe a poached egg with some smashed avocado? Oh, and another coffee, please.' He replies, holding out his cup.

'I think I can just about manage that.' Cassie laughs, taking the cup from his hand.

As Cassie leaves to fix breakfast for Gray, she notices me at the breakfast bar, nursing my coffee.

'Morning Cassie.' I start with a false brightness in my voice.

'Morning.' She replies coldly. 'I'm making Dad breakfast. Do you want anything?'

'I'll stick to coffee I think, thanks.' I reply nervously before adding. 'If you want to talk, I'm more than happy to answer any more questions that you may have.'

'We'll talk later.' She replies, conversation closed as she busies herself in the kitchen. I take my coffee and join Gray outside.

Later, Cassie arrives with Gray's breakfast and coffee, and we all chat about the day ahead.

'When was the last time you cooked for me? This breakfast is amazing. Your culinary skills are definitely improving.' Gray remarks to Cassie as he takes his first mouthful.

'Mum taught me how to cook the perfect poached egg. You have to remember to add the vinegar.' she replies, as I think, well at least I'm good for some things.

'Why don't you see if Will's awake? We've got our

kayaking at eleven-thirty, and we need to get there about fifteen minutes early for a safety briefing.' Gray remarks.

I'm pleasantly surprised when Cassie agrees without a huff, an eyeroll or any backchat.

Cassie returns with Will, and she even offers to make breakfast for him. Perhaps we've turned a corner?

Kayaking is a great success, with Gray and I in one kayak and the children in another. Will almost tips them into the inky water, but thankfully they both manage to right themselves without too much squabbling. We get into quite a rhythm with our paddles and manage to kayak around the lake quite easily without any mishaps. Thankfully, the rest of the day is uneventful and come the evening Cassie and Will have retreated to their rooms and Gray and I are enjoying a final glass of wine outside.

'What day is Maura flying out here?' Gray asks me again. I've already told him, but he hasn't remembered.

'Saturday. She's getting the lunchtime flight, so she'll be here quite late. I said you'd pick her up from the airport. I hope that's ok?' I reply.

'Of course. It will be good to see her.' Gray says. 'Just let me know her flight number, and I'll track her flight.' He swills the wine around in his glass. 'I've been thinking about when we first met in that bar in Brighton that Maura used to manage.'

'Oh yeah?'

'How did you end up in Brighton?'

'My friend at the church recommended it as quite a cool place to go to, that was easy enough to get to but far enough away from Bournemouth.'

'Oh, yes, I remember you mentioning her to me. What was her name again?' He asks casually.

'Emma. Emma Hadfield. She was the only person in Bournemouth who ever showed me any kindness. She'd seen me at church and then we started talking because I took my exams at her school. She knew what Mother and Auntie Maureen were like from seeing them at church. She even gave me some of her savings, so I had a little bit of money behind me to get me away from Bournemouth.'

'Did you keep in touch?' He probes further.

'No. I felt it was better to reinvent myself, hence my name change to Genie. Milly was gone, and I had absolutely nothing to keep me in Bournemouth. Can you believe that Mother and Auntie Maureen had me volunteering at the church?'

He nods because he knows what my Mother is really like. Despite her being an amazing grandparent, she's never cared as much about me, my beliefs or my wants.

'It was torture.' I continue. 'Even after giving my baby away, they still had control over me, as I had no money and they were always with me, even at the church. It was incredible how I ever managed to get away, to be honest. I waited until Dad came to visit, as I wanted to see him one more time before I left and as per usual, he slipped me some money on the quiet. Once Dad returned to London, I pretended I was unwell so I didn't have to do my shift at the church. Mother ended up taking my shift and I then put a load of laxatives into Auntie Maureen's cup of tea which I'd found in her bathroom cupboard. She was in the bathroom when I left. Looking back, I should have made sure she wasn't in the bath... she could have drowned. But I didn't care at the time. I was so desperate.' I finish the last of my wine and sit back, breathing in the night air.

'I called Emma the morning that I left from a phone box. I didn't call her again to let her know where I was staying, as I didn't want to get her in trouble. Her parents were also quite big in the church, and they would have been horrified to hear that she had helped me. I could never have done it without Emma's help. I do wonder how life has treated her. I've been lucky with my choice of friends, but I do feel guilty that I lost touch with both Emma and my friend Ginny from school. Thank goodness I still have Maura and you.' I say, leaning over and kissing Gray firmly on the lips.

Gray suggests another glass of wine, which I happily agree to, that last glass of wine has taken the edge off and I'm hopeful that things with Cassie will improve.

31

ED

Now

I'm at a bit of a loose end, so I've arranged to meet Jez in one of my local pubs. We manage to secure a table in the pub garden and we both go against Toby's special pre-tour diet plans, and both opt for the speciality burgers with a couple of pints. It's about 5:30p.m. and the pub is already busy, full of yummy mummies making the most of a midweek glass or two of prosecco with their various bored and tired offspring. There's also a selection of office workers getting stuck into some post-work drinks.

Jez rarely gets noticed by the public, but as the front man of the band, people know my face and I'm aware that I'm attracting a bit of attention, despite me wearing my obligatory sunglasses.

'God I'd forgotten what it's like going out with you. All the attention. I don't know how you put up with it all.' Jez remarks, indicating with his eyes at a couple of yummy mummies who are constantly nudging each other and looking over in our direction. We order a couple more beers, to hell with Toby and his diets. We have a brief tussle over the bill, with Jez being quicker than me as he uses his Apple watch to settle up, so I insist on leaving an extra tip in cash for the extremely attentive and attractive young waitress. Jez nips to the bathroom and I wait for him at the table, when one of the yummy mummies staggers over, dragging a somewhat grubby and tired-looking little boy behind her.

'I have to say, I really do lurve your music.' she slurs, placing her hand on my arm. 'I've got tickets for your tour, you know.

Her lipstick is smudged and she's desperately trying to steady herself on her overly high heels.

'Oh, um, thank you.' I reply modestly.

'Any chance of a photo?' the drunk yummy mummy continues. 'Otherwise, the girls at Pilates won't believe that I met you.'

'Sure, why not?' I reply with a fixed grin.

The woman sidles up to me, putting her arm around me. Her equally sozzled friend takes the photo. I'm used to this kind of attention, and I've learnt to always be pleasant to people, especially the drunk ones.

'Thanks sooo much. I really do appreciate it. It'll really make my husband jealous too!' She laughs, something that resembles a loud cackle, as she takes her phone back from her friend, eager to look at the photo.

'No worries. Have a great evening, ladies.' I reply with a well-practiced smile.

Jez returns to the table with a big grin on his face.

'You been spotted again?'

'Yup!'

'They both looked like they'd put a few away.' Jez observes.

'You could say that, but you do get a much better class of drunk around Teddington.' I joke. 'Fancy coming back to mine for a bit. I've got some beers in the fridge. You haven't been over for ages.'

'Yeah. Why not? It's not like I've got a gorgeous girlfriend waiting for me at home, is it?' Jez says as we leave the pub, the earlier yummy mummies gossiping away, as they try in their inebriated state to work out how to post the picture to Instagram.

We're back at mine within minutes and Jez and I sit out on the balcony sipping a couple of beers.

'God you could never get tired of this view.' Jez enthuses as he looks out admiring the manicured gardens and river views.

'I know that's what sold the apartment to me; the views and the double balconies.' I reply.

'What are we like? We sound like a couple of estate agents minus the tight shiny suits!' Jez blurts out, almost choking on his beer.

'I think we're a bit long in the tooth for a career change just now, don't you?' I reply, which sets us both off laughing hysterically.

'Fancy a night out in Soho? I've got a couple of tickets to a new club opening. It'll be a right laugh. We haven't been out just the two of us for ages and there are no more rehearsals until Monday!' Jez suggests. 'You know I don't drink that much, but I really fancy a good night out with one of my best mates. What do you reckon?'

'Yeah. Why not?' I reply, impulsively. 'I'll just change my t-shirt. Do you wanna borrow anything?'

'Yeah, go on, if you've got a t-shirt that will fit me.' Jez replies, flexing his muscles. 'Since I've been working out again my arms have become almost too big to fit in any of my tops.'

'That's a nice problem to have.' I banter.

Jez and I have a good look through my wardrobe and

come up with a few possibilities for Jez's newly pumped-up arms.

T-shirts chosen; we are on our way to the re-opening of the St Moritz Club on Wardour Street. It's a refurb job but Jez and his plus one gets us into the club and the night is full of possibilities. It's a free bar in exchange for having a few photos taken. I've spent worse evenings.

It's an underground bar and club and we climb down the stairs to be greeted by a couple of hostesses, giving full on Heidi vibes complete with cute plaits. The owners have certainly paid a lot of attention to detail. A good looking waiter in the tightest, full leather lederhosen, complete with embroidered braces bib emblazoned with the club logo offers us both a glass of champagne which seems kind of out of place in this German styled club although on closer inspection there are a selection of German beers and schnapps on offer too.

Jez knows Lottie, one of the PR girls and she spots him straight away through the crowded room. She's blonde, extremely well-spoken and aged about thirty so in reality far too young for either of us.

'Jez, darling. So great to see you! It's been ages.' says Lottie as she greets him with a double air kiss. 'And you don't need any introduction.' Lottie says to me with a big smile on her face, as she holds out her hand to greet me.

'Great to meet you at last.' She enthuses, knowing immediately the power of two Mountaineers at a club launch could be dynamite PR wise.

'Well done, Lottie. You've doing a great job tonight.' Jez says kindly, giving her a hug.

'Thanks Jez. I'll introduce you to the owner later. His wife is a big fan of yours.' She replies.

'Sounds great.' I say faking enthusiasm.

We switch from champagne to a couple of bottles of

German beer and then get persuaded by one of the shot girls to have a Schnapps. Thankfully the earlier hearty burgers soak up most of the alcohol and we find ourselves chatting to a couple of radio DJs who are always supportive of our work, and I also bump into Ethan and Rachel from Wake Up and Smell the Coffee. Rachel greets me like a long-lost friend, and I introduce her to Jez to take the heat off me as I can see Ethan making a beeline towards me. He's slightly pissed and is swaying ever so slightly as he approaches.

'Well, if it isn't Mr Ed Nash.' He slurs.

'Hi Ethan. How's it going?' I say jovially.

'It was going ok until I saw you. My Rachel seems to be your number one fan.'

'We appreciate all our fans.' I say, remembering my media training. 'And you guys on Wake Up are always so welcoming and supportive.' I cleverly retort.

'Is that so? My Rachel hasn't stopped banging on about you since you last appeared. Isn't it about time you found that old girlfriend of yours?' He mutters under his breath.

'No luck as yet.' I reply thinking it was probably time Ethan went home. I manage to extricate Jez from the clutches of Rachel, and we make our excuses that the club owner wants to talk to us.

'Thanks for rescuing me.' Jez whispers in my ear. 'Lovely woman but her husband's a bit full on, isn't he?'

'Tell me about it. I would have lamped him one in my previous life but he's not worth the hassle and we don't need that sort of publicity right now.' I agree.

Jez steers us away from Rachel and an ever increasingly pissed Ethan and we pose for some photos for Lottie with the club owner Hector Ferrantes and his wife Sofia who is the huge Mountaineers fan, which pleases Lottie. Sofia looks like she is going to self-combust with excitement as she cosies up to us both in a series of photos.

The evening is a great success, and we finally leave around 2:00a.m., slightly worse for wear, stumbling up the stairs as we hit the night air. Surprisingly, there are no paps waiting for us outside which is unusual as since all #the-girlinthesong hysteria we are constantly bombarded by the press, our previous lives as regular jobbing musicians a distant memory. We walk up Wardour Street, winding our way to Bar Italia on Frith Street joining the many other revelers who aren't quite willing for the night to end, for a strong coffee, before grabbing a cab back to Jez's in Chiswick.

I know Jez's flat almost as well as my own, having stayed here on many occasions. I lived here with Jez about five years ago when no one else would tolerate me when my drinking and drug use were at their worst. Jez is like a brother to me; he's always had my back and has often got me out of many a scrape along the years. I've always been the one with the short fuse, whereas Jez is the definition of chilled. It probably has something to do with his dabble with Buddhism after Poppy died. It changed him as a person. He's always been the mature one out of the two of us. He holds a black belt in karate but wouldn't hurt a fly and I'm proud to call him my friend.

My old bedroom, which is now the spare bedroom is made up and I gratefully crash out as soon as my head hits the pillow as it's almost 3:30a.m. One thing that I'd forgotten is that Jez is an early riser as later I glance at the bedside table to see the illuminated numbers showing that it's 8:30a.m. My head is fuzzy, and I drink a mouthful of water from the bottle that Jez has thoughtfully left out for me and grab my t-shirt and jeans and once dressed, I go through to the kitchen to find Jez drinking a green tea. He silently pushes a few buttons on his all singing all dancing coffee machine, and about a minute later hands me a cup of hot, steaming coffee. I gratefully swallow the coffee down, feeling the caffeine, my drug of choice nowadays, coursing through my veins.

'Thanks for that.' I say cupping the coffee mug with both hands, as the welcome caffeine works it magic.

'Thought you'd need a coffee this morning. Sorry if I woke you up but I went for a quick jog when I woke up. It's a habit I picked up when I lived in Thailand. Pounding the streets of Chiswick isn't quite the same though.' Jez explains.

'How come you're full of the joys of Spring this morning?' I ask Jez, as I'm sure he had as much to drink as I did.

'I started drinking water after we had that Schnapps. Can't be doing with hangovers at our age.' Jez confesses with a wry grin.

'Sensible. I feel awful. Wish I'd done the same.' I say with a groan as I rinse the rest of my coffee.

'I'll fix you some breakfast. How about scrambled eggs with smoked salmon on sourdough? That should do the trick.' Jez happily suggests with a smile.

'Sounds perfect, if you're making it.' I say, returning his smile.

Five minutes later we're tucking in to our relatively healthy breakfast and Jez thoughtfully tops up my coffee. I sit back in my seat and finish up my second cup of coffee and almost feel ready for the day.

'I'd best get going soon.' I say, getting up from the table.

'Before you do, you might want to see this.' Jez says, passing his phone over to me.

It's the website for The Daily Mail in the Showbiz section.

Callum Baker, ex-husband of Virginia Baker, formerly Ginny Weathers and childhood friend of Evie Del Rio has released some more explosive photos from Ed Nash and Evie Del Rio's scandalous past!

I frown and click on it to read it, not quite believing what

I'm seeing. Callum, the shitty ex himself, has sold another story to a newspaper. I read through Callum's outrageous lies about how Virginia had met up with me recently and that we knew all along where and who Evie is. My anger increases with every word, my hands shaking as I struggle to scroll down the page. He's topped everything off by somehow getting hold of some more of Virginia's old Polaroids and these are ones that I haven't seen. There's one I *really* don't need people to see: me and Evie and Virginia and Jamie back at my house after Virginia's party. We all look extremely drunk, and Uncle Paul is in the background, taking a puff from a huge spliff. God knows how Virginia is going to take this latest bombshell being revealed by her ex-husband, let alone Evie. There are many, many lows people can reach. Selling a fake story on the mother of your child is surely right down there – but if I stop and think about things maybe I'm no different to Callum Baker, quite happy to sell music and do interviews off the back of my ex-girlfriend who may just be the mother of my unknown child.

Things with Evie would probably never have worked out. We've been apart for a lifetime, and I have no idea what she's like now. She's made her life without me, and I really should have respected that, but I still need to know if she had our baby. At one time, we all thought that Paul was so cool. My mother had been right all along. He's a complete waster who ingratiated himself into my group of friends, manipulating us all for his own gain. The paper has named him in the photo, so it won't be too long before they're knocking on his door for his side of the story.

Jez lets me process that I've just read.

'You ok?' He finally asks. I nod as I try to take in what Callum has said.

'Don't worry too much. Toby's dealing with the press. There's a message to all of us, instructing us not to comment on this story. To be honest, any publicity in his eyes is good publicity for the tour. By remaining silent, it will all die down.' Jez says calmly. 'Get yourself together and I'll drive you home.'

We drive back in companionable silence as only lifelong friends can. Back at my flat, the photographers are back but have been forced to move further down the road by Sid, but their cameras click and flash at us as Jez drives towards the car park. He parks up, and Sid's waiting for me, eager to talk.

'They're a ferocious lot out there today, aren't they? People shouldn't believe everything they read in the press, you know. Well, I don't anyway. Today's news is tomorrow's fish and chips paper.' Sid advises me.

'Thanks, Sid. I really do appreciate all your help. You're a lifesaver. You remember my mate Jez, don't you?'

Sid and Jez nod at each other and Sid calls the lift for us.

Back in the sanctuary of my flat, I take a shower and then Jez and I sit out on one of the balconies, catching up on the headlines. Social media is awash with comments about Callum's latest revelations:

X is particularly vocal:

@EdNash deserves everything he gets @CallumBaker is just giving him a taste of his own medicine! #TeamEvie

@EdNash deserves to be happy. He also deserves to know whether he has a child #UsedToBe

There's no point in reading any more. It's all out there now. There's a message from Toby on WhatsApp, just to me this time: *Hey, Ed. Great publicity for the tour with the headlines this morning! I couldn't have organised anything better myself. Just remember not to make any comments to the press. See you next week for rehearsals.*

It's all about the headlines with Toby. Always has been and always will be.

32

GENIE

Now

This first week in Jonesy's villa is rapidly running away with itself. In just a couple of days, Maura is joining us for the final week. It will then be time for me to let someone else in on my secret. I already feel Maura will be the easiest person to tell, as she's never critical or judgmental. She obviously knows about all the rumours, but she deserves to hear the truth from me. When I escaped from Bournemouth, a kind girl on the bus told me about the job at The Hidden Snicket. A job that came with accommodation. Maura took me on based on a "good feeling" when I first arrived in Brighton and gave me a chance, originally as a cleaner. If that's not fate, I don't know what is. She's always joked that I was a far better barmaid than a cleaner.

Gray's jetlag has finally settled down, and it's me who's now awake early, alone and lost in my thoughts. I sit outside with my phone, checking for messages from back home.

I grab my iPad and check the gossip sites. Ginny's ex-husband has sold another story about how Ed and Ginny knew all along where I am and indeed who I am. Surely that can't be true? But Ed has been relentless in exploiting our relationship to further his career and Ginny always had a soft spot for Ed. And there in technicolour is an awful Polaroid of us all back at Ed's house after Ginny's birthday party. I examine the photo – there's me, Ed, Ginny and Jamie. We all look extremely drunk and stoned, and Ed's Uncle Paul is in the background, taking a puff from a huge spliff. That man still gives me the creeps. I never felt safe whenever he was around after that unsettling afternoon. Examining the Polaroid I only feel shame, embarrassment and regret as looking back now I have a feeling that may well have been the night I got pregnant, the very first time we properly had sex. I was so naïve and stupid back then. I also feel sorry for Ginny, for being betrayed by her ex-husband although it's no different to what Ed has done to me. But out of everyone, I'm the one who has committed the biggest betrayal of them all, denying Ed the right to know that he has a daughter out there somewhere.

I spend the next half an hour poring over the photos that accompany the article. There's Ginny with her ex-husband Callum on their wedding day, then a more recent one of Callum with both of Ginny's daughters.

I continue to search online for photos of the old gang, but all the stories are a repeat, including the photos of Callum's revelations. I send Maura a quick WhatsApp. I can't wait to see her. I don't have to wait too long for Maura to respond due to the time difference. She's busy finishing off some last-minute work things. Maura, who has worked and managed pubs for years, now advises failing pubs and bars on how to push their businesses forward.

She's included her flight details for Gray so he can pick her up from the airport. I've just sent another message to Maura, saying how much we're all looking forward to seeing her, when Gray joins me outside.

'Morning. You're up early. Everything ok?' Gray asks, gently brushing my neck with a kiss as I try to stifle a yawn.

'Yeah, I just couldn't sleep. Maura's sent through her flight details. I'll forward them to you.' I reply, pushing my hair out of my eyes.

'It'll be great to see Maura. What do you fancy doing today?' Gray asks, scratching the last few days of stubble coming through on his chin.

'Umm I don't mind, but I did want to show you the latest on the press front. It looks like Ginny's ex-husband has sold another story. There are also some dodgy photos of me and the gang looking very out of it.' I warn Gray.

I bring up the story on the iPad, and he has a good look through the article, dismissing it almost immediately.

'Nothing to worry about there,' he says, giving me the iPad back. "It's just a disgruntled ex getting his pound of flesh. Are you ok with it all?'

'I'm not particularly happy about the photo with me in it being used.'

'I know, but we're lucky to be away, as we're in a bit of a bubble here. I was wondering if you fancy a trip to the beach today. Go for a swim and feel the sand between our toes?' Gray suggests.

'Yeah, why not? I know the kids will love it,' I enthuse, needing a day away from the UK gossip sites.

It takes us just under two hours to get to the beach, and we park in the car park attached to a big surfing shop selling an eclectic range of beach towels, surfboards, beachwear and typical must-have seaside souvenirs, which we almost have to drag Cassie away from.

We secure a couple of cabanas on the beach, complete with sun loungers for the day, and set up camp.

'Fancy a dip, Cassie?' Will asks.

'Sure.' she replies, removing her sarong to reveal a stunning, but very small, silver bikini that really doesn't leave much to the imagination. I almost gasp but button my lips instead. Now that Cassie and I are kind of back talking, I really don't want to upset things between us by criticising her choice of swimwear, as much as I want to.

Our beautiful daughter certainly turns a fair few heads as she sashays towards the crystal-clear sea, closely followed by Will. Gray and I watch as Will attempts to playfight with Cassie, making it his mission to dunk her. And it's only a couple of minutes before he succeeds, Cassie completely disappearing underwater for a split second, jumping up quickly, her mouth wide, Will laughing.

Cassie stomps back towards us, water trailing from and behind her. 'He's such a pain, Mum. He's ruined my hair.' she moans, bottom lip jutting out in a sulk.

'You still look gorgeous. I love your bikini. Is it new?' I ask, hoping my attempt at complimenting her choice of swimwear is working, when all I really want is for her to cover herself up.

'Yes, I bought it at Westfield with Mel.' Cassie replies, lying on her sun lounger to dry off.

I put my sunglasses on, lie back and drift in and out of sleep as my early start begins to catch up with me. I dream of my carefree days with Ed, when nothing more than having a good time mattered before the sadness of living in Bournemouth with Mother and mean-spirited Auntie Maureen almost finished me off. And then I dream of my new life in Brighton, where I was finally accepted into a group of people, who, despite having no blood ties to me, only ever showed me love and kindness, all held together by Maura.

I wake to the children arguing again as Gray unsuccess- fully plays peacemaker.

'Wha—' I begin.

'It all started because Will's hungry and his irritability is annoying his sister, as per usual.'

Cassie shoots me a look, confirming Gray's words to be true.

'I noticed a McDonald's over the road. I thought it might fill the gap in Will's empty stomach.' Gray suggests.

'Sounds like the perfect idea.' I reply.

'Great. Just WhatsApp me what you both want.' Gray says. 'I'll come with you, Dad, as I'm not sure what I want yet.' says Will.

'Probably the whole menu.' Gray mutters as they wander off.

'I think I'll have a quick swim later.' I say to Cassie, Will and Gray now out of earshot.

'The water really is lovely. It's like being in a relaxing bath.' The thought draws me in further to the idea.

'Do you fancy joining me after lunch?' I ask, trying to make an effort.

'You're not planning to try and drown me, are you?' she replies with a smile.

'Not unless you try and drown me first.' I laugh.

There's silence for a while as we both close our eyes and soak up the sun, but then I hear a small, reluctant voice.

'Mum?'

I turn to Cassie. She's looking at me like she's got something to confess. I can tell it's on the tip of her tongue.

'Yes?'

'Did you see that Virginia's ex-husband has sold another story?" Cassie blurts out. 'And there's a right dodgy photo of you and your friends looking really drunk.' she adds, removing her sunglasses so she can look straight at me.

'Yes, I saw it this morning.' I reply. My throat feels as if it's closing up, so I swallow before I answer. I sit up on my sun lounger.

'Obviously it doesn't show us in the best light, but in the grand scheme of things your dad and I don't think it's too much to worry about.' I say, hoping Cassie will be reassured.

'I like that we're talking like we used to.' Cassie says with a genuine smile. 'I'm beginning to realise that you didn't really have any choice about keeping your baby, and that makes me feel really sad and also so shocked and angry with Grandma and Grandad.' she adds, reaching over to touch my hand.

'It was more grandma than grandad as the driving force behind me getting my baby adopted. The way I acted was a disappointment to grandad, but *I* was the disappointment to grandma.' I admit, gaining comfort from her touch.

'Sometimes I can't believe some of the things that you did when you were young?'

'I regret all the mistakes I've made but back then, times were so different to how they are now. I suppose I rebelled against my mother, as she was so strict. As you know, as a teenager, you always think you know best.' I say as Cassie rolls her eyes at my comment. 'And that's why I'm hard on you and Will sometimes - because I want the best for you both. I don't want you to make the same mistakes I did. I'm still suffering the consequences of making wrong decisions.' I'm getting fed up with apologising for my youthful mistakes, so I'm glad she's not mad anymore and I get to take the explaining route instead.

Cassie nods and is about to say something else just as Gray and Will return with our food, the moment now lost.

The rest of the afternoon is one of the most relaxing times we've all experienced together for ages, and once the beach starts to clear as people leave to go back to their hotels to get ready for dinner, we gather our things and walk along the pier in the late afternoon sun. We watch the fishermen fishing and marvel at the opportunist birds swooping down to see what the fishermen have caught. As we make our way back down the pier to go back to the car park, the evening stallholders are starting to set up, much to the delight of Cassie, who insists on buying a couple of handmade friendship bracelets for herself and Mel.

The drive back to Orlando is easy enough, and after having had a full day of sun, Cassie and Will nod off in the car. Once back home and showered, I fix us some scrambled eggs on toast and then we all go to our bedrooms to watch TV. Gray, bless him, crashes out almost immediately after all the driving.

I spend the next half an hour alone just googling images of Ed Nash. Looking back at photos of us together when we were young still make my stomach do a little flip, but looking at the grown-up Ed, I feel absolutely nothing. I think it's more the nostalgia that has a grip on me and I have come to the realisation that Ed needs to know that he has a daughter out there somewhere and deep down in my heart I have a burning almost primeval desire to find her too.

33

ED

Now

The recent piece in the paper from Callum seems to have only ignited the search for Evie and now unfortunately Paul is in the mix too. TikTok sleuths are out in force after spotting Paul in the background of one of the photos smoking a big fat joint. They're close to finding him too, as someone has done a TikTok saying that he's a familiar face on Hayling Island, although he hasn't been seen for a while. I'm just waiting for that call from him. I haven't tried the last number I have for him as I don't want to re-establish contact if I can help it. He'll only be after money. And the subject of underage drinking and smoking has reared its ugly head again and the criticism that our parents have been faced with has been quite vitriolic.

X

From @therealJaniceJ

Where were the parents when their children were out partying? Why would you leave your children in the company of a known drug user? #disgustingbehaviour

From @theguitarmonster

Saw Paul Nash in a pub on Hayling Island only last week. He's unemployed and lives in a caravan but will help clear the glasses in the pub for a few drinks. Seems harmless enough #liveandletlive

There were hundreds of assorted posts on X; some criticising our parents, many criticising Paul and many more wondering if Evie was indeed pregnant and that's why she left. That article has opened a can of worms, and I'm not coming out of it very favourably. There were many women chastising me for trying to ruin Evie's life by naming her publicly (especially if she was the mother of my child). I still wasn't completely sure if Genie McNamara really is Evie as apart from those hazy photos at Heathrow Airport, I can't seem to find anything else about her as her social media accounts are private.

Amira Malik has just done a TikTok saying that tonight at 6pm she will be dropping some scandalous facts about the identity of #thegirlinthesong. I have a dummy TikTok as well as an official account so at least I'll be able to view it without people realising that it's me. I don't know how she does it, but Amira has a knack of always finding out the truth. I have no idea who her sources are, but she's nearly always spot on. Roll on 6:00p.m. I think with bated breath, just as my phone beeps with a series of notifications.

There's a text from Virginia:

Here I am again apologising for Callum's kiss n tells! I'm so sorry, I really am. None of us are talking to him if it's any consolation. If you ever do find Evie, then please do apologise to her for me. V

I do feel sorry for Virginia. It's not her fault that her ex is a dickhead, but I'm probably called worse by Evie and her family. I shoot a quick message back, telling her not to worry and yes of course I will apologise to Evie if she ever reaches out. Fat chance of that happening.

As predicted, there's a message from Paul, swearing blind he hasn't said a thing to the press about me or Evie, as he appreciates our relationship too much but there it is at the end of the message – *If you could help me out a bit, I'd really appreciate it. I've fallen behind on my rent on the caravan. Just £500 would help me out. As you know I'd never say anything about you to the press. My bank details are still the same. Cheers*

Paul's message is followed up by one from Dad.

Hello Ed, Just to say your mother is extremely stressed with all the recent publicity about Paul. Have you heard from him? I don't think I've got his up-to-date number currently. She's also hoping that she's got a grandchild out there somewhere. Any news from Evie? I don't suppose she's reached out? All the best. Dad

My Dad's messages always make me smile. They're always so formal. Like he's writing a letter. Mum doesn't bother to contact me. Everything comes through Dad but it's interesting to hear that the possibility of me providing her with a grandchild would please her. Funny old world.

I ponder over the best course of action to take with Paul. I've constantly drip-fed money to his account over the years to keep him ticking over, to keep him away from the press and up until now it's been a good arrangement. I guess I've only got myself to blame by agreeing to do the Netflix documentary as that's what really started the whole thing off. But it's not the done thing to turn down Netflix, now, is it?

I reply to Dad, passing on Paul's number for him. They're brothers and Dad deserves to be able to contact Paul if he wants to. Who am I to deny him that? Years back Dad and Paul were so close but as Paul's drug use intensified Dad felt the need to take a step back. It's just as well my parents don't know half the stuff that I have got up to over the years, but if the price is right for Paul, then the whole world will know absolutely everything. I open my banking app and transfer him £700. I've given him a bit more than he asked for to keep him onside. I glance at the time. It's 4:00p.m. – just two hours before Amira's big reveal.

34

GENIE

Now

Gray awakes early. It's 5:30 a.m. when he goes downstairs. I lie in bed listening to him pottering around the kitchen, making the coffee and once that's done, he goes outside to watch the sun rise over the pool. It's another beautiful day in paradise. I reach for my dressing gown and pop downstairs and pour myself a coffee as I watch Gray sitting at the table completely engrossed in his phone. I'm furious to see that it's his work phone! I open the patio doors, and he jumps and hastily shuts down his phone. He looks guilty.

'Sorry did I wake you?' Gray says, trying to act as normal as possible.

'No. I couldn't sleep and thought I'd join you.' I reply bluntly. 'You're working! You promised this holiday would be different.

'I'm not working. Honestly.' Gray replies, somewhat sheepishly.

'That's a lie!' I almost hiss at him. 'I saw you using your work phone.'

'Ahh. There's another reason for that.' He starts to explain.

'I would never ever want to go behind your back, and I usually don't but I can't sit back and do nothing knowing there's a guy out there who doesn't know he has a child and a woman who doesn't know her real parents, so I've been doing a bit of research of my own.' He starts before I interrupt him.

'Without telling me?' I shout. 'I wish you'd asked me, Gray! You can't just do things that concern me and not consult me.' I feel my face flushing bright red with complete outrage.

'You didn't exactly want to give your child up, so what's stopping you from forming a bond now? Imagine the relief you could give to your daughter, her knowing that she was and still is wanted. Imagine the happiness you could give to Ed knowing he isn't childless, after all.

'I've done a bit of research on the adoption service associated to the church and I think I've tracked down your friend Emma on FaceBook.' Gray confesses.

I sit and stare at my husband. This caring man who would lay his life down for me. He's always looked after me and has my best interests at heart but is this a step too far?

'You shouldn't have done it!' I protest again, tears threatening to pour down my face. 'You can't keep trying to fix me!' I shout at him.

'I'm sorry Genie but I just want to help you and as much as I'm not a fan of Ed Nash particularly after what he's done, he does still deserve to know he has a daughter out there somewhere and knowing you as such a wonderful and loving mother, I know deep down you want to find Milly.' Gray replies stoically.

'Of course I do!' I sob. 'But I want to be in control of finding her.'

'I'm sorry. I just wanted to help. Do you want me to share what I've found out?' He tentatively asks, fearful of another emotional outburst most probably.

I nod and he passes me his phone. There's an article on a local Bournemouth newspaper website which reads:

St Joseph's Catholic Church in Bournemouth has been linked to an adoption scandal with a local Catholic adoption agency. The Bournemouth Chronicle has evidence that many of the adoptions through this agency were mishandled and the agency itself was closed down in the late 1980s because of this.

There was evidence found that many of the adoptions had been illegal with many birth certificates having been fabricated together with rumours of cash bribes between the church and the adoption agency.

'Shit.' I grumble, running my hand through my hair. 'If the agency was shut down, does that mean that all the files are gone too and finding Milly will be impossible.'

'I know. It's frustrating to get this far and to come to a dead end. But the good news is that I've found Emma and she might be able to shed some light on things.' Gray replies, trying as ever to be optimistic. He's shows me screenshots from her various social media accounts. She appears to be married with two grown-up sons and still lives in the Bournemouth area, going by the name of Emma Hadfield-Jones.

I spend ages looking at the various photos of Emma and her family.

'She looks just the same. Well, obviously older, but I'd recognise her anywhere. I'm going to contact her .' I say decisively. 'I'll send her a direct message on Facebook.'

'Look, I just wanted to help.' Gray says apologetically but I can tell he's also happy that in some way he has helped me possibly find my daughter. 'Am I forgiven?' Gray asks me with a cheeky smile, but I'm not letting him get away with taking control.

'Not really. Please stop making decisions for me, Gray. You've always done it ever since I met you, and I've always allowed you to do it. But I want to be able to make my own decisions, especially on the possibility of finding my daughter.' I reply, my cheeks flushing again with the little anger still left inside me.

Gray nods, accepting what I've just said, as he knows that he's spent the whole of our marriage trying to protect me. I know I'm right. It's time for me to take back control.

Gray leaves me to my own devices, offering to do a coffee and doughnuts run, anticipating Maura's arrival later. I'm in a world of my own again, back with Ed and my friends.

Gray returns and the children descend on the food like a plague of locusts, even Cassie has forgotten about her diet. We have a pool day, and I busy myself making sure that Maura's room is ready for her arrival. Gray decides to leave a little bit early to go to the airport to collect Maura and I stay at the villa, to put a little distance between us. I'm still smarting from him doing his own research without telling me first but in hindsight I'm thrilled that I potentially could be back in touch with Emma. I don't know why I never thought of contacting her sooner, but I guess it all comes down to not wanting to surround myself with people who know that I had a baby all those years ago. But I've sent her a message privately via Facebook so I'm hopeful she'll be in touch.

I lounge in the sun with Cassie while Will divebombs in and out of the pool and then finds a small, squeezy ball which he throws at his sister, using her as target practice.

She shrieks, he laughs, and I ineffectively play referee. Gray is so much better at this type of parenting than I am.

Eventually even Will tires from annoying his sister and we all go inside to shower in readiness for Maura's arrival.

Gray messages me to say that Maura's flight has been slightly delayed, so by the time she clears immigration and locates her luggage, and they are on the road, it's early evening and it's getting dark. I hear the car arrive and open the door to greet Maura, hugging her tight, not wanting to let her go. It's only a week since we've seen each other, but it seems like longer.

I let Maura unpack and then we enjoy a Thai takeaway with the children, and we catch up on our holiday news. Once we're stuck into our second bottle of wine, the children make their excuses and go to their rooms. Maura looks tired what with the time difference between London and Florida. Maybe tonight isn't the night to let her into my secret.

'Thanks, guys, so much for inviting me. I can't tell you how much I've been looking forward to this break.' Maura says, settling back in one of Jonesy's comfortable leather recliner chairs, sipping her wine.

'We're thrilled you could join us.' I begin. 'But there is something I've been wanting to talk to you about for ages.' I say, placing my wine glass on the table.

'Can I presume it has something to do with a certain Mr Ed Nash?' Maura replies, looking at both of our faces for a sign that she's right 'Social media has been awash with gossip.'

'Spot on.' I say, nodding, before continuing. 'As you know by now, Ed and I did date as teenagers, and yes of course it's all true that I was the inspiration behind a lot of his early songs. And it wasn't too long after that that I ended up in Brighton.'

She nods, slightly misty eyed, remembering me as a young, broken girl who found my way to her and the pub she was managing all those years ago.

'Well, I think it's time I told you the reason I ended up in Brighton.' I say.

Afterwards, I look to the floor, the last word of my secret finally spilled.

'Oh, Genie. I had no idea, darling, no idea at all.' Maura says, shaking her head in disbelief.

I look up at Maura, while Gray just sits there with his arm wrapped around me protectively.

'I'm a dreadful person, aren't I?' I say, wiping my nose with a tear-sodden tissue.

'Not at all. You were so young to have to deal with all of that: being taken away from your home, your boyfriend, your friends and being forced to give away your baby.' Maura says kindly, trying to console me. 'I just wish you'd told me when you first came to Brighton.'

We spend the rest of the evening talking about the adoption agency being forced to close and how I was going to try and find my friend Emma and of course my baby, who by now is in her thirties. We stay up late, drink far too much, we laugh, and we cry until our tiredness finally gets the better of us.

35

AMIRA

Now

It's almost time for my big reveal and I'm sitting in my North London flat waiting to go live on TikTok. Bang on 6:00p.m., I'm live:

Everyone I know, including myself have been fascinated and invested in Ed Nash, lead singer of indie rock group The Mountaineers and his search for his muse Evie Del Rio, #thegirlinthesong who inspired the iconic indie love song "Used to Be" and indeed all the songs on The Mountaineers debut album Past Times.

I use the usual TikTok trick by repeating what people know already to hook more viewers in, being careful enough not to give my audience too much waffle and padding, knowing how impatient viewers become waiting for a big reveal and for me to reveal something they don't know.

As you know I managed to narrow down some possibilities of women who matched Evie's profile and demographic, one of those being Genie McNamara from West London. I now have it on good authority that Genie McNamara was in fact formerly known as Evie Del Rio and did leave London

unexpectedly in the mid 1980s, never to be heard of again –
until now.

I can also confirm that Evie Del Rio did leave her
London home due to getting pregnant with Ed Nash's baby,
as per all the recent rumours. I ramp up the tension as "Used
to Be" plays softly in the background.

Evie and her family left London as soon as they knew
that she was pregnant, and she went to live with her aunt in
Bournemouth to see the pregnancy out in secret.

Evie, along with her aunt and her mother were frequent
visitors to St Joseph's Catholic Church and she would often
be seen helping to keep the church clean during and after
her pregnancy. She became very close to another young girl
who always attended the church services. Her name was
Emma Hadfield my source has revealed. Evie gave birth to
a daughter and was forced to give her away to a now
defunct Catholic Adoption Service. The baby was appar-
ently adopted by a local childless couple who used to attend
St Joseph's.

Emma Hadfield somehow helped Evie Del Rio leave
Bournemouth, and I have been told that she ran away from
her aunt's home in Bournemouth and was last heard of
travelling to Brighton. I would like to point out that I will
under no circumstances reveal my source of this informa-
tion, but I do categorically deny that Emma Hadfield is my
contact and has had nothing to do with this latest
revelation.

I hope that Ed and Evie are watching my TikTok today
and perhaps they can now talk to each other and be
reunited with their daughter? Perhaps you were adopted
and are in your early thirties? You could be the daughter of
the woman who inspired one of today's most iconic indie
love songs and the man who wrote such heartfelt lyrics.

Reach out if you think you are the daughter of #thegirlinthesong

I'm Amira Malik. Take care until next time, when I'll be revealing some further information from someone very close to Ed Nash!

I've managed to track down Ed's uncle, Paul Nash, who has promised to reveal all about Ed's druggy past. And all for the price of a few beers! My followers are going to go wild with these new revelations and my TikTok popularity will continue to take the world by storm!

36

GENIE

Now

My relief in telling Maura my long-kept secret has finally brought me a kind of solace. Maura being Maura doesn't judge or criticise; she only offers comfort. She mourns with me for being denied a lifetime with my daughter. And just like Gray, I can see how devastated she is about not knowing and not being able to help me all those years ago. When I finally got away from Bournemouth and arrived in Brighton, it was my chance to start again and block out all that had happened. The only person that I remotely missed was my dear old Dad. Maura was instrumental in helping me build a new and happy life, and I will always be so very grateful to her for that.

Despite the initial tears that my revelation caused, we do manage to have fun in our remaining week Stateside. Maura insists on treating us all to swimming with dolphins at one of the nearby theme parks on one of the days - something the children have always wanted to do. We all take delight from our up-close encounter with such captivating creatures. We sunbathe, snorkel, swim and take it in turns trying to get into a hammock and not fall out. Will is the most skilled and successful in staying put, whilst the rest of us prefer the static comfort of a sun lounger.

Later, Gray catches up on some much-needed sleep under a shady palm tree, Will enjoys sampling a selection of the all-inclusive food that's on offer and Maura, Cassie and I find ourselves mesmerised by the aviary, where colourful birds fly down to take food from your hands. We couldn't have asked for a more perfect day together.

With Maura here, the shopping trips have increased, and Gray finds himself being somewhat of a taxi service, but he never complains, often just dropping us off, giving him and Will some time together to play crazy golf, go to the movies or just chill at the villa. Everyone is happy doing things that please them. Surely that's the point of a good holiday; getting away from the usual routine, experiencing new things, having fun and relaxing. For us, for the first time in ages, we feel like a normal family again.

We fall into a new routine, and most evenings after dinner, Gray often nods off or goes to bed early, all those jetlagged early mornings clearly catching up with him. Maura and I usually grab a bottle of wine, relax in the pool and just talk, reminiscing about times gone by, just as we are tonight.

'Who'd have thought old Jonesy would have made such a success of himself?' Maura observes, taking in the beauty of the illuminated pool and lush tropical garden, which both seem even more magical at night.

'I know what you mean. Even before I met Gray, Jonesy would always have a different woman with him at the bar.' I agree.

'He never settled down, did he?' Maura asks.

I shake my head, reaching for my wine glass. 'He just can't seem to, but he's such a good friend to us as a family.

And I owe him a lot. He was the one who persuaded me to invite Gray for an after-hours drink the night we met.'

'I never knew that.' Maura confesses. 'But then, there were a lot of things I didn't know back then…'

'I'm sorry that I didn't tell you sooner about what I'd been through. I guess I just cast everything bad that had happened to me away because I needed a new life. Looking back now, I realise I was most likely suffering from postnatal depression, and I had kind of shut down emotionally as a way of dealing with everything that had happened to me.' My eyes are unable to hold Maura's understanding gaze for too long, the guilt too much.

'I guess I would have liked to have had the opportunity to help you, look after you in some kind of way.' she explains sadly, full of regret about what she might have been able to do if I'd perhaps given her the chance.

'But you did help me.' I try to reassure her. 'Together with Rudi and his incredible food and lovely, patient Dom who taught me everything about being a good barmaid, who never tired in telling me about the stories behind his numerous tattoos, you became my new family. We were all there because you took a leap of faith with us and gave us all a chance.' I say with such conviction and love for a woman who I have no blood ties to but who loves me more than my own mother ever has.

Maura smiles at me through her tears. 'We had such a good gang there at The Hidden Snicket back then, didn't we? I still get emails from Rudi and Dom to this day, and they always ask after you.'

'I'm sure Rudi finding success with his restaurants back in Germany and Dom finally becoming a bar owner in Ibiza all has something to do with you. Dom always said you had a knack of finding the right people to take a chance on. I would never have met Gray if it wasn't for you…'

'And I've always believed that you all had your own way of finding me because I needed you all as much as you needed me.' Maura says as we both raise our glasses, celebrating our enduring friendship.

And just as we clink our glasses, we notice a group of fireflies lighting up and sparkling in the night sky. Their beauty is enchanting and mystical as they move together with their shining light. I remember once reading that the sight of fireflies is a symbol of light entering your life, and that's exactly how I feel right now, here with Maura. After a lifetime of holding back, keeping secrets from my loved ones, it's now my time to light up and shine and push forward to try and find my missing daughter, with the help of my ever-loving family and best friend.

37

ED

Now

I awake with a start, momentarily unaware of what day it is and then I remember that it's Saturday and I have the day to myself. I think back to Amira's most recent revelation and wonder if Evie has watched it. I'm trying not to worry too much about who Amira has dug out of the woodwork to reveal more about me. My guess is that it's most probably Paul. Perhaps I should have given him more money in return for his silence, but it's a slippery slope to keep drip feeding his bank account. I shower, make myself some coffee and have some cereal on my balcony, just watching the world go by. One of the Australian girls I often say hello to in the lobby area is busy doing some exercises in the communal garden. She's my usual type: young, pretty, athletic and blonde, but what on earth would I have in common with someone her age? Perhaps I'm finally growing up. Laughable, considering I'm almost fifty.

I finish my breakfast, lock up and take the lift down to the garage, bumping into Sid, who's carefully checking for anything untoward.

'Morning, Ed.'

'Morning, Sid. Everything ok with you today?'

'Not too bad, thanks. I still can't believe how some people live, leaving their litter in the car park like this.' he says, shaking his head whilst picking up several abandoned crisp packets with his litter grabber.

'You'd think if you could afford to live somewhere like this, you would know how to behave.' I agree.

'It beggars belief, it really does, but enough of my woes. How are things with you?' Sid asks.

'Not too bad, thanks.' I reply.

Sid stops litter picking and uses his litter picker in the same way people who talk with their hands do, as he starts turning the conversation to a fuller one. 'Did I tell you that me and my Janice have been together for nearly forty years. I'm going to take her on a cruise to celebrate. She's always fancied going on one. You ever been on one of those cruises Ed?'

Time for me to leave before I'm here all day. 'I've never been on one myself, but my parents have, and they loved it.' I say with a smile, getting into my car.

I have a lot of time for Sid. He's old-school, with a heart of gold, and his Janice is lucky to have him.

Mark and Rosita are getting Baby Luna christened tomorrow and I'm being wheeled out as Luna's godfather. Rosita's friend Manuela is the godmother. Together with Jez, Mark and I went to a Catholic secondary school but that's as far as the Catholic bit goes for me, but Rosita is just happy that Mark was able to find at least one Catholic friend to be involved, albeit an extremely lapsed Catholic. Jez couldn't do it really as he's now atheist after his little dabble with Buddhism after Poppy died. Manuela and Isabella who are Rosita's best friends from her school days have just flown over from Spain for the celebration. It's a big Catholic baptism and Mark has flown over Rosita's entire immediate family over too.

I decide to drive to Kingston to buy a suitable christening gift for Luna, having typically left it a bit last minute. I park up and begin aimlessly perusing the baby department in John Lewis trying to find inspiration for a gift until a kindly and motherly shop assistant, who thankfully has no clue who I am, takes pity on me and suggests some suitable gifts. We settle on a tiny sterling silver bracelet, a hand knitted blanket with Luna's initial embroidered on it and a piggy bank. The kindly shop assistant even reminds me to put some cash into the piggy bank which I duly do, as apparently, it's a sign of good luck. What do I know about babies? She arranges for everything to be gift wrapped to be collected later. I thank her profusely for all her help and say goodbye just as one of her colleagues says to her in a loud whisper.

'Oh my God, Dorothy! Do you realise that you just served Ed Nash?'

'Who dear?' Dorothy replies as her colleague then gives her a potted history all about me.

'Well, you know me, I just like to help the customers, whoever they might be. And I have to say he was a very polite man!' Dorothy replies. Clearly Dorothy wasn't on TikTok!

I decide to get some lunch and choose a discreet pub along the river, opting to sit in a corner booth away from prying eyes and order a chicken salad and sparkling mineral water as I'm driving, and I also know that tomorrow will be a heavy one after the christening. Mark and Rosita have been planning this christening for ages and Mark is looking forward to letting his hair down after all the recent sleepless nights he's had since Luna was born whereas Rosita is just looking forward to having all her family with her to celebrate her daughter.

I finish up at the pub as it's getting busy now and word has got round that I'm here. A couple of customers take a few snaps as I leave. Hurriedly I make my way back to John Lewis to pick up the gift-wrapped gifts for Luna. I drive back through Richmond Park and instead of heading home, I pop by to see if Mark needs any help for tomorrow and it's a good opportunity to drop off the christening gifts. I love it at Mark's house. Throughout the many years of us being gigging musicians Mark always had an interest in property and together with his dad they would buy up the worst house in the best street in an affluent or upcoming area, do it up and flip it. It worked well for ages until he fell in love with the Richmond house and his parents helped him buy it, as they felt that he had put so much of his heart and soul into this particular project. I park up on Mark's expansive drive and ring the bell to be greeted by who I can only assume to be Rosita's mother. She is highly confused as to who I am or indeed why I have called by, so she calls Mark.

'Hello mate.' Mark calls out with a whisper, as he comes down the stairs carrying a sleeping Luna over his shoulder.

'Sorry, have I called at a bad time? I just wanted to drop off my beautiful goddaughter's christening gifts.' I say, apologising profusely.

'No probs Ed. Just pop them in the front room and I'll let Rosita know about them when she gets back from the hairdressers.' Mark says, rubbing the small of Luna's back. He then remembers his manners and introduces me to Carmen.

'Carmen, this is my friend Ed who is the singer in our band. He's also going to be Luna's godfather.' Mark says in a combination of broken Spanish with a few English words thrown in for good measure.

'Si, Si. Buenas tardes Ed.' Carmen replies with a big smile, kissing me on both cheeks.

'Buenas tardes Carmen.' I reply, as Carmen holds me in a

vice like grip. She then starts making a kind of shooing noise in Mark's direction and swoops in to take the sleeping Luna from Mark's arms.

'Gracias, Carmen.' Mark replies, leading me towards the back of the house and into the garden and ushers me to the summerhouse which also doubles up as Mark's man cave. It's equipped with a selection of gym equipment and weights with a fully fitted bar and a screen. There is also a vintage juke box in the corner which I can never resist taking a look at.

'Choose a tune. I purposely haven't added any Mountaineers' tracks on there, if that's what you're looking for, though!' Mark comments, stifling a snort of laughter.

'I'm not that egotistical, you know!' I reply, digging Mark in the ribs. 'What about some Clash?'

'Yeah. Go for it. Do you remember when we used to cover their songs?' Mark asks, remembering that not too long ago we were a covers band, before our breakthrough with "Used to Be."

'I was never going to be as good as Joe Strummer, now, was I?'

'You found your own voice and we eventually found our own sound and if our recent popularity is anything to go by, we're not doing too badly, are we?' Mark says with a sense of pride. 'Now get that tune on and I'll fix us both a drink.'

'I've got the car, better not have a drink.'

'Ah come on. I've bloody earned a couple of beers after the week I've had with Rosita's extended family and friends being here.'

Are they all staying here?' I ask.

'No, thank God. Just Carmen, who you've just met, and Rosita's dad Enrique and Rosita's best friends Isabella and Manuela. Her cousins are in a local hotel.' Mark explains. 'I reckon you and Jez will really get on with Isabella and

Manuela. They're both gorgeous and you'll be spending a lot of time with them tomorrow.'

'Don't worry, I'll make sure I'm nice and polite to Rosita's friends. I'm sorry I'm so distracted with all this #girlinthesong business but I'm hopeful that Evie will reach out before too long.' I try to explain.

'You've got to let it go mate. Don't you think if Evie wanted to be found, she would have reached out by now?' Mark says pragmatically.

'Yeah. I know. But I've just got a feeling she'll be in touch. I just want to know if I'm a dad really. Ever since Virginia showed me those photos of your pool party all those years ago, it's just got me thinking that that is the most logical reason for her leaving.'

'I know it's hard mate, but have you ever thought she might be married, and her lack of comment is her way of responding?' Mark replies.

'Yeah. I guess you could be right.' I say somewhat despondently, knowing that Mark is most probably right.

'Are you sure you won't join me? You can always just leave your car here, you know.' Mark says encouragingly as he takes a sip of his beer.

'Yeah. Go on. Let's wet the baby's head or whatever the saying is.' I reply, finally giving in and accepting a bottle of beer from Mark.

'Cheers.' We say in unison and clink our bottles.

'Here's to a very successful christening for my beautiful goddaughter.' I toast, as Joe Strummer sings out from the jukebox. I end up having a few more beers with Mark and we're already on beer number three when Rosita knocks on the door of the summerhouse and Mark calls through to invite her in.

'Hola Ed. How are you?' Rosita says, doing the same

double kiss routine that her mother had greeted me with earlier.

'Hi Rosita. I'm really looking forward to tomorrow. It's a big day ahead for Luna.' I reply, wanting to put Rosita at ease as I've always liked her, and I know that sometimes she finds it difficult with Mark being in the band, often being away from home and her not having a real support network in London as her family all still live in Spain.

'Yes, yes. It will be such a wonderful day with us all together.' She replies, her face breaking into a beaming smile. 'Would you like to eat with us? Mama has made big paella so plenty food for all.'

'Are you sure? I don't want to intrude on your family time.' I reply, placing my beer on the bar.

'Yes, of course. Mama makes food for everyone. You also meet my friends. Manuela is godmother. Yes?' Rosita persists, as I now realise that I am indeed staying for dinner and meeting her friends, whether I want to or not!

Rosita stands on her tiptoes and kisses Mark on the lips which he reciprocates.

'Your hair looks great.' Mark says noticing that her hair has been freshly cut and coloured her trademark burgundy. 'Where's Luna?'

'Thank you mi amor. She sleep now, so we eat, yes?' Rosita says, smiling up at her husband.

'Ok. We'll be with you n five minutes.'

Rosita nods and leaves us alone.

'Bloody Hell! Paella again. It's nice, don't get me wrong, but it's the third time since they got here!' Mark says trying to make a joke out of it. 'Luna will be awake in about an hour or so, so that's why we eat so damned early. Sorry.'

'No problem. It'll be nice to have some company for a change.'

'You'll be only too happy to return to your nice quiet flat after a night with us!' I'm not so sure I think to myself.

Mark picks up our empty beer bottles and pops them in a carefully placed recycling bin, just outside the summerhouse and we make our way back to the house.

Carmen greets me with more double kisses and seats me in between Rosita's friends, Mark is next to Rosita with the cousins opposite him. Enrique is at the head of the table with Carmen to his left. Enrique quietens everyone down and says grace at the table in Spanish before we eat. Carmen busies herself serving everyone and finally we dig in.

The cousins, Pedro and Juan seem pleasant enough, and they chat quite animatedly to me about the band and how they are looking forward to seeing us on tour. Isabella and Manuela are delightful and even a year ago, I would have been interested in pursuing things with either of them but my heart's just not in it. My infamous womanising seems to have left the building and looking around me, seeing Mark so settled with Rosita, totally enchanted with Baby Luna, despite his extreme tiredness, I realise I want what he's got – a family. He somehow shares his love and his time between his other daughters and maintains a civil relationship with each of his daughters' mothers and is an integral part of our band. Apart from the band, I feel isolated and alone without a partner or a family. Is Evie and our potential child the answer to all my problems?

38

GENIE

Now

The holiday was just what we all needed but now we're back we've got Cassie's GCSE results to deal with and #thegirlinthesong media storm has only intensified with Amira Malik, the major TikTok influencer, who has now named me as #thegirlinthesong and revealed that I was indeed pregnant when I left Bournemouth. The children have had to lock down their social media accounts to private to avoid the vile trolling and incessant media requests they have been bombarded with.

I don't really check my Facebook account very often but since I contacted my friend Emma via messenger, I've been obsessively checking it. She obviously didn't check hers much either because it wasn't until we were back home that it showed that she had even read it.

Gray was at work when the message came through, so I had time to really digest what she said.

Wow! I never expected to hear from you again Evie (sorry can't think of you as any name apart from Evie!) But since all the recent publicity from the Netflix documentary I

218

put two and two together and realised that it was you that Ed Nash was looking for. In answer to your question about your daughter, there was a new family that appeared at church with a baby not long after you left, and the dates seemed to add up. I don't really think it's safe or secure to talk over messenger. Is there any way that we could possibly meet to discuss further. I swear to you that it wasn't me that told that Amira Malik that you were pregnant, but I have a feeling I know who did. Sorry to sound mysterious but I would like to tell you what I know face to face.

All the best – Emma x

I re-read Emma's message repeatedly, looking for clues as to exactly what she really meant. She was such a support to me in Bournemouth and always seemed trustworthy. Can I really trust her now? I like to think that I was a good judge of character back then and indeed now, so to hell with it, I will meet up with her. I quickly compose a quick message back.

Thank you, Emma, for getting in touch and I appreciate any help that you can give me and just like you did all those years ago, I really do value your discretion. Send me your mobile number and I'll message you suggestions of where to meet.

Thanks again

Genie x

This time Emma responds almost immediately with her mobile number, and I carefully word a WhatsApp message back to her with our address and an invitation to stay the night. I haven't bothered to check the arrangements with Gray as since the holiday I have decided to start to take control of my life. I know that Gray only ever has my best interests at heart but ever since we first met, he has always tried to fix me, to smooth away my upsets and worries, but on this occasion, it's me that needs to make the decisions that ultimately could reunite me with my daughter. And both Gray and Cassie are right that Ed does deserve to know that he really does have a daughter. I'm not sure how or when I'm going to reach out to him, but I do know that he is going to be part of my future, whether I like it or not. But for now, I'm excited about meeting Emma again. She was always such a support, and I feel bad that I never got in touch over the years, but I felt that I needed to protect myself as well as Emma at the time.

I spend the rest of the day indoors as Cassie has gone to meet up with a load of her friends on Richmond Green, a kind of pre results gathering before they all go their separate ways. I've let her take a few beers from the fridge with her. I know she's only sixteen, but I like to parent in a different way to my mother, so I turn a blind eye to a little bit of underage drinking. If I keep saying no, she'll just rebel - like I did! Will is at Tommy's as usual. Tommy's mum has a houseful of sons, so she always says one more doesn't make a difference. Both children have been sworn to secrecy about not discussing the recent media revelations. We did tentatively think about keeping them home, but I know from bitter experience how that can backfire, so we have put our trust in them instead. Only time will tell if this has been a wise move.

I busy myself by working my way through the holiday washing. It's a boring and repetitive job but it keeps me off social media. Cassie has even set up an anonymous TikTok account for me, so I've been able to catch up on the latest gossip from Amira Malik.

Although my life is in free fall, I find myself humming along to the radio, finding solace in the humdrum of ordinary life. That's all I've ever really wanted. An ordinary life. A happy life with a loving husband and children and a close friend who you could depend on in a crisis. And of course, I have all of that, but my long-kept secret seems to be out there now. I've been ignoring the phone calls from my dad, which I know will have been instigated by my mother. The Daily Mail has repeated details of Amira's recent revelations. I feel bad not to speak to my dad, but I'm petrified that my mother will intercept the call and it'll be like when my she realised I was pregnant, and I never want to feel like that ever again. And at the grand old age of forty-nine, why should I?

I cast all thoughts of my mother out of my mind and concentrate my efforts on getting the guest room ready for Emma's visit. Only two days to wait and I still need to break the news to Gray. Knowing Gray, he'll be a bit taken aback at first, but I know he'll come round eventually if I explain my reasons for meeting up with Emma. I choose a pretty floral duvet set for Emma and make up the bed in readiness for her visit. I'm intrigued by her recent message, and I start counting the hours off in my head until we are finally reunited.

39

ED

Now

I finally leave Mark's around 10:00p.m. as everyone looks tired and are stifling their yawns apart from the cousins and Rosita's friends who look like they want to continue the night, so Mark recommends a couple of bars in Richmond to them, and they leave around the same time as me. It takes me a good ten minutes to get round the table to say goodbye to everyone what with all the obligatory double kissing going on and I order a taxi from a local firm and then I'm back home, do a last-minute check of what I'm wearing for the christening tomorrow and then hit the sack.

Jez is pressing the buzzer to my flat bang on 10:30a.m. the following morning. We're due at the church at midday. I buzz him in. Jez looks good in his suit. He's clutching a beautifully wrapped present in his hand.

'Looking sharp.' I say, admiring his new threads.

'Cheers. Likewise. Are you sure we don't look like a couple of bouncers?' He says, laughing as he looks at our suited and booted reflections in the hallway mirror.

'Well, it's a special occasion, isn't it? The cab is on its

way so we'll be early, but I think Mark will be grateful for the company. He's feeling a bit outnumbered by Rosita's family. I popped by to drop off my present yesterday and to see if Mark needed any help, and they insisted I stayed for dinner.'

We leave the flat and pick up our cab from outside. The resident paps are there and snap away at us both as we get in our cab. We're at the church in plenty of time and some of the guests accumulate at the entrance to the church for a bit of a smoke but being reformed smokers Jez and I decide to just mingle as I introduce Jez to both the cousins and Rosita's friends with Isabella taking quite a shine to Jez. He's as polite as ever and chats quite happily with them all.

Just before midday Mark, Rosita and Luna arrive at the church in Mark's huge station wagon, driven by Enrique. Rosita gets out of the car, as Mark passes Luna to her. Luna is dressed in a white silk christening gown, her dark hair, accentuated with a tiny rose attached to a matching headband. Mark is dressed in a dark, tailored suit and Rosita wears a beautiful red floor length silk gown.

They greet all their guests including Mark's other daughters and we are quickly ushered into the church. The service goes smoothly, and Luna sleeps all the way through the ceremony until the priest anoints her with the holy water when she lets out a loud, lusty cry which breaks the tension of the seriousness of the service conducted by the somewhat stern priest, who has the worst halitosis I have ever had the misfortune to be up close and personal to. Manuela and I take our godparental duties very seriously and everyone claps now that Luna is a fully-fledged member of the Catholic church. It's a relief once Manuela and I are allowed to step away from the priest and his rancid breath. Our shared experience breaks the ice between us, as we chat quite amicably. We move outside and have some official photos taken and then we travel back in a series of cabs and cars to Mark and Rosita's house to start the real celebrations. The paps have quite a field day, capturing the assorted christening guests as we leave the church. As soon as I'm outside, the shades are on, as I try to ignore the photographers and concentrate on being present and in the moment for my goddaughter's christening.

Back home, Rosita immediately takes charge of Luna and rocks her to sleep while the rest of us accept canapés and champagne from the wait staff who have been employed to make sure we have everything that we need.

I hang with Jez, Manuela and Isabella for most of the time until Isabella steals Jez away for a dance. She's got the wrong guy there as Jez has never been much of a dancer but three songs in, Jez is still stepping the light fantastic on the temporary dance floor in their conservatory. Manuela and I continue the small talk.

'You boys in the band have all known each other for years, haven't you? You met at school, didn't you?' she asks, fiddling with the stem of her champagne glass with her blood red painted nails, obviously having done her homework on us all.

'Yeah. That's right. You and Isabella met Rosita at school as well, didn't you?' I reply, trying to remember my manners. As gorgeous as she is, I can't be bothered with finding all about yet another woman.

'Yes. In fact, we first met at kindergarten.' Manuela says her chocolate brown eyes burning straight into mine.

Mark ditches the champagne and gets stuck into some beers, joined by Rosita who sips a much-needed glass of champagne, as she's finally managed to put Luna down for a sleep. Carmen oversees the wait staff, and Enrique holds court with the cousins and other assorted family members.

'Shame your dad couldn't make it.' I say to Mark.

'He's too poorly to travel from Spain since his last bout of chemo.' Mark replies, sadly.

'How's he doing?' I ask with concern. Mark only lost his mum last year. A sudden heart attack at their Spanish villa, which they'd moved to just the year before, having sold up their family home in Barnes, wanting to, ironically, have a better quality of life. Her death was totally unexpected as it had been Mark's dad who had been diagnosed with cancer and had just started his chemo. His health has deteriorated since then, but he has struck up a friendship with a widowed neighbour, Helga, who basically moved in with Mark's dad, just six months after his mum died. Mark is grateful that his dad has someone to care for him in his latter years, but it still felt like a betrayal to his mum. Carmen and Enrique live about a half an hour drive from Mark's dad's house, and they often pop in to check up on him, but Helga is somewhat possessive and keeps their visits to no more than half an hour.

'He's weak to be honest. Helga sends me updates, but I feel that she's the one that prevented him coming over. I said that I would pay for a nurse to travel with him, but she put the kibosh on that, I'm afraid. We FaceTimed him last night with Luna in her christening dress and he was quite overcome, bless him. I'm not sure how long he's got, to be honest.' Mark replied, helping himself to another beer from a nearby server.

'I'm sorry mate. I shouldn't have asked. Didn't want to upset you, today of all days.' I apologise, pulling him in for a blokey hug.

'Don't be. I'm grateful you asked. Rosita tries to encourage me to talk more about what's happening with my dad, but you know how us blokes try to decompartmentalize things.' Mark answers. I nod in agreement knowing how closed we can all be with our feelings.

'Jez and Isabella seem to be getting on well. She hasn't let him leave the dance floor!' I say, trying to lighten the mood.

'I noticed. Rosita will be delighted that some of her

matchmaking has worked.' Mark says with a twinkle in his eye. 'I'd better go and check on Marnie and the twins. I promised Marsha and Frida that I would make sure they all eat properly and get to bed at a reasonable time!'

'Good luck with that.' I say, marvelling at Mark's blended family set up.

With Mark gone, I find myself alone, so I help myself to yet another beer before I'm joined by a slightly breathless Jez.

'That Isabella wouldn't let me escape! I told her I'm not much of a dancer, but she wouldn't take no for an answer. I'm so hungry.' Jez says as he helps himself to a canapé from a passing server.

'I didn't know you could dance like that?' I say, grinning from ear to ear. 'We might have to incorporate some of those moves into our Reunion Tour!'

'Give it up. You know dancing isn't within my skill set. I'll stick with playing the bass thank you!' Jez replies, as he demolishes the canapé.

The party is a joyous occasion; there's a DJ playing a selection of music (tonight is a Mountaineers free zone!) and people dance, drink and eat from a delicious buffet with both English and Spanish food including another of Carmen's paellas which I notice that Mark gives a miss and to top it all little Luna makes a sleepy appearance for the cutting of the christening cake, before Carmen takes hold of her again and whisks her away, leaving Rosita and Mark to have some time to party.

It's good to see both Mark and Rosita enjoying them-selves so much after the last difficult few months of having a newborn. I notice Isabella tapping her phone number into Jez's phone before persuading him to take to the dancefloor once again. He's a willing dance partner, despite his earlier declarations. Manuela tries her best to encourage me to dance and I feel obliged to keep her happy after all the effort she's made. The music is uplifting or maybe it's the many beers that I've consumed but I really enjoy the feel of Manuela's toned body next to mine, as the tempo of the music slows down and I hold her close, so it's no surprise that we spend the rest of the evening together.

The party comes to a natural end as daytime drinking catches up with most people and Jez and I effusively thank Mark and Rosita and the immediate family for a wonderful day. Somehow, I find myself suggesting that Jez and I continue the night together with Isabella and Manuela at a discreet members' club in Soho. This wasn't really the plan I had, but I'm feeling relaxed for the first time in ages and I'm having fun. All things #thegirlinthesong seem a million miles away as I enjoy the feel of Manuela's leg pressed up against mine as we laugh and flirt in the back of a black cab, while Jez and Isabella are lost in conversation.

As we reach the club, I realise that I don't have my member's card with me but the bouncers on the door know my face and welcome us all inside. We are ushered to and are seated in the VIP section, so I order a couple of bottles of champagne, not caring about the cost, just feeling the need to impress. Isabella takes Jez's arm, and they check out the dance floor, leaving Manuela and I alone. The waitress brings us our champagne and pours out two glasses and I remember us clinking our glasses and then later ordering another bottle. We seem to have lost sight of Jez and Isabella and somehow Manuela and I are in yet another taxi leaving the club, and then there is nothing...

40

GENIE

Now

Gray gets back from the office late and he seems vexed. Gone is my nice, relaxed husband from our holiday. He seems like a distant memory.

'You ok Gray? You seem grumpy.' I say, wanting him to know that his foul mood has been noted.

'Yeah. Sorry. Just work stuff.' He replies curtly as he unpacks his laptop from his work bag and sets it up on the kitchen island as he perches on one of the bar stools and starts looking at the screen intently. It's not until I go past him to get something out of the fridge, I notice that he's actually watching TikTok!

'What the..' I start, as he slams his laptop shut. 'You're on TikTok!'

He knows he's been caught out and there is absolutely no point in trying to lie.

'I can explain..' He says, his usual confident voice, faltering slightly.

'Ok. I'm waiting.' I reply, my cheeks feeling flushed as I

put my hands on my hips, hoping that I look more confident that I feel.

'I just wanted to see what the general consensus is about you on TikTok. I want to know exactly what people are saying about my wife! I want to be prepared for the next media storm, so I'm reading absolutely everything that people are saying. I just want to be armed with all the relevant information so that I can protect you. That's all.' Gray finally reveals defensively, crossing his arms in front of his chest as if to further distance himself from his earlier betrayal.

'I know you always have my best interests at heart, but has it really come to this?' I say, shaking my head in disbelief.

'I'm sorry Genie but you know what I'm like, I always like to be forearmed with information, especially if it's something to do with you.' He replies, looking suitably remorseful.

'Well, I have some more information for you to digest.' I boldly state.

'Oh yes?' Gray replies looking suitably interested.

'You know I was in touch with Emma?' I start, as Gray nods. 'Well, she's responded, and she wants to talk to me in private as she's got some news, so I've invited her to stay!' I blurt out as quickly as possible, so Gray can't get a word in with his normal barrage of questions.

'Is that wise do you think? You haven't seen this woman for over thirty years. She might be trying to sell a story on you by promising you some information to gain more content for a story by staying here.' Gray poses a question that had briefly crossed my mind, but I'm convinced that Emma, who had only known me as a very pregnant teenager for such a short amount of time, would never betray me in that way. She only ever offered me comfort and friendship when I really needed it.

'I know Emma. She would never do anything to hurt me.' I snap back at Gray.

'Ok but I just want to protect you and if by inviting Emma into our home helps you, then so be it. I will welcome her with open arms.' Gray replies being as reasonable as ever, despite my snappy response.

I wrap my arms around his neck and place an apologetic kiss on his lips and he kisses me back, all our cross words immediately forgotten.

'I know I've been a nightmare recently with all this Ed stuff going on, but now you all know about Milly, I feel stronger with all your support.' I confess to Gray as he rubs my back.

'I'm just glad that we as a family know about Milly. I'm not so keen on the recent revelations on social media and I can't believe I'm even going to say this – but I really do think it's probably about time that you contacted Ed Nash. Even though he's exploited your past relationship for his own good, I really do think he deserves to know the circumstances about why you left and of course the fact that you both share a daughter who is out there somewhere.' Gray says somewhat magnanimously.

'You're right. As per usual. Ed's been on my mind recently and he does deserve to hear the truth from me. I've just got to work out how to contact him discreetly and indeed what exactly to say.' I reveal truthfully, hoping that my words don't hurt him, although I'm beginning to think that man has a Teflon coated heart with everything that I have put him through.

'Whatever you decide to do, just know that I'll always be here for you.' Gray says with such love and conviction, I can feel my eyes smarting.

'What would I ever do without you?' I say in almost a whisper.

'Let's not think about things like that.' Gray replies,

brushing any negative thoughts away. 'Do you need any help in getting things ready for Emma?'

I shake my head.

'I take it that the guest room is immaculate!' Gray says, a huge smile spreading across his handsome face. He knows me so well. Sometimes I think he knows me better than I know myself.

'I'm surprised you even need to ask!' I reply with a smile, all previous tensions between us now resolved. That's the beauty of a long lasting and happy marriage; compromise and not holding a grudge for too long.

'Well, it looks like you have everything under control Mrs McNamara! How about a celebratory bottle of wine with our dinner?' Gray suggests with a wink.

'Yes. Definitely. I think we both deserve it!' I reply as I start serving us dinner. 'Can you call the children? It's lasagna, with home-made garlic bread.'

The children were clearly hungry as they both appear at the table just minutes later. It's satisfying for us all to eat together as a family as this happens quite infrequently as the children grow older. They're getting to that age when they start to pull away from us, forge their own lives but as long as they know that we are always here for them, should they need us, well that's the real skill of parenthood; getting the right balance of nurturing but letting them fly…….

We explain to the children about Emma coming to stay and again swear them to secrecy about her visit. Being Gen Z children they are fully aware of the pitfalls of social media, having never known a life without it. They still marvel how our generation managed without the internet or mobile phones!

With dinner finished, the children clear the table unprompted and even stack the dishwasher and uncharacteristically they join us in the living room as Gray pours us both another glass of wine as Cassie is furiously scrolling on her phone. 'You'd better have a look at this Mum!' she says, thrusting her phone into my hands.

My finger hovers over play on a TikTok post and there's a series of unflattering photos and a video of Ed stumbling out of a west end night club, looking quite worse for wear, accompanied by an attractive dark-haired woman who was desperately trying to hide their faces from the camera.

Is the search for Evie Del Rio aka #thegirlinthesong finally taking its toll on indie rocker Ed 'Nasher' Nash? the headline screams on TikTok and indeed every other media outlet. I listen to the post that Cassie has seen and then switch to a tabloid website to read what they have to say.

Ed 'Nasher' Nash is spotted leaving the West End night-club Blaze, accompanied by an unknown brunette beauty, the article starts.

Earlier in the day, Ed Nash had attended his fellow band member Mark Fordham's daughter's christening, and we believe, even stepping up for godfather duties. He was then spotted later that evening with fellow Mountaineer Jez Carter and two stunning unnamed brunettes. It appears that Jez Carter, 49, left Blaze about an hour and a half later than Ed Nash. Jez Carter is no stranger to heartbreak himself, becoming a widower on his honeymoon back in the early 90s when his childhood sweetheart Poppy Burrows drowned under mysterious circumstances in Thailand. Jez Carter has been plagued by rumours of their heavy drug use ever since, although it is understood that Carter spent some time at a Buddhist retreat and is now drug free.

I study the crystal-clear photo of Ed coming out of the club with his mystery brunette trying to hold him up while at the same time shielding their faces. He looks extremely drunk, and his normal chiselled good looks are nowhere to be seen in this opportunist photo. And because of all the furore about #thegirlinthesong, poor Jez has had the death of his wife dragged up all over again. It wasn't fair, but if you play with fire, you are bound to get burned at some stage.

I pass Cassie's phone to Gray, and he has a cursory glance at the latest gossip, rubbing at the stubble coming through on his chin, deep in thought.

'Nothing for us to worry about. I think Ed's just had a big night out, had too much to drink and because of all the recent publicity, the paps are all over him.' Gray replies, handing Cassie's phone back to her.

'Is it ok if I stay at Mel's tonight?' Cassie casually asks.

'I don't see why not but just be wary of talking about Ed.' I reply, finishing off my glass of wine.

'Yes. Your mum is right. The less people that know about mum's side of things, the better.' Gray adds, before topping up my glass.

'Thanks. You're the best and honestly, I promise not to utter a word about you and Ed Nash. Mel knows me well enough to know that that subject is out of bounds.' Cassie replies earnestly, but knowing what her and Mel are like, I already wonder if Mel knows more than what Cassie is letting on. I guess I'll just have to trust her on this one.

'If Cassie's allowed to see Mel, is it ok if I go to Tommy's?' Will asks, realising that there is certainly room for negotiation here.

'Yeah. Go on. But the same applies to you with regards to responding to any gossip.' Gray warns him.

Within seconds each of our children are back on the phones; Cassie taps back a message back, which I assume is to Mel and Will leaves an almost inaudible voice note for Tommy.

"I can give you both a lift if you like? I've only had one glass of wine, so I'm fit to drive.' Gray offers jovially.

'Are you sure you don't mind, Dad?' Cassie says in her most persuasive voice.

'Course not. Hurry up before I change my mind.' Gray replies, knowing that Cassie will take ages getting everything ready for her overnight stay.

'You'll be ok here on your own for a bit, won't you?' He checks with me.

'Yeah. I've got wine so I'll be more than ok.' I reply with a grin, looking forward to the prospect of an evening to ourselves.

Ten minutes later, the house is silent, and I find myself pouring a third glass of wine, enjoying the feeling of relaxation that it gives me, and my mind returns to thoughts of Ed. I know that Gray is right that I do owe Ed some sort of explanation and that he needs to know first; away from the media, away from the cameras and TikTok. He deserves that much at least.

41

ED

Now

I awake with a start and notice that I'm in my own bed. My brand-new suit is a crumpled mess, half-heartedly thrown over the chair in my bedroom. I glance down, relieved to see that I'm at least wearing pants, and I'm alone.

I start getting flashbacks from last night. I remember the christening and that all seems like a clear memory and then I remember taking a cab with Manuela, Jez and Isabella and buying champagne and then I think I remember another taxi. My head is thumping with that awful pain that you only get from drinking too much champagne. I reach for a bottle of water on my bedside table and drink almost half of its contents before running to my ensuite bathroom, promptly throwing up as the water hits my empty stomach. I feel better almost immediately apart from cramps from an empty stomach. I brush my teeth and pull on a t-shirt and joggers and walk towards the kitchen to fix myself a coffee. And as I walk through the sitting room there is Manuela, asleep on the sofa, covered by a throw. She looks peaceful so I continue through to the kitchen. I clearly underestimate quite how noisy my coffee machine is, and I'm soon joined by Manuela.

'Good morning, Ed. How is your head?' Manuela enquires with a kind smile.

'Umm. Yeah. Err better than when I first woke up. Coffee?' I reply, wondering if I need to apologise to Manuela for my behaviour.

She smiles and nods in answer to my offer of coffee and I shudder as to what else I may have offered her in the early hours of this morning.

My hands shake as I pass her a coffee and point towards the milk and sugar, which she declines.

'Thank you. How are you feeling this morning?' she continues.

'As I said earlier, better than first thing. The coffee's helping.' I reply with a fake smile.

'No, I don't mean your head. I mean how is your heart? You were so sad last night, and I think you just wanted to drink more to forget all about Evie.' she says with a real look of concern.

'Oh, to be honest, I don't really remember much about last night. I'm so sorry. I do hope that I didn't do anything to upset or offend you?' I ask tentatively, hoping that somehow, she can help fill in the blanks. She shakes her head.

'Of course not. I believe there will be some, er, how you say, some paparazzi photos of you today, I tried to cover our faces but I'm not so sure that it worked, and my phone is out of charge, so I haven't been able to check.' she further elaborates.

'There's a charger here.' I say pointing towards the charger, next to the Alexa. 'Pass it here.'

Hands still shaking, I just about manage to plug her phone in while I search for my own phone, which is on the coffee table. Surprisingly it has some juice left in it, so I take a look at the showbiz headlines to be greeted with photos of myself and Manuela stumbling out of Blaze nightclub. They're not particularly flattering photos of me, but I've seen worse.

'Sorry, Manuela that you've been dragged into my mess.' I say as a way of an apology.

'It's fine. I like you, but I have realised that you need to find some closure with finding your ex-girlfriend. I know from Rosita what a good friend you are to her and Mark. She says that you always make time to talk to her and she is forever grateful.' Manuela replies.

'Thanks. I love Rosita. She's good for Mark and I know how settled she makes him feel.' I start to explain as I pass my phone over to her. 'And don't worry about the photos. You look gorgeous. Nothing to be ashamed about, apart perhaps from the company that you keep.' I say, trying to lighten the mood.

'You are funny Ed Nash.' Manuela replies with an amused smile as she drains the rest of her mug. I think carefully about what she has said about needing to heal my heart and although we have only just met, I realise that she has got the measure of me perfectly.

'Can I offer you some breakfast?' I ask, when all I really want to do is drag myself back to bed, my champagne hangover really starting to kick in.

'No. I'm ok thanks. I really should be getting back to Rosita and Mark's house.' She replies as if reading my mind.

'Let me at least pay for a taxi.' I offer, feeling that I really do owe her for looking out for me last night.

'Yes. Ok. I would appreciate that. Thank you.' She replies, reaching over and chastely kisses my cheek.

Once Manuela has left, I grab a bottle of water and a couple of paracetamol and return to bed and toss and turn for about an hour as my hangover threatens to take over. I shoot Jez a message and he tells me about Isabella staying the night

– in the spare room – he hastens to add. I explain that Manuela crashed on the sofa as I was in no state to even show her to my guest room!

Jez casually mentions the recent photos and I kind of shrug them off and Jez knowing me so well, doesn't pursue things but suggests meeting for a healthy lunch the following day, more for my benefit than his I think, and I jump at the chance to meet up with him. I could take a leaf out of his book with doing all things in moderation.

42

GENIE

Now

I probably shouldn't have drunk all that wine last night, as I'm regretting it this morning. By the time Gray got home from dropping off the children at their friends' houses I was just about ready for bottle number two. I just seemed to have my drinking boots on last night which is so unlike me. We had a good evening, reminiscing about when we first met, our joyous mood buoyed up by watching numerous, fuzzy 80s music videos where rara skirts were the height of fashion and day-glo ruled!

Gray is up already, and I can hear him happily whistling away to himself in the kitchen below. I shouldn't waste too much time dawdling in bed as Emma is arriving late this afternoon to stay with us. I've offered to pick her up from Richmond Station but she insisted on getting a taxi. Gray said he would try and finish work a bit earlier than usual to join us. We're not going anywhere tonight, just staying at home to eat.

Gray pops upstairs to say goodbye and to wish me well

before he leaves for work. Later, I potter around the house, cleaning as I go. The house is immaculate. I've cleaned it twice already, but I just want everything to be perfect and the compulsive cleaning is keeping my brain occupied.

Emma arrives promptly at 5pm as we'd agreed. I've been obsessively watching out for her through the shutters in the sitting room. As soon as I spot her, I smooth down my carefully chosen pale blue linen dress and go to open the front door to greet my long-lost friend.

As soon as I see her, it was as if we had never been apart as we effortlessly chat away like a couple of schoolgirls.

'Oh, it's so good to see you again.' Emma exclaims.

'I feel the same!' I reply, and I really mean it. 'You have two sons, don't you?' I ask. 'Yes, I have two sons, Andrew, my eldest, is at uni in Manchester and my youngest, Matty stayed close to home at Bournemouth University. I miss them both, but it means that my husband Matt and I get to spend more time together without the constraints of family life. Tell me all about your family. I've thought about you often.'

'Well, I had my baby, not long after my exams and she was given away to a 'nice' Catholic family as was the arrangement and as you know I then left for Brighton.' I begin. 'I'm married to Gray. I met him not long after I arrived in Brighton and we've got two children. Cassie who is sixteen and Will is fifteen. And out came my story to yet someone else. Emma was probably one of the easier people to speak to. She knew only too well what my life had been like in Bournemouth with both my mother and my aunt.

Gray arrives home early for once, keen to protect me potentially from Emma and her revelations. Thankfully, Gray warms immediately to Emma.

'It's so good to finally meet you. I've heard an awful lot about you recently.' he says pleasantly.

'It's great to meet you too, and to finally catch up with Genie, although I still think of her as Evie, but I completely understand her wanting to reinvent herself!' Emma replies, warmly, touching me reassuringly on my arm. 'Sorry about all the cloak and dagger messages but I'm just very wary of my socials being hacked. I don't really take much notice of the tabloids and celebrity gossip doesn't interest me at all but over the last year I began to think that Evie my friend from Church all those years ago was #thegirlinthesong from the Netflix documentary. It took me a while to realise it was you, but when the press identified you, I then saw the resemblance. You've obviously changed quite a bit over the years, I guess we all have to a degree, but I knew it was you, so it didn't really come as much of a surprise when I got a DM from you.' Emma continues.

Gray and I sit and listen while Emma tells her side of the story of what happened after I'd left. When Auntie Maureen had recovered from her laxative laden tea she contacted my mother at the church. Mother was enraged and later Auntie Maureen had recognised Emma from both school and church, so she was interrogated by both her parents and my mother and my aunt. Emma remained loyal to me and told them that she was as shocked and surprised at my disappearance as they all were. For weeks afterwards she was quizzed by everyone about my whereabouts and although she had recommended that I should go to Brighton, Emma really didn't know where I was, so technically she wasn't lying. Eventually they stopped quizzing her as they had come to realise that she really didn't know my whereabouts, or if she did, she was a very good liar.

It was a couple of months after I'd left that she noticed that a middle-aged couple who came to our Church had suddenly acquired a new baby. Most babies to teenagers all look the same but one Sunday when her mother was admiring the baby Emma took a closer look. The baby didn't have much hair and was always asleep whenever she saw her at Church, so she never saw the colour of her eyes. One day she plucked up the courage to ask the baby's name. The slightly harassed mother said her name was Frances, named after St Francis of Assisi. The couple attended Church for at least a year before they disappeared. Emma's father said that they had relocated to London, due to work and that was the last she ever saw of any of them.

Gray took notes as Emma spoke. She did stress to us both that she had no proof that the baby was mine. It was probably just a romantic notion from an impressionable teenager, but I knew in my heart of hearts that it was Milly.

After dinner, Gray makes his excuses to do some work and retires to his office, leaving Emma and I to catch up some more and then that was when Emma drops a bombshell.

'I just wanted to let you know face to face that I had nothing to do with the TikTok reveal on Amira Malik's account.' Emma says solemnly.

'I know you didn't. Amira was quite adamant that you hadn't spoken to her.' I reassure her, placing my hand on her arm.

'But I've recently found out who it was.' she reveals, taking a breath, as if waiting for me to say something.

'I don't understand what you mean.' I reply, not quite knowing where this line of conversation is going, as my heart races.

'I'm just going to come out and say it.' Emma blurts. 'It was Hetty, my sister who contacted Amira Malik. I'm so sorry, Genie. If I could have stopped her, I would have. You've got to believe me.'

'Hetty?' I say. 'It was her....'

Emma just nodded.

'I'm so sorry. I had no idea that she even remembered you from Church, but she was always such an observant child.'

This was not the revelation that I had been expecting. Emma shakes her head sadly.

'She's always liked being the centre of attention and I'm not sure that Amira even paid her anything for her revelation. These TikTok people don't realise how they are destroying people's real lives with all their revelations and speculations, but Hetty has always been a bit of an attention seeker so in some ways it doesn't surprise me that she'd want to be in the thick of things.' Emma further reveals, wiping a tear away from her right eye that is threatening to fall.

'Thank you for telling me. At least I know now. I've just got to decide what to do next.' I reply, although I'm completely blindsided that it was Hetty behind the story. We hug and I feel such gratitude towards Emma for telling me the truth although I can tell that she is heartbroken.

'I guess you'll contact Ed?' Emma suggests, leaning back on the sofa, looking so much more relaxed now that she has shared the information about Hetty. I nod, knowing that I can't put off speaking to Ed any longer. Gray and I both agree that he deserves to know that he does have a daughter out there somewhere.

'Despite everything, Ed does deserve to know the truth.' I reply.

Emma stays for a couple of days. Any thoughts that Emma was 'in it for the money' disappear from both mine and Gray's minds as Emma simply delights everyone that she meets. The children love hearing our stories from school; Emma reminding the children that once upon a time I was a young and feisty girl who followed her own rules. I also introduced her to Maura, and they got on like a house on fire.

Initially two strangers who, in their own ways were both sent to me in my hour of need.

When Emma finally returns home, the house feels empty without her, and I spend the rest of the day daydreaming about how on earth I'm going to contact Ed and tell him that all the rumours about him being a father are in fact true.

43

ED

Now

True to his word, Jez calls round to pick me up in his car to take me out for that promised healthy lunch. He's discovered a new authentic Thai place in Twickenham, close to where his parents live. We leave the car in his parents' drive and walk into the high street. The owner greets Jez like an old friend and seats us at a table overlooking the high street, handing over a couple of menus. Jez orders a Som Tum and a Thai ginger green salad for us to share with a couple of citrus infused sodas whereas I was hoping for an extra hot red curry and a nice cold beer to wash it down with. But today is all about things in moderation according to Jez and after my recent big night out, who am I to argue? Jez chats a little in Thai (picked up from his extensive travels in South East Asia) much to the delight of the proprietor and before long we are both tucking into our Thai salads. I'll be wanting cheese on toast when I get home I think to myself but I've promised myself and Jez that booze and unhealthy food are off the menu, so I'll just have to take a leaf out of Jez's book and try to make more of a conscious effort to lead a healthy life, especially as the tour starts in the next few months.

'The food's so good in here. And so healthy too.' Jez says enthusiastically tucking into his salad.

The salad hasn't touched the sides for me as I hear my stomach rumble. A full English breakfast would have done me better and helped to soak up all the booze from the last few days. But I know this is the way forward if I'm to get in proper shape for the tour. It's harder as you get older to bounce back after a few heavy nights out.

'It's great.' I reply, I hope sounding convincing enough.

'You're still hungry, aren't you?' Jez observes. 'I'll order some chicken satay. Lots of nice protein for you. That'll perk you up.'

'That'd be great.' I reply, feeling and probably looking relieved that Jez can practically read my mind.

Jez orders the extra food, and I demolish it like I've been starved for days but it does the trick. Afterwards, Jez settles the bill, and we walk back to his parents' house.

'Fancy popping in to say hello to mum and dad?' Jez asks.

'Of course. It's been ages since I've seen them.'

Jez opens the front door, and we walk through to their familiar sitting room where Jez's mum is engrossed in a crossword and his dad is enjoying forty winks, with Geronimo their large black cat cuddled up contentedly on his lap.

'Hello Mum. Look who's come to visit.' Jez says gently as his mum looks up from her crossword.

'Well, if it isn't Ed.' she says with a genuine smile.

'Hello Sylvie.' I say, leaning in to give her a kiss, inhaling her ever familiar Rive Gauche perfume.

'Come sit next to me Ed. Let me see you properly, it's

been such an age since I last saw you.' she says, patting the seat beside her.

I obediently do as she asks. Sylvie was always like a second mum to me growing up and I would often decamp to Jez's house when my mum was on one about my behaviour. I loved the slight chaos and homeliness of their house and there was always a home cooked meal to be had, whoever you were.

'Well, I swear you look younger every time I see you. Life is definitely treating you well.' Sylvie says, taking my hand in hers.

'Aw thanks Sylvie. And you look as gorgeous as ever. How's Bill?' I say, looking over at Jez's dad asleep in his favourite armchair with Geronimo.

'He's doing well, despite his last fall. That'll teach him, trying to clean out the gutters himself just to save a few pounds.' Sylvie replies, slightly chastising her husband.

'Hello darling. And hello to Ed.' he replies, opening his eyes. 'Don't take too much of what Sylvie says to heart. Geronimo nodded off on my lap and I couldn't bear to move him, so I just took the opportunity to rest my eyes for a bit. And as for the gutters, I like to keep my hand in with a bit of maintenance while I still can.' he blustered.

'Dad, I can always help out. You only have to ask.' Jez interjects.

'I know, but you're busy with your own life and I like to be useful.' Bill retorts.

'You're not much good to me, if you hurt yourself and you know we've got that trip to Australia to see Lyla early next year once that baby comes.' Sylvia scolds. Lyla, Jez's younger sister had met and married an Australian guy, and they were expecting their first baby in the new year.

I stand up and shake Bill's hand.

'What have you two been up to?' Bill asks with a twinkle in his eye. 'Up to mischief I should imagine…'

'Not at all, Dad. We just tried out that new Thai place in the High Street. You know, the new healthy one I was telling you about. Ed and I are getting ready for the upcoming tour so we're starting to have a look at our diets.' Jez explains patiently as Bill still thinks of us as young men, even though we're all in our late forties.

'Ah yes. I remember now.' Bill replies, running his hand through his thick greying hair. No chance of Bill ever going bald as he had a better head of hair as most men half his age.

'I think it's time for a cup of tea, don't you boys?' Sylvie announces walking towards the kitchen before anyone answers. 'I've got a freshly baked lemon drizzle cake that you simply must try Ed. And I won't take no for an answer, despite what my son says about keeping it healthy. You look like you could do with a bit of feeding up.' she continues.

'How can anyone refuse an invitation like that?' I enthuse. 'Can I help with anything?'

'If you could fill up the kettle for me. I find a filled kettle a little on the heavy side nowadays.' Sylvie replies as I take the kettle from her and fill it up. Sylvie and Bill still prefer to boil their kettle on the gas stove and while we wait for the kettle to whistle to say it's ready, I nostalgically remember back to our school days when Sylvie would make us hot sugary cups of tea from a kettle similar to this one, after we'd played our hearts out for the school football team. We hardly ever won but we would always end up at Jez's house as his mum worked from home, writing the occasional article for the local paper and she was always delighted to have a houseful of children to look after while the other parents worked, and we were always spoiled with some sort of home baked treat. Although Jez lived the furthest away from our school, the field that we played foot-

248

ball on was in Richmond, so it made sense to all go back to his.

Sylvie insists on getting out her good china cups and teapot, complete with matching sugar bowl and milk jug. I notice that her hand shakes a little as she pours the hot water into the teapot and then she searches for some matching side plates and some linen napkins.

'Please don't go to too much trouble.' I begin to say, but my protests are batted away by Sylvie.

'I like to make it a special occasion when we have visitors and today is one of those days.' she says as she busies herself slicing the lemon drizzle cake into generous, hefty slices.

'Jez. You must try a slice of cake. You look like you've lost too much weight recently with all your faddy diets.' Sylvie scolds her only son.

'Go on then mum, I'll have a piece. I haven't lost weight. I've just toned up at the gym. That's all.' Jez replies, almost reverting to a sulky teenager again whenever his parents start to criticize. I'm the same with my parents. It's just that I choose not to see them too often.

I feel comfortable sitting here with Sylvie and Bill and as we sit and drink our tea and all marvel at Sylvie's incredible baking, that I realise I miss family life. Before Paul outstayed his welcome at our house, my parents would always have a house full of people, drinking and making music together. It's what got me interested in playing music as my dad relished in teaching me how to play the guitar properly and encouraged me to form a band with my mates.

Despite being full of tea and cake, Jez and I do a few jobs in the house for Sylvie and Bill. Jez is much more handy than I am, but I make quite a good apprentice, handing him the relevant screws and tools as he fixes a couple of shelves that look in danger of collapsing and we fix their garden gate to make it more secure. Bill is now banned from doing any DIY after his fall much to his dismay as he hovers beside us as we work, keen to get involved.

'Any news on that Evie one?' Bill asks out of the blue.

Jez shoots his dad a look, but I feel happy to reply to Bill. I like it that the older generation almost don't have any filter and say what they really mean.

'No. Not yet unfortunately. But I'm hopeful in time she'll reach out.' I reply as Jez stands back to admire his handy work of securing the garden gate.

'She was quite feisty if I remember correctly.' Bill continues. 'Wasn't her mother somewhat religious? I'm sure I remember her trying to get Sylvie to help at the church. Sylvie always managed to come up with some excuse or other.' he says remembering back to our school days.

'Yep. Evie was quite a character, and you've remembered Felicity Del Rio perfectly! A religious nut is how we all described her. Even her sister contemplated being a nun!' I add as Bill nods, pleased that his brain does still work properly and that he still remembers things.

Jez and I tidy up a bit and put the assorted tools that we've used back in their rightful places and go to walk inside. Geronimo shoots past us like the clappers and jumps over the newly fixed gate, off to explore.

'You've got the cat's approval!' Bill jokes as he walks back into the kitchen.

'All sorted?' Sylvie asks.

'All sorted.' Jez replies kindly.

'Fancy staying for dinner?' Sylvie asks, her eyes looking hopeful.

'No. Sorry. I must get Ed back home as we both need an early night. We've got rehearsals coming up.' Jez says, closing down the suggestion of staying which is a shame as I love being part of Jez's family here with Sylvie and Bill and the thought of one of Sylvie's delicious home cooked meals really does appeal.

'Oh, ok but you know how much I enjoy having a house full.' Sylvie replies before adding,

'Ed. Let's organise a date when you are both less busy for dinner.' she says compromising with Jez.

'Definitely. I've really enjoyed seeing you both.' I reply swiftly for the both of us.

We both kiss Sylvie and hug Bill goodbye, and they insist on waving us off, as Jez backs out of the drive.

'You didn't have to accept another invitation.' Jez says as he drives away.

'I wish I had the same kind of relationship with my parents that you do with yours.' I say sadly.

'I suppose because my parents are so present in my life, I maybe take them for granted. I know I'm lucky to have them, but they do try and take over a bit, especially with people like you. I'll organise another visit.' Jez replies trying to appease his guilt for taking his parents for granted.

'That'd be great. The only way I'm going to get back in my mum's good books if my supposed long-lost child suddenly appears! Dad says that mum keeps asking if there's any news on the grandchild front!' I reveal to Jez.

'My parents are the same. Desperate for me to reproduce! Thankfully Lila has taken the heat off me for a while with her pregnancy.' Jez explains as he drives along Cross Deep towards my apartment.

'Fancy coming up for a drink?' I casually ask, knowing what the reply will be.

'Not tonight. I'm going for a run when I get home. I hope you haven't forgotten that we start back rehearsing in a couple of days.' Jez explains to me as if I'm a child. I haven't forgotten about the rehearsals but I'm keen to continue the night, but I realise it's not happening, at least not with Jez!

'Yeah, of course and don't worry, I certainly haven't forgotten about the rehearsals!' I say as jovially as I can. 'And thanks for today. Seeing both Sylvie and Bill was a bonus!'

'No problem. I'll organise dinner with them soon. See you at rehearsals.' Jez says as I get out of his car and walk towards the entrance of the flats, as Jez reverses and drives off. Thankfully the paps seemed to have given up for tonight.

I take the lift upstairs and then take a shower and change, doing anything to resist consuming any alcohol. I open the patio doors that lead out from the sitting room and enjoy watching the light fade over the manicured gardens and relish the stillness, hearing the slight hum of people talking outside, enjoying the warmth of the evening. It's idyllic here; if only I had someone to share it with.

44

GENIE

Now

Since Emma left, I've spent so much time almost tying myself up in knots trying to work out the best way to contact Ed. Gray thinks that I should maybe try and message him via Instagram which is the probably the best idea so far. I think he lives in Teddington as it's been mentioned in a recent magazine article, so he's quite close by but I don't know his exact address, so a letter is out of the question and imagine if the letter got into the wrong pair of hands. I'm just grateful that I've never bumped into him at the supermarket over the years, but I don't see Ed as a kind of weekly shop kind of guy. We've ruled out contacting his management company as I would like to speak to Ed face to face. He deserves that much. Gray thankfully, as always, is supporting me in my need to speak to Ed and finally put to rest my long-kept secret which unfortunately thanks to TikTok and Amira Malik is now public knowledge.

After a somewhat robust media campaign of trying to find #thegirlinthesong things have quietened down a little and the

TikTok sleuths have turned their thoughts to another poor family to investigate whose daughter has disappeared on her first girls' holiday in Spain. So now poor Daisy-Mae Jackson's pretty face with her blonde bobbed hair is plastered all over social media. I just can't stop thinking about how her parents must be feeling and for a moment I feel sorry for the grief that I caused my parents when I left Bournemouth all those years ago. Not so much my mother but my dear dad who has spent a lifetime trying to make my mother happy, sometimes to the detriment of his own happiness. It was only when I met Gray that he encouraged me to reach out to my parents again; to mend bridges as we were planning on getting married. They were impressed by Gray making me a respectable woman and he had a good job too. Then, when after years of trying to conceive, my parents were finally rewarded with a legitimate granddaughter in Cassie who has remained a favoured grandchild ever since. I remind myself that I had a very good reason for leaving whereas Daisy-Mae seems to have disappeared into thin air, after leaving a nightclub alone, having been separated from her friends on a night out. Every parent's nightmare.

I feel so agitated and fidgety and can't seem to settle on any one task. The cleaning is up to date, and I've already put two loads of washing outside on the line. I've emptied the dishwasher, the kids are out, Gray's at work so I'm left with my own thoughts. I seem to be in cognitive overload; as my brain flits from memories of those happy, carefree days of being with Ed, to my pregnancy with Milly and then the utter heartbreak of having to give her away, my postnatal blues and having to deal with my milk coming through but having no baby to feed and then feeling the relief and the freedom of escaping from Bournemouth, away from my mother and aunt and their religious mania. And then for the first time in ages having security and feeling accepted and safe in Brighton with Maura and the gang. And finally feeling cared for and cherished and almost 'fixed' by Gray coming into my life and the pure joy of having a proper family with him with the arrivals of both Cassie and Will.

I start listening to the radio and momentarily I'm distracted by an 80s radio station and then I'm right back with Ed and the gang and I remember all the fun we had back then when the most important thing was being allowed to go to the next party or gig as the radio station plays songs which make up the soundtrack of my youth. Being with Ed had been such a buzz back then and I do remember the pure magical thrill when he played the song that he'd written for me for the very first time at Ginny's birthday party. He was my first love but if I hadn't got pregnant, we would probably have split up eventually, I expect. It's very rare that you stay with your first love. And then of course I met Gray, who must be the most tolerant and loving man ever, who has taught me what true love really is; it's passionate, raw and loving, where your partner accepts you for your authentic self and that is just how Gray treats me. I, on the other hand seem to have brought complete chaos into Gray's life but I do wholeheartedly love him with every bone in my body. Despite everything that has happened I feel that we are stronger than ever, and I can cope with anything that life throws us, if I have him by my side.

I search for my iPad and open the notes part of it and start writing an open letter to Ed. I write a few sentences, and I know that the words just aren't flowing. I'll discuss it with Gray when he gets back from work. His advice is always that less words are more effective, but I think in the first instance I just need to establish contact with Ed. I can then hopefully explain everything to him face to face if we decide to meet.

I make myself a cup of tea and lose myself in social media as I watch video after video where numerous people post their theories about my life and Ed's, and I realise that from now on our lives will always be stringently linked – not just through the numerous social media posts that are out there but ultimately through our daughter. It's quite a sobering thought.

With Gray still at work until at least 7pm and the children are out with friends, still enjoying the untethered freedom of the never-ending summer holidays, I continue my frenzied search for all things #thegirlinthesong, remembering to use my dummy TikTok account to watch some of Ed's recent posts which somehow have passed me by. He's taken to posting videos outlining the meanings of all the songs on their debut album Past Times. And then in one of his posts, there it is, his plea for me to reach out to him. As I watch his video on repeat, his words seem quite heartfelt, and I now know that contacting him is the right thing to do.

I sit under the shade of the umbrella on our sunny patio feeling grateful for all that I have, as I look around our beautiful garden with its carefully mowed lawn (which is Gray's one and only job to do at home) but one that he does to absolute perfection and although I'm overwhelmed by all the recent revelations, I also feel the most secure in my marriage now that there are no secrets between us. My worry was once Gray knew everything about me, he would start to feel differently about me but if anything, it has strengthened our relationship, and I feel happy and very much loved and cared for. I once again start to compose a suitable message to Ed. This time my mind seems clearer and before long, although brief, I've now got an idea of what I want to say to Ed.

Now that I have a clear plan of contacting Ed, I start to feel more relaxed than I have done in ages, and I reach for my current read and spend a good half an hour just enjoying getting lost in someone else's story. As the sun starts to set behind the trees at the end of our garden, I glance at the time and gather up my book and cup and walk inside to start dinner. The oppressive heat from yet another hot day still hangs in the air, so I've decided to keep things simple tonight with a chicken salad. There's no point slaving in a hot kitchen. I made some potato salad – Gray's absolute favourite – earlier in the day so if the children return from their friends' houses, there's plenty of food for everyone should they want it.

I set the table and wait for Gray to return. I check my messages, and he says that he's on his way home, but he missed his usual train. I'm not particularly hungry so I decide to wait until Gray gets in but instead, I open a bottle of wine and pour myself a small glass and return to the garden and light a citronella candle to keep the midges away and place it on the patio table.

My thoughts turn to my old school friend Ginny, and I search online and reread the damning newspaper articles where her ex-husband sold her photos of all of us to the press and made up a load of lies about us all. She must be mortified to be betrayed like that. Although Ed has exploited our romance to enhance his career, at least he hasn't sold any photos of us and now all he seems to want is clarity over whether he is a father or not. I'm not going soft on him but I'm slowly appreciating how it must have been for him when I left. When I was in Bournemouth before I had Milly all I thought about was him and I was desperate to talk to him, but once our baby had been given away, I knew it was best for everyone for me to remain silent and to keep my distance.

Ginny looks stunning in the newspaper's accompanying photos. Life has been kind to her, despite her ex-husband revelations. Would there be some time in the future where we might be friends again, I ponder. From the articles, it seems that she is in touch with Ed. She'd always had a soft spot for him but as soon as Ed and I met, we were inseparable. I think about maybe getting in touch with her again, but I really need to talk to Ed first. I take another sip of my wine, enjoying the delicate fruity undertones as it slips down my throat somewhat too easily. I hear the notification of our Ring doorbell and see Gray's handsome face show up on my phone.

Moments later he pops his head round the patio doors.

'Am I glad to see you. it's been one of those days where I haven't stopped.' Gray says, loosening his tie and undoing his top button taking a seat at the table.

'Fancy joining me?' I say, holding up my almost empty glass.

'I certainly do.' Gray replies with a weary grin as I walk towards the patio doors. 'On second thoughts, bring out the bottle!'

'Will do.' I call back.

I pick up a glass for Gray and bring out the rest of the bottle. I place them both on the outside table and pour him a generous glass and top mine up too.

Gray clinks my glass before taking a generous sip from his, as the strain of his day starts to lift.

'Thanks for this Genie. You're a lifesaver. Hope your day has fared better than mine.'

'I've felt so discombobulated today; thinking about everything, processing what Emma told us and missing having her here and wondering what to do for the best and then suddenly things became clearer.' I explain.

'Ok. I'm all ears.' Gray says, willing me to carry on talking.

'I'm going to send a message to Ed via Instagram as you suggested recently.' I continue as Gray nods in agreement.

'And I've been looking through social media on some posts that we've somehow missed. Ed's been posting videos himself being quite open and honest. He's said on two separate occasions; he just wants me to reach out.' I explain.

'It's the way forward. Your message will go straight through to him, hopefully without being intercepted by anyone else and then the rest is up to him I guess.' Gray says quietly. I'm concerned that by reconnecting with Ed again that it will hurt Gray, but he has been the one constantly pushing the idea of restablishing contact.

'Are you sure you're ok with it? It potentially could open a can of worms.' I say, as I reach over to touch his hand, wanting reassurance that he really is ok with this.

'It's the right thing to do Genie.' he says softly, squeezing my hand gently. 'Despite how I feel about the guy, he does have a right to know that he is a father. Perhaps together we can all help find Milly.'

'Thank you.' I whisper, the words almost stuck in my throat as I feel so much love and gratitude for my soulmate.

'You're welcome. You know I've always got you.' he replies, smiling straight into my eyes and I know that he really does mean it.

'I think it's time to eat before we demolish this moreish bottle of wine.' I suggest, lightening the mood.

'Agreed. Especially as you're a whole glass or so ahead of me.' Gray jokes. 'Need any help?'

'No. You're good. It'll give you an opportunity to catch up with me.' I say, blowing him a kiss as I walk to the kitchen to bring out our food.

Gray and I heartily tuck into our food and Gray hoovers up the remainder of the potato salad. Luckily, I've made extra for the children, which is tucked away at the back of the fridge, just in case they come home hungry. What I really mean is I've made extra for Will as that boy is always hungry. He seems to be going through yet another growth spurt. Gray says he was just the same at Will's age.

We've almost finished our drinks, and I feel so buoyed up with confidence and hope that I now feel ready to contact Ed. And it's not just the alcohol that is feeding my need for contact but for the first time in ages I no longer have that feeling of fear, of being found out. When the one thing about me that I never felt ready to share with anyone is out there for everyone to know and despite everything, I'm still standing, then surely, I'm strong enough to meet Ed again and tell him the truth face to face.

Gray helps clear the table and we decamp inside as despite the heat of the day, it's starting to feel a bit chilly to still be outside. I start to load up the dishwasher, but Gray distracts me by opening another bottle so we leave the rest of the kitchen and relax in the sitting room.

'Obviously now is not the time to send a message to Ed as I've had far too much to drink, but I'd like you to take a look at what I propose to send to him.' I say casually, as I pass my phone over to him.

He reads it and nods.

'It's perfect. It's simple and straight to the point. There's no reason to elaborate.' he says, handing back my phone. 'To be honest, you could easily send it now. You wrote it when you were sober, didn't you?'

'Yes. Of course. Despite being the shortest message I've ever written, it took me ages to get it right.' I say, smiling at Gray. He knows that he could use far fewer words than me to say the same thing!

'No time like the present. Copy and paste it into a message' Gray says convincingly.

'You don't think it's too late?' I ask, hesitating.

'Of course not. You'll tie yourself in knots wondering if it's too late or too early. He'll respond in his own time.' Gray says decisively.

'Ok. Here goes.' I say as I copy and paste the text from

my notes and copy it into an Instagram private message. I hesitate before pressing send.

'Done!' I announce somewhat breathlessly to Gray.

'Good. You've done the right thing. I'm proud of you.' he replies, as he pulls me in for a kiss. I kiss him back and hold him close, relieved that he's got my back.

45

ED

Now

The temperature outside has just taken a slight dip, and I shiver, put my phone in my back pocket and go inside. I busy myself by tidying up a bit. I've been out so much recently; I haven't really spent much time enjoying my beautiful apartment that costs me an arm and a leg each month. I thankfully do have a cleaner, Tanya, who comes in once a week that Sid kindly arranged for me. She's one of Sid's many nieces and she lives just off Teddington High Street. She's lovely; nice and discreet and not into music or celebrity, so she is the perfect person to have around.

I'm just loading up the dishwasher when I feel my phone vibrate in my back pocket. Jez and Mark are always telling me to take my phone off vibrate as I so often miss calls and messages.

I notice that there a few other cups and plates that need to be washed so I spend a few minutes finishing stacking up the dishwasher before I sit down on the sofa. I pick up the remote and idly flick through the numerous channels before settling on the news. As Clive Myrie reads the headlines, I remember that my phone beeped earlier, and I probably have a message. I glance at a WhatsApp message from Jez, sending me another healthy breakfast recipe! I'll read it properly later but send a thumbs up back to him. I then look at my social media feeds, starting with Instagram first and there are my usual @ notifications. They are mainly complimentary but with every positive comment there's always a few from the trolls who hide behind anonymous accounts. But there almost hidden in between a load of message requests offering me all manner of things is the message that I've been waiting for. A message from Genie McNamara. It's brief, but straight to the point.

Hi Ed, I've been watching a few of your recent TikToks where you said to get in touch. So, I'm here if you want to talk.

Kind regards, Genie/Evie

I read and reread the message, wondering if after all this time, is it really her? The message doesn't give much away. It's been years since we had any contact. She must be almost fifty now, the same as me. Her Instagram account @geniemc is the same as the one that Amira Malik identified, so surely it must be her. I hesitate before replying. I've waited for a life-time for this message, so I need to think about exactly what to say. Of course I want to see her; to look her in the eyes, to hear the truth once and for all from my Evie who so didn't want to be found, she even changed her name. All I want to do is open a bottle of beer to bolster my confidence in replying to her, to find the right words. Ask me to write a love song and I'll have no problem but replying to a message potentially answering all the questions that I've ever wanted to know seems impossible. Was that what it was like for Evie when she composed her message too? Is that why her message was so vanilla. I would have to respond in the same manner, keep it light, keep it simple.

I resist opening a beer and pour myself a sparkling water

and gulp down a large mouthful, eager to quench my parched throat.

Hi Genie, Thanks for reaching out. I know that must have been difficult after all these years and the recent publicity. Of course I'd like to talk – in person preferably, as I'm never sure how safe these messaging services are. I'll message you my number in a separate message.

Thanks. Ed

I send the first message and then follow it up with a second one containing my mobile number. And then wait......

Now that the message has been sent, I find myself pacing up and down the apartment. I feel a trickle of sweat run down the back of my spine and my hands feel clammy. I don't have to wait too long before my mobile vibrates and there is a message on WhatsApp from Genie.

Hi Ed, I suggest that we meet up somewhere discreet. You are welcome to come to our house if that suits. We're in Richmond so not too far from you.

Genie

Meeting at Genie's house could be an idea as long as no one sees me. I could ask Jez to drop me off nearby and then walk the rest of the way. I reply to Genie agreeing to meet at her house in a couple of days and she shoots me a message with her address in Richmond. I sit back on the sofa. This is really happening. I'm finally going to find out the truth.

46

NOW

Genie

Both Cassie and Will are staying with friends as tonight is the night that Ed and I finally reunite. Gray has taken a half day and is due home imminently. The house is immaculate. Not that I'm bothered about what Ed thinks of our home but cleaning calms me and it gives me something to do as I await his arrival. We've arranged for him to come over at 8:00p.m. Gray and I have eaten early but I could barely swallow a mouthful of my food, the tension and anticipation of finally seeing Ed face to face after all these years, gnaws away at my throat.

We both sit bolt upright on the sofa as if awaiting a visit from royalty as the minutes count down before 8:00p.m. At precisely 8:00p.m. we hear the crunch from the gravel as Ed walks up our drive and then rings on the doorbell.

'You ok to go?' Gray asks me gently, touching my arm for reassurance.

'Of course.' I reply, nodding as I make my way to the front door. I need to see Ed face to face on my own.

The walk to the front door seems to take an age and I

glance briefly at my reflection in the hallway mirror, take a deep breath and open the front door.

Standing in front of me is a stranger, albeit a slightly familiar one. He's wearing a baseball cap, jeans and a hoodie, obviously trying not to stand out too much.

'Hi Ed.' I say, the reality of seeing him standing here on my doorstep hits me hard, as I experience some sort of adrenaline rush, not quite sure how to communicate with the person who has gone from the love of my life to practically a stranger.

'Hi Evie…' He starts to say before correcting himself. 'Sorry. Sorry. I mean Genie… He says, seeming somewhat flustered, his cheeks flushing.

'It's fine, Ed. Come on in.' I say to him sounding much more relaxed and confident than I feel.

He follows me through to the sitting room and Gray immediately stands up.

'I'm Gray, Genie's husband.' Gray says confidently putting out his hand towards Ed's as they shake hands. 'Please, take a seat.'

Ed sits down on one of the single armchairs and I sit back down next to Gray.

'Thank you both for agreeing to meet me. I really do appreciate it.' Ed starts.

'I'm going to leave you two to talk, but in the meantime can I get you a drink Ed?' Gray says.

'A water would be good. Cheers.' He replies. This is all so awkward I think to myself. My husband and my ex-boyfriend making small talk in our sitting room.

Gray leaves us and reappears moments later with a water for Ed and then makes his excuses leaving us alone properly for the first time in over thirty years.

'You look well.' I say as the nerves now start to kick in. And he does look well. Age has been kind to him, despite that rock n roll lifestyle that he supposedly leads, if the tabloids and social media are anything to go by.

'Thanks. You do too.' he replies, his voice no more than a hoarse whisper. He takes a sip of his water, and I notice that his hands are shaking. Despite all his rockstar bravado that he presents to the world, he's just as nervous as I am. Ed clears his throat.

'I have to know why you left. It's been eating away at me for a lifetime.' he implores.

'I'm so sorry. I really am sorry for leaving you….for leaving everyone.' I begin and that's when my tears start to fall.

Ed looks mortified that I've started to cry and passes me a nearby box of tissues.

'Please don't cry. The last thing I ever wanted to do was hurt you. I know that probably doesn't sound true when I know I've capitalised on our relationship in the press to further my career. But all I've ever wanted to know is why you left.' Ed says, as he gets up from the chair and sits next to me on the sofa.

'Please, please tell me the truth.' He pleads, looking almost deep into my soul.

I take a breath and wipe my eyes. Once I say these words, they can't be unsaid. I've got to get this right.

'All the rumours are true. I was pregnant.' I whisper. 'My parents found out the evening of Mark's pool party. I had no idea.'

Ed looks poleaxed.

'So, you left because you were pregnant?'

I just nod. My well-rehearsed words fail to come out of my mouth.

'We could have brought up the baby together.' Ed continues but we both know that his suggestion at that time in our lives is a ridiculous idea.

'You think I wouldn't have told you at the time if I'd had the chance?' I reply quietly. 'I didn't get a say in anything after my parents found out. They drove me straight to Bournemouth to stay with my aunt. They didn't want anyone to know. They were ashamed of me.'

Ed looks broken to finally have the rumours confirmed as I'm not so sure that he was ready for the truth.

'Why didn't you call me? Why didn't you call Ginny?' He asks.

'They had me under lock and key. Between my mother and my aunt, I had no chance.' I reply, looking directly into Ed's eyes, willing for him to understand what it had been like for me.

'If only I'd known, maybe I could have helped you? Maybe made your parents see sense?' Ed says, reaching for my hand. I immediately pull back, the intimate gesture unnerving me. He looks hurt by my response.

'You couldn't have helped. My mother despised you. She put all the blame on you for the pregnancy, as if I had nothing to do with it.' I say, laughing at the complete irony. I brace myself for his next question and I'm ready for it.

'Did you have the baby?' he finally asks.

'Yes. I did. She came early. We were both very poorly.' I say, as my carefully applied makeup starts to run as I try to wipe away my tears with my tear sodden tissue.

'It really is true. We've got a daughter?' Ed says jubilantly.

'She's almost thirty-three. I only saw her briefly when she was born, as I was so out of it. The midwife told me she had masses of fair hair and the bluest eyes she'd ever seen.' I say as I smile, thinking about our beautiful daughter who I was forced to give away. 'I named her Milly. But I don't know what her actual name is now. My mother had arranged for her to be adopted by a 'good'

Catholic family, who could give her a better life than I ever could.'

'I'm sorry that I've caused you so much pain since that documentary aired.' He apologises and I feel that despite everything that has happened, he really does mean it.

'Thank you. I can't deny that I've hated the attention. But I'm also sorry that you didn't have the opportunity to see our daughter grow up. Being forced to give her away is my biggest regret.' I reply remorsefully.

'To be honest, my life meant nothing when you left. I was coasting for years, and when the song started getting popular, I just kind of seized the opportunity I'd been given. I had nothing else.' Ed reveals and I can feel that his regret is true and honest. I thought it would be difficult talking to him after a lifetime of separation, but it feels natural, almost organic. 'I dreamt about seeing you every day after you left. I had so many questions that needed answers, but there was a big fat nothing.' Ed continues, his words almost now in freefall.

'When I was in Bournemouth, I wondered what you were thinking and what you were doing all the time. It was heart-breaking.' I reply, wanting him to know how much he meant to me at that time. 'At first being pregnant with our baby gave me comfort, even though it was also the reason that we were apart. Once I realised that my mother was planning on having our baby adopted, I tried not to think about you too much. Mainly because I knew that you would be devastated to think that I could allow our baby to be taken away. But I didn't have a choice.' I say as my tears continue to fall and I don't even have the strength to wipe them away. 'I thought you'd hate me. And that's why I never got back in contact with you. It seemed easier to keep my secret that way.'

'I would never have hated you.' Ed replies solemnly, touching my hand once more and this time it feels natural, despite the lost years between us there was once love and a true connection. The contact is fleeting but a necessary action. We've both made choices that we've later regretted but reconnecting after a lifetime apart finally feels cathartic. My whole truth has now been shared with the one man who always deserved to be told the truth as to why I left, and I finally feel free of the burden of keeping my long-kept secret.

Ed and I spend the next half an hour just catching up on over thirty years of our very different lives and missed memories. It feels easy talking to him and now that he knows exactly why I had to leave, he appears to feel no malice towards me for the decisions that I've made and I in turn can now see things from his point of view too.

47

ED

Now

My meeting with Genie is surprisingly going well, despite me calling her Evie the moment I see her. What an idiot I am. Seeing her up close for the first time in over thirty years, there are still signs of the 'Evie' that I once knew. I've dreamt about seeing her for a lifetime and now here she is, right in front of me, introducing me to her husband. We talk a bit of small talk before he disappears on the pretext of getting me a drink and then magnanimously says he'll leave us alone to talk.

Once alone, I realise that I know very little about grown-up Genie, just what the gossip and news sites say. Gone is the wild, young, carefree girl I knew. She's been replaced by someone I hardly recognise; her once rebellious spiky blonde hair is now immaculately cut and coloured, she has fine lines near her eyes, but…those mesmerising blue eyes…they're still the same. There's some sort of familiarity there, but in some ways, I feel like I'm talking to someone I met briefly a long ago.

And so, after apologising to her for dragging her into the

media spotlight, as I have relentlessly exploited our relationship, I just come right out and ask her exactly why she left, and she finally tells me that truth that I've been wanting to hear for over thirty years. Although I have always hoped that there was a possibility that we had a child together, I've mostly brushed off that possibility, afraid to believe in it, afraid of how I would feel if it wasn't the case. My heart is racing, as if I've just taken a line of speed, my head spinning. I feel lightheaded but I also have a feeling of calm, finally knowing the truth. As Genie explains what life in Bournemouth was like for her and although it's hard to hear that she too was hurting in some ways it's also a comfort that our relationship wasn't one-sided and that I really meant so much to her too at the time.

Genie apologises for denying me the chance to know our daughter, but I only feel sadness that we have both missed seeing our daughter (and my only child) grow up. We chat a bit more companionably about our mutual friends and I remember to pass on Virginia's good wishes to her and Genie says that she owes Virginia a message as they have reached out briefly over Instagram. I fill Genie in on Mark and Jez's news and she in turn tells me about her children with Gray.

Having sat next to Genie on the sofa when she was upset, I decide to sit back on the armchair that I sat on when I first arrived, not wanting Gray to think that I was muscling in on his wife, especially when he seems cordial towards me.

Moments later, he pops his head around the door.

'Need anything?' He asks politely. He's obviously been dying to know how we've been getting on and rightly so.

'All good.' Genie replies, her face lighting up as she smiles at him. He returns her smile and makes some excuse about needing to make some work calls.

Genie tells me about the closure of the Catholic Adoption Service who had handled our baby's adoption and the likelihood that her adoption along with many others had been mishandled.

I tell Genie that I had been contemplating hiring a private detective to find her but now that we've reunited, I feel perhaps we should choose one together to find our daughter. She wholeheartedly agrees and I feel the tension that I felt at the beginning of the evening starting to lift, and now I just feel buoyed up by pure optimism in finding our daughter with a future full of possibilities. I don't outstay my visit, despite being made to feel very welcome which is so much more than I deserve. Gray reappears and we shake hands once again before he leaves Genie to walk me to the door.

'Thank you for being so honest.' I say, hesitating, not quite sure how to say goodbye, but Genie thankfully makes that decision for me and pulls me in for an innocent hug.

'Thank you for being so understanding about why I left. Hopefully together we can find Milly.' Genie says as she opens the door.

'I'll be in touch with a couple of private detectives to choose from.' I say as I start to leave.

'It's always good to have a plan.' Genie replies as a small genuine smile spreads across her face, accentuating those familiar blue eyes.

'Take care.' We both say in unison as I walk away.

I walk down Richmond Hill, away from the McNamara's impressive home, pulling my baseball cap further down to cover my face and uncharacteristically decide to walk over Richmond Bridge to take a bus back to Teddington, enjoying the anonymity.

I was pleasantly surprised by the whole outcome of my meeting with Genie. We realised with hindsight that we have both made mistakes and choices that we have later regretted. But that is now in the past and we have kept in touch over the last few weeks with our continued search for out lost daughter. Together with Genie and Gray, we have instructed a private detective to investigate the adoption. Every now and again, he has a lead, but as the adoption service has been closed for quite some time, due to the mishandling of many of the adoptions, the search is seemingly futile.

Life goes on and the preparation for the tour only intensifies, filling my days and nights. I check in with Genie every so often for updates on finding our daughter although the trail seems to have run cold. Our relationship is cordial, and I find myself looking forward to our regular updates. Occasionally Genie and Gray invite me over for a drink if a lead looks particularly promising and it feels good to have reconnected with Genie. Any animosity that there may have been has faded away. Despite the original publicity that started my search for #thegirlinthesong we manage to keep our reunion a secret from the press. How long that will last, I'm not so sure, as Netflix who initiated all the media interest are about to start filming our Reunion Tour and the irony isn't lost on me. Possibly one day Genie and I will reveal that we have reconnected and are indeed parents of a grown-up daughter, but for now we want to keep things as private as possible.

48

GENIE

Now

Despite the slight awkwardness of when Ed and I first reconnected where he mistakenly called me Evie (I guess I'll always be Evie to him) and then when he first tried to hold my hand to comfort me when I got upset revealing exactly why I left London, we have thankfully formed an amicable relationship and surprisingly Ed and Gray do get on reasonably well, all things considered. Cassie and Will were slightly star struck when they first met Ed, but they are now quite used to seeing him at the house when we all catch up for updates in our continued search for Milly. The children have both been sworn to secrecy about our search for their half-sister, although I'm sure that their best friends Mel and Tommy have been privy to a lot more information than we'd like. They're both good kids so we'll just have to hope for their discretion.

The Mountaineers' Reunion Tour seems to be a roaring success, and Ed has mentioned that Netflix are currently filming some of their rehearsals and gigs. He's suggested that we possibly give a joint interview about our renewed friend-ship and our search for our daughter in the hope that the media exposure might lead us to our daughter. I'm hesitant for the moment as I'm just getting used to reuniting with Ed. Gray also thinks it's a good idea, but I'm still not convinced. I'm just not ready to have that amount of media intrusion in our lives right now. Media wise we have managed to keep our 'relationship' a secret. When Ed comes to see us, Jez drops him off around the corner from the house. Ed always wears his standard anonymous uniform of jeans, hoodie and a base-ball cap and depending on the time of day, a pair of dark sunglasses. Knowing our somewhat robust neighbourhood watch round here they probably think he's a potential burglar casing the joint!

I'm still hoping that Ed will bring Jez with him one evening as I'd love to see him again. I often ask about him and Mark who were all such a part of my early teenage years. The good news is that Ginny (or Virginia) as she now goes by, and I are back in touch and have plans to meet up for lunch next week. She's still so apologetic about her ex stealing her photos and selling them to the tabloids. With everything that has happened, a few unflattering photos being published is the least of my worries. I'm so excited to see her again and find out all about her, away from the tabloids. We were as thick as thieves at one stage. Being identified by Amira Malik as being #thegirlinthesong seemed at the time to be the worst thing that could ever happen to me, but it's in fact been almost cathartic. My husband and children now know the real me and despite everything, they still love me unconditionally.

Seeing Ed again hasn't been as terrifying as I had first thought. He's always had that void in his life as to why I left and the not knowing almost destroyed him. But he rose above it and although he possibly didn't go about things completely the right way we have now managed to reunite without any recriminations. And of course, the search for our daughter continues…..

49

FRANKIE

Now

As I leave the hall, I can almost feel the pity in their eyes. Another aspiring singer who has failed to make the grade. Billie and Gracie are patiently waiting for me outside the hall on some seats in the corridor, happily watching cute kitten videos on my phone.

'Did you get the job Mama?' Billie asks, momentarily looking up from my phone when she hears me open the door.

'I'm not sure honey. They said they would let me know.' I answer my first-born daughter. I say first-born as she's just thirty minutes older than her twin sister.

'We did good sharing Mama when you were singing.' Gracie says, wrapping herself around my legs.

'I'm so pleased Gracie. You're both such good girls. Shall we treat ourselves to some fish and chips tonight?' I say, ruffling her golden curls, hoping that someone, somewhere would just give me a chance with a singing job. Since the twins' father left me when he found out that we were expecting not just one baby but two, it's just been me and my girls. I've long since cut ties with my parents. They didn't really agree with my choice of career and being a single mum of twins didn't quite fit in with their idea of how their daughter should behave. Singing in a band is what I've always wanted to do. Having the girls has put my career back somewhat but now they're about to start school, I can get back to performing again. I've always loved singing and I'm lucky enough to have secured a job at the girls' school covering for the music teacher while she's on maternity leave. It's brilliant that I'm going to finish work the same time that the girls finish school, so I'll always be there to collect them. But it isn't enough. I want to be in a band again, to write my own lyrics and music and get that buzz that only a live gig can give you. I'm almost thirty-three, so I'm not old but there are a lot of much younger singers out there without the added complication of having four-year-old twins. Billie is the outgoing one, her hair so much darker than her still blonde sister. Billie is fearless whereas Gracie is much quieter and depends almost completely on her big sister. Thankfully the school are going to let them both be in the same class at school which is much more for Gracie's benefit than Billie's. And to Billie's credit she always has her sister's back.

We pick up our fish and chips from our local chippy and walk back home where we have a picnic supper outside in our shared garden. We're still enjoying a really hot summer which makes up for the fact that I can't afford to take them on holiday. It won't be long before the girls are at school full time, I'll have my part-time job at the school and lovely Mina who lives in the flat above us and absolutely adores the girls has promised to babysit if ever I need to work at night, so life is looking up. I think back to my earlier audition and hope and pray that I've done enough as Billie and Gracie hoover up the rest of the chips.

EPILOGUE

CAMDEN ROUNDHOUSE

Now

The build-up to The Mountaineers' final tour date at Camden's Roundhouse is electric. The tour has been a great success and Ed and the boys are on fine form. Every single night is a sellout.

Despite being invited to The Mountaineers' final tour date Genie and Gray have decided not to attend, giving their tickets to Cassie on the condition that she goes with Maura. She didn't need to be asked twice. A changed girl from the summer after a good selection of passes in her GCSEs, Cassie is now happily at college studying Drama. Will is in his final year at school, keen to get his GCSEs done and looking forward to next summer's Reading Festival with all the boys.

Ed is enjoying having a laugh with Mark, Jez, Andy and Simon before it's time for them to go on stage. Chyna and Cindy are busy getting ready in their dressing room with Toby nipping in from time to time to make sure they have everything they need.

Virginia's ex-husband Callum has thankfully run out of stories to sell to the tabloids, begging his current wife Amy to take him back which she did briefly before he had another affair, this time with one of the recent Love Island's contestant's mothers, having met her at one of his numerous tacky nightclub personal appearances. It didn't last long as she reunited with her husband soon after their son ended up leaving the island for fighting. Callum is currently living with his mate Jimmy, seeing his daughter Lauren every other weekend which is so much more than he deserves.

Paul has been caught for drug dealing again. His caravan was raided which coincided with the discovery of a selection of historic photos of teenage girls in various states of undress and a series of inappropriate WhatsApp messages between Paul posing as a fifteen-year-old boy and a very impressionable thirteen-year-old girl. He is finally going to prison for a very long time.

Amira Malik is absolutely livid that her planned secret exclusive interview on TikTok with Paul Nash will now never happen due to his arrest. He had promised to spill the tea about Ed and Evie's early relationship and Ed's subsequent drug use to her. It would have been pure TikTok dynamite but she's not about to give up on #thegirlinthesong story quite yet...

Virginia and Genie have met up for lunch a couple of times, enjoying resurrecting their teenage friendship.

Genie and Ed continue to meet up with Gray's blessing, although less so now that the Reunion Tour is in full swing. There is always that glimmer of hope that they will one day finally be reunited with their daughter. There's a buzz in the audience as the time comes nearer for The Mountaineers to take the stage for the very last night of the tour. Ed and the band huddle together for a final time before going on stage; their excitement and energy almost palpable.

Ed is incredible, despite it being the final date of the tour he has the energy of a thirty-year-old thanks to the personal trainer that Toby hired for him. He owns the stage, and his voice is the best that it's been in years. They give the audience just what they want, and the hits just keep on coming. Chyna and Cindy really earn their money and their added harmonies on some of the newer numbers only accentuate Ed's voice. They have just finished performing their most recent single, No More Tears, enjoying the sound of the crowd singing along with all the words.

'Good evening, Camden!' Ed shouts as the band plays and the crowd cheers. As it's almost Christmas we thought we'd get you in a festive mood with our rendition of Fairytale of New York. The audience starts to clap as Ed moves towards the front of the stage with Chyna who starts singing Kirsty McColl's part, her voice pitch perfect. It's a great success and just as they finish, Ed addresses the audience once more.

'No Mountaineers gig is complete without this one! This is 'Used to Be' which I'd like to dedicate to an old friend of mine!' Ed shouts.

The crowd goes wild as the band do what they do best, with the audience happily singing along with all the words. Cassie holds hands with Maura as the band plays on, happy in the knowledge that her mother, 'The Girl in the Song' is finally coming to terms with her past but also embracing her future too. Somewhere out there is a missing part of their family but of course there was always the chance that she didn't even know that she was missing. Both Genie and Ed hope that she has made a good life for herself and that maybe one day she might just come looking for them.

Just up the road from the Roundhouse, a new indie band are playing their first ever gig in a rundown pub which up until recently had been a strip joint. The pub, The Canterbury Arms is under new management now and they are keen to give new bands a chance. The third band on that night are a newly formed band called Pulse. Their lead singer Frankie takes to the stage, at first competing against the general chatter of a rowdy Saturday night crowd but once she starts singing, they all take notice of the pretty blonde with the husky voice as she sings her heart out. Frankie owns the stage, delighted that she is back singing live and that someone has finally given her a chance. She lied about her age at her audition, cutting five years off her real age, but needs must. Any money earned tonight was going straight into her Christmas fund to make sure her daughters have the best Christmas ever. Their setlist is a variety of covers with a couple of original songs thrown in for good measure, their final song is Christmas Wrapping by The Waitresses which the crowd go mad for, clapping continuously all the way until the end. As they leave the stage all Frankie can hear is the audience shouting 'One more song! One more song!' She's finally back where she belongs...

The End

ACKNOWLEDGEMENTS

Writing can be such a solitary experience but getting a book ready to publish is a team effort.

First of all would like to thank Jamie Taylor (@jtayauthor) for all her wonderful advice in helping to bring The Girl in the Song to publication. She has been such a constant support throughout the whole process, suggesting major plot and structural changes. Her humour and patience has kept me going, especially throughout my ill health, operations and Bell's Palsy when at times I couldn't even see the computer screen properly!

Big thanks also go to my wonderful beta readers, my life long friend and general good egg, Jane Coggins and to Zarah Moores who is always there with her positivity, support and a glass of prosecco!

Thank you to all my early readers; the wonderful book bloggers and Instagram friends and writers for taking time out of your busy days to read my book. It is so appreciated.

And to the readers out there who have taken a chance on an unknown author like me. If you enjoyed the book, please do leave a review. Reviews are the life blood for any author - even just a line or two makes all the difference in being seen.

Finally thank you to my family; my husband Jay and sons Jack and Harry and my dear mum (who thankfully is nothing like Felicity Del Rio!) for your support throughout the writing process and helping me get through a couple of tough few years health wise.

If you would like to know what happens next to Genie and Ed, please follow me on Instagram- @sarahwattswrites and consider visiting my author page on Amazon and pressing the 'Follow' button to receive updates on my next book.

Printed in Dunstable, United Kingdom